RAIN DRAGON

A Novel

Jon Raymond

BLOOMSBURY

New York   Berlin   London   Sydney

Published by Bloomsbury USA, New York

All papers used by Bloomsbury USA are natural, recyclable products made from wood grown in well-managed forests. The manufacturing processes conform to the environmental regulations of the country of origin.

LIBRARY OF CONGRESS CATALOGING-IN-PUBLICATION DATA
HAS BEEN APPLIED FOR.

ISBN: 978-1-60819-679-1

First U.S. Edition 2012

1 3 5 7 9 10 8 6 4 2

Typeset by Westchester Book Group
Printed in the U.S.A. by Quad/Graphics, Fairfield, Pennsylvania

RAIN DRAGON

Livability

The Half-Life

For my dad,
a remarkable man

And always,
for Emily, Eliza, and Josephine

I saw my head laughing
rolling on the ground
And now I'm set free
I'm set free
I'm set free to find a new illusion

"I'M SET FREE," LOU REED

SPRING

ONE

THE OWL WASN'T that big—the size of a cat, maybe. Its face was round and flat, and covered in downy plumage, with a little peanut-sized beak, and its body was like a puffy football, spattered cutely with white spots. There was no menacing horned brow on the forehead. No snake coiling in its deadly talons. In fact, the only really spooky, owlish thing about the creature that had appeared in front of our car at the end of the cul-de-sac in the pre-dawn gloom, as far as I could tell, were its incredible round eyes.

The eyes were eerie—perfect glassy circles of blackness ringed in bands of yellow, tufted on top with delicate, angry gray eyebrows. They stared unblinkingly at Amy and me, taking in everything about us in one long, cold glare—seeming to comprehend every thought and action we'd ever had, every thought and action yet to come, and tabulating all of it against dry, firsthand knowledge of the black hole where all time leads in the end. There were tiny flecks of color in the irises, lit by the sunbursts of the car's stopped headlights. Framed in the windshield, perched on the crossbar of a rain-slickened jungle gym, the bird seemed like some kind of apparition from another world.

Amy sat beside me in the passenger seat, wrapped in her pilling wool blankets, her lap speckled with split pistachio shells. For the last half hour she'd been complaining steadily about a litany of minor grievances—her lack of decent coffee this morning, my poor navigational decisions, the musty funk that had settled into the car over the last two days of driving—but suddenly, now that we'd stumbled onto the owl, her mood had turned. I could read it in the new tension in her posture, the subtle smirk that had settled on her lips. But most of all I could tell by the way she'd been trying to convince me that we'd been delivered some kind of terrible sign.

"It's a sign!" she said, for at least the fourth time, and for the fourth time I denied it. That was my role in the moment—the voice of jaundiced optimism.

"It's here for a reason, Damon," she said. "Or we're here for a reason. This isn't just an accident."

"We invaded its territory," I said. "It's probably here every morning. This is its regular place."

The rain hammered steadily on the roof, streaming over the glass on every side of us. "Our first day, our new life," she said, "and we get lost and see an owl. How can you say this isn't a sign?"

I shrugged, the idling grumble of the engine vibrating in my bones. What could I say? I'd already told her that I didn't believe in signs, that I doubted that God, or the Goddess, or whatever you called the organizing consciousness under the teeming colors of the visible plane, played these kinds of games of hide-and-seek with Its creation. And furthermore, even if the universe did decide to send out messages from time to time, coy little missives, I didn't see the point in trying to decode them. Why tempt fate? was my thinking. Anecdotal evidence suggested it was better to avert one's eyes when owls or black cats or white elephants crossed one's path. But then again, I was the kind of person who'd probably walk past a sword in a stone without bothering to test my luck. Amy was the kind who'd push right to the head of the line.

She husked a pistachio and dropped the shell in the brown bag at her feet. "In Greece the owl is a symbol of untimely death," she said.

"Why would you say that right now?"

"I thought you weren't superstitious. Why do you care?"

"A pillar of flame. A dead Indian on the road. Those are signs. An owl on a jungle gym, though. I don't know what that is. We're in good shape, all right? Don't worry about it."

"Look at that thing, Damon! It's staring straight at us."

"A burning bush. A triple rainbow."

"When was the last time you saw an owl? Have you ever seen an owl?"

"It's only a bad sign if you think it's a bad sign."

"Oh. So I'm the bad sign."

The dashboard vents hummed and rain thrummed on the Camry's roof. Our headlights beamed over the bird, only to be swallowed in the pitch-darkness beyond. For a second, as the owl's flat face cocked in a new direction, it almost did seem like it was on the verge of telling us something—like it might open its beak and utter some cryptic prophecy, some gnomic riddle. But of course nothing happened. It just stood there gripping and regripping the crossbar, until finally, awkwardly yet elegantly, it unfolded its wings. From the small body unfurled almost six feet of dappled brown feathers. The gorgeous royal robe ruffled and shook, spraying sparks of rain, and with a slight hop the owl lifted off into the early-morning gloom.

And we were alone again, sitting at the edge of an elementary school somewhere east of Portland, in the town of Clackamas or possibly Gresham, thoroughly lost. The rain kept falling, soaking into the bark dust, drizzling from the glazed swings. The chains clanged on the tetherball poles, tossed by the fits of wind. When we were finally sure the bird wasn't coming back, I pulled a sloppy three-point turn and aimed us back toward the main road, and soon wooden fences and grassy fields were rushing by again, the wipers bashing thick sheaves of water from the windshield, blurring the occasional lights into mangled haloes of white and gold and red.

I could tell by the way Amy stared at the road, though, gnawing on her lip, that the owl was still with us. She sighed under her breath, contemplating the mystery of its significance. Already the high of the sighting was fading, and a gloomier spirit of worry and vague doubt was rising into view. The owl demanded some kind of stock-taking, some kind of weighing of fates, and for a moment all the decisions we'd made over the past year came flocking back into the car for review. All the subtle signals we'd chosen to regard or disregard, all the research we'd half done. We were now obliged to sift the evidence again, to figure out why the plan we'd so enthusiastically conceived of in the fall—Go north! Simplify! Return to the land!—was proving so hard to manifest in real life.

As we cruised along, inches above the licking asphalt, rain crackling on the windshield, the case for pessimism was getting harder to ignore. Of the five places we'd visited so far—a boutique winery; a seed farm; a flower-growing operation; an alpaca ranch; a natural corn chip factory—all had been busts, deemed too small or too remote or too elitist or too disorganized, and in one case, the chip factory, going bankrupt in a matter of weeks anyway. None had proffered the copious learning opportunities we'd been promised over the phone, and none had even been particularly friendly, an attribute that was extremely high on Amy's list.

Not that we were exactly surprised by any of this. It wasn't like we'd expected everything to work out perfectly from the start. We were trying to give ourselves a choice, after all. But as the wipers flapped and the heater blew, I couldn't help but worry that maybe we'd set our standards a little too high. We hadn't even made it to the border of our next destination—an organic farm in the foothills of the Cascades called Rain Dragon—and already I could feel the disappointment settling in, the color draining from the fantasy.

Rain Dragon sounded fine, on paper. But then again, they'd all sounded fine on paper. They were all sustainable, bike-friendly, certified organic. And in the case of Rain Dragon, long-lived, too. For three decades now, the company had been churning out excellent yogurt and yogurt-based products, with wide distribution up and down the coast. It created award-winning cheeses and holiday eggnog and was lauded regularly by magazines as a progressive and fun-loving work environment, nestled in a location of great natural beauty. Our friend Jaeha had been there for years and was always trying to get us to come check it out. On paper, almost every bullet point on our life list stood checked.

Sadly, you couldn't trust the magazines and Web sites in these matters, and sometimes you couldn't even trust your friends. The magazines would say anything to fill their pages, and friends had their own tastes and motives. It might be that Rain Dragon was nothing like its online photos suggested. It might cheat on its sustainability practices. Its finances might be precarious. The people might be boring or paranoid. Who knew where the flaw would come in? And if a major flaw did appear, the question of what came next remained uncomfortably open. There was still an herbal tea factory up in Bellingham to check out, but it didn't seem very enticing. After that, the options dwindled significantly.

We hadn't discussed the absolute worst-case scenario. Namely, we found nothing, and just kept driving until we were demoralized or our money ran out, whatever came first. It was possible we'd even wind up right back where we'd started: Amy working at the voice acting agency in Pasadena, me at the ad firm in Venice Beach, living in our same apartment, shopping at our same Safeway, having the same fights we'd been having the last two years, if not more. It was a fate that to Amy sounded only barely better than death.

I could have lived. But it was with her in mind that I sent a little prayer to the universe. Please, I thought, let this be the place we've been looking for. Let this be the new home we've been wanting, or at least a pit stop where we can quit driving for a while. Please, let this be where Amy's Laura Ingalls Wilder fantasy finally blossoms to life, where she starts jarring pickles, churning butter, building a sod house, whatever. Let all her creative impulses finally take root. Because if Rain Dragon failed to deliver on these hopes, if this, too, was a bust, we very well might be lost for good.

Amy rested her forehead on the rain-streaked window, and her breath silvered the glass, retracted, and silvered the glass again. Her faith was wobbling. I could tell the time had come for some kind of pep talk.

"It's going to be fine," I said, patting the mound of blanket approximately where her thigh would be. "We're just a little off track is all. And that owl, whatever."

"Yogurt," she said, drawing out all the strangeness of the

word in her mouth. "What are we thinking, Damon? We have no idea what we're doing."

"It's more than just yogurt," I said. "It's also ice cream and cheese and other stuff. It's a whole philosophy of how to eat and live. We're doing exactly what we wanted to do."

"It all just seems so arbitrary."

"It's important," I said, which was what she'd been telling me for the past six months, and which I'd come to think was almost definitely true. "And anyway, what else is there to do?"

She sighed again, and we fell into silence. The car arced along a wide curve between two dark fields of mud, and for a second I had the feeling we might be getting close to the freeway again, and with it, I hoped, the reignition of a more positive mind frame, but sadly the road dead-ended at a cow pasture and the headlights banged into a reflective placard telling us the street would one day be extended with new development. The bell of safe travel dinged as our momentum jolted out. Cold rain swept over the long grass behind the fence.

"Where the sidewalk ends," Amy said. "You can't argue with that sign."

"I thought this would go through," I said. "Fuck."

I stared out the window. Fifteen minutes earlier I'd claimed to know where I was going, and I'd ended up leading us to the lip of an abandoned stone quarry. This time I decided not to make any promises. I just backed up and drove us along the same road yet again—through the woods, past the school, over the bridge, and alongside the acres of sod farm barely visible in the morning twilight—still hoping we would stumble onto the on-ramp but having to admit that nothing looked very promising anymore.

Amy's reflection appeared on the passenger window, black

shadows carving her warped features. The longer we stayed lost, I knew, the more her mood was prone to crumble. Pretty soon it would dip down to the level where it threatened our whole day's experience. So much depended on a right mind in this kind of situation. An old barn could be construed as charming or dilapidated. An inarticulate farm manager could be hilarious or incompetent. And because Amy's first impressions were usually unshakable, these mood questions were not insignificant. If she was still unhappy by the time we rolled into Rain Dragon, our future there might be doomed from the start.

It was under this gathering cloud that we emerged at the two-block commercial zone where we'd made our first major navigational mistake almost an hour before. This time we turned left at the Kmart and glided past a lumberyard, a garden supply store, the loading bay of the backside of a Walgreens, on the lookout for any street signs but not finding any. Traffic was still almost nonexistent, only rain and fog in alternating belts, and soon the buildings again tapered off, leaving us at a blank four-way intersection. The scene seemed to hover in some purgatory between day and night, each road banked by humps of trimmed grass and leading off into foggy obscurities. Out of nowhere a trio of cars swept by, blurring inside hazy auras of rain, leaving crimson trails on the wet asphalt.

"Stop thinking about that owl," I said, gripping the wheel.

"Don't think about an elephant," she said, and then, as if to taunt me, "God. We never should have left L.A. I knew it. What a waste."

"Last week you said L.A. was the engine of all false desires," I reminded her.

"At least it was home."

The bleary morning landscape fuzzed out and snapped back into focus, the wipers veiling and unveiling the cold, gray, wet world.

"We could still go back," I said.

"No we can't."

"Why not?"

"Give me a break. We just can't."

I didn't argue. She was right, as usual. After all our bon-voyage parties, garage sales, and days of packing, to slink back into town would have been humiliating. And God knew what it would have meant for the two of us. Could we survive going back? I wasn't sure. The prospect of our future together was predicated on this choice we'd made, this risk we'd taken. To change course now would mean changing our whole tacit agreement, to admit failure not only in the plan but in each other, too. We'd come to the end of something down there. And if we didn't find something new up here, we might just have to part ways for good.

When the light turned green I just sat there and rubbed my kneecap while Amy shelled another pistachio and dropped the husk in the brown bag. I scanned for a gas station, or any other place to ask for directions, but I didn't see anything. If we could just get back on track, I thought, if we could tap some luck, we still had a chance to enter our day with trumpets sounding. It just seemed like some kind of gesture was necessary, some ritual.

The light changed back to red.

"What if the freeway is right over this hill?" I said, nodding at the road rising most steeply into the fog. "If we make the right choice here, would it count as a good sign? Would that cancel the owl?"

Amy followed my gaze into the fog. "What do you mean?" She was suspicious of my logic, if logic was the right word.

"If we ask the universe for the freeway to appear, and the universe gives us the freeway, would that count as a good sign?"

"Gambling with the universe," she said. "That's dangerous stuff, Damon. I don't know if the universe works like that."

"I'm willing to test it."

Amy turned her eyes onto me. In the low light, framed by the hard cut of her black bangs, her face almost seemed to glow. Her small, pale eyes; her fine, delicate mouth; her blushing cheeks—all were expressionless. She didn't say anything, but just watched me, mentally scrutinizing my intentions. I didn't say anything either, and I tried sending back strong pulsations of optimism. I was on her team, I projected; I had utter confidence in her powers of judgment; I saw her as a talented, self-possessed woman on all levels. We kept staring at each other, and I kept emanating the positive thoughts: She could do anything. She'd been right to walk away from the winery. She was a creative force to be reckoned with, at the beginning of a long, satisfying career of some kind.

I couldn't tell if she was receiving everything I was putting out there, but the way she kept staring at me made me think she got most of it. Her lips lightly pursed, her eyes narrowed. Her response could go either way. Sometimes her negativity was intractable, and other times it was tissue-thin. I was lucky this time—my silent display of conviction tore it away.

"Okay," she said at last. "If we make the right choice here, everything is wonderful forever."

"Good!" I said, "Then let's take a second to visualize."

"If you say so."

We closed our eyes and summoned our most hopeful images to mind. Dewy hills, newborn animals, sunlight through maple leaves. At least that's what I summoned. I wasn't sure what she summoned. When I opened my eyes, her eyes were still closed, and I watched her for a second longer in the half-light, watery shadows coursing over her skin. I patted her on the knee, and her eyes fluttered open.

"So?" I said. "Ready?" She squeezed my hand, nodding.

"So this is where it starts," I said.

"Right . . . ," she said, ". . . now."

I could almost hear the click of the switch in the metal box outside. A heartbeat later the red lens extinguished and the green lens brightened, limning the little awning that protected it from the rain. I glanced both ways, and gave the car some gas.

We passed through the intersection and rolled out into the darkness, gathering momentum, and soon we were passing low warehouses fronted by rows of young, naked elm trees on either side. A Subaru zoomed by in the opposite direction, piloted by an invisible driver, and as its taillights disappeared behind us we headed higher up the road.

We were both quiet, scanning for signs. In the first minute or so, no turnoffs appeared, and we kept climbing. Another minute went by and still nothing. At three minutes, I began getting worried. We should have gone right, I realized. Higher up was obviously the wrong idea here. We needed to get lower if anything. The highway ran along a valley floor, after all, not up in the hills. I hadn't thought it all the way through.

By the fourth minute I was fabricating excuses as to why this gamble wasn't to be considered a real loss, why it should be disqualified as a meaningful event. We hadn't really put our minds to it, had we? We hadn't made a genuinely sincere effort. I was so busy building my case that I barely noticed when the hill crested and we began dropping downward again, or when the fog began thinning, and it was only when Amy leaned forward, squinting into the silvery sheen, that I realized something was happening.

Off in the distance, a fir-covered ridge was resolving into view, mist caught in the black trees like torn cotton. The fog kept thinning. In the still-dark basin of a valley, a river of headlights became visible. The highway.

Soon we were able to make out the construction site that had snared us in the first place, the group of tiny men huddled alongside the flatbed trailer strapped with an enormous drainage pipe. A Caterpillar scooped a load of wet dirt from the shoulder, scattering rocks pointlessly on the ravaged ground. As we headed for the on-ramp, Amy leaned over and kissed me on the cheek.

"You know what a group of owls is called?" she said, attacking her pistachios again. The trough she'd fallen into was already a memory.

"Nope," I said.

"A wisdom. A wisdom of owls. That's pretty good, right?"

"A delusion of owls. That would be better."

"Ha. A figment of owls."

We hit the on-ramp, and we were still riffing. A mistake of owls. An illusion of owls. A big, huge boner of owls. Soon the sound of the wet tires and the grinding engine and the wind over the Camry's hood rose into a single, mighty vibration, like the roar of a fiery, atmospheric reentry, and we merged into the world's traffic again, a stream of angelic white lights flowing west, against us, and a smattering of demonic red lights heading east, our way.

TWO

OVER THE YEARS, I'd heard most of Amy's stories many times, and vice versa. We had our little set pieces we trotted out, our old favorites we always found some new context to deploy. For me, the main ones were usually about traveling in Mexico when I was a teenager—seeing a dead body in the countryside outside Chiapas, bribing Federales in Mexico City—and generally designed to make me seem at least mildly, if formerly, adventurous. For her, the big anecdotes were mostly comical: the one-night stand she'd spotted the next afternoon climbing out of a cop car in handcuffs; the drunken projectile vomiting at her sister's wedding; the time she'd tried burning a mole off her dog's stomach, thinking it was a deer tick. The number of airings she could squeeze out of her theory that humans would one day evolve tiny hands on the ends of their fingers in response to digital culture's ever-smaller keyboard manipulations was kind of amazing.

It was only in the last couple years that I'd started hearing talk about her farming fantasy, though. It had started up sometime around the first American outbreak of mad cow disease, which had coincided with the appearance of the gorgeous rainbow chard at the local health food store, and by the end of the season, between the incredible frittatas she was making and the specter of cannibal cows, she was an evangelist for the glories of small-scale agriculture.

Growing up outside Phoenix, she claimed, she'd always found the idea of farm life exotically alluring. The wind, the rain, the denim, all of it. To hear her talk, major tracts of her childhood had been spent just staring out the back window of her family's duplex, imagining the desert as a field of windblown golden wheat, the cars in the distance covered wagons hauling barrels and blankets to their pioneer homesteads. In fourth grade, she'd taken to wearing calico bonnets and prairie dresses to school, carrying her books in what she thought was a gunny sack, but might not have been one, and come high school she'd wanted more than anything to sign up for 4H, but sadly there hadn't been a chapter in her town. It was only because her parents had talked her out of the idea that she hadn't applied to agronomy programs going into college, and the fact she'd ended up at Berkeley studying psychology was in retrospect basically a fluke.

I was happy for that fluke. It was at Berkeley that we'd first met, and where we'd enjoyed the brief fling that had laid the groundwork for our subsequent, serendipitous reunion at the L.A. DMV. Since then we'd been together almost constantly, sharing apartments, spending holidays with each others' extended families, marching ever farther down the road toward eventual mortgage and matrimony, not that we ever spoke openly about such plans.

At first I'd doubted the farm talk. I'd chalked up the new-found interest to a broader cultural fascination, a response to all the farmers' markets springing up in town, the new restaurants with walls of preserve jars and strange organ meats on the menus. But Amy was adamant that her interest in food and the politics of food pre-dated the current obsession. It had only been dormant all this time, awaiting a rekindling spark.

"Food is the center of everything," she said, perched on the railing of our Echo Park patio for our traditional, exhausted glass of wine after work. "I've always said that. Class, ecology, animal rights. Eating is the most fundamental thing humans do. If we can't get that right, then we don't really have a right to exist."

"You've got a problem with corn syrup?" I said. "That's all this country's got anymore. Corn syrup and video games."

"Obesity. God. If we could start teaching kids where their food came from. Most of them don't even know that a potato grows in the ground. We should be digging up parking lots. All those lights out there. See those pretty lights? Energy from some river hundreds of miles away, just pouring out onto the streets. What a waste."

She read all the books on the topic of food, followed the locavore blogs. And the more she read, the more convinced she became that some major life change was necessary. She started out making her own granola and baking her own no-knead bread. She apprenticed with an artisanal butcher, which led to the testing of her own tofu meat substitutes and an exploration of fried tempeh. She took a plot at the community garden, and within a few months she was managing the whole spread. And all the while she was amassing data, researching options for a more full-blown commitment.

It wasn't the first such obsession that had gripped her. In the past, labor organizing, prison literacy, women's self-defense, and urban planning had all consumed her for spells, until eventually falling away due to disillusionment or scheduling problems. From a certain angle, it was possible to see Amy as a little fickle in her commitments, never quite able to unlock her passion, never quite satisfied with the reality of work, love, and landscape as they had to be lived. But to call her uncommitted or capricious or inconsistent was not quite right, either. There were always real principles leading to her changes of heart, real, divergent intuitions being grappled with. To me, her restlessness was the very thing that was so admirable. It was life itself, and I wished I had more of it in me.

Rain Dragon might offer the next great project. Who knew how far it would take us? Arriving at the property's entrance—a barely visible gartersnake road off Highway 26, marked by a hand-engraved wooden sign—our hopes were again rising. The owl had left us a little giddy, and since then the sunrise had laid out a pyrotechnic welcome mat—a melting spectrum of hot fuchsia, bruised purple, deep gold, and pellucid, mountain-fresh silver that briefly spotlit every blade of grass and beaded water droplet in the visible world. The last strip malls of the city's edge had given way to rolling farmland mixed with evergreen woods, and we'd found decent coffee at a hardware-store java hut. The good signs kept coming, even as we moved into the realm of hard, irrefutable evidence.

Our hopes were goosed a little further by the sight of the company's main headquarters hewing into sight over the naked trees: a giant Georgian Revival mansion backed by the mountains, buttressed by rhododendrons and lilac bushes. It was a handsome building, with a row of stately pillars lining the front porch, a phalanx of dormers studding the roof, a swath of solar cells capping the south wing. Funky, fading paint gave the whole place a lived-in, unprecious feel.

"So how late are we?" Amy asked, watching the weathervane bob against the clouds, and keeping any enthusiasm she might feel under wraps.

"Not that late," I said.

"How late?"

"An hour or so."

"Nice building."

"Yep."

The road plunged downward, gathering itself for the final, muddy ascent, and we entered a patch of raking sunlight strobing through the trees. Up ahead a delivery van materialized, frozen at the lowest point of the road's dip. I slowed down, and slowed down some more. Drawing closer, I could see there was a holdup of some kind. In the middle of a battlefield of gouged earth and water, the van wasn't just stopped but trapped, struggling to get out of the muck.

We came to a halt. To either side, ghost fern and mossy spruce closed in tight. The van was an old milk delivery truck, and three mud-spattered men were pushing heavily against the rear bumper. On the left, a gigantic Frankenstein of a guy, sporting a long blond ponytail and pink cheeks fringed with mutton chops. In the middle, a normal-sized guy, notable mainly for his crazy, kinky hair and beautifully sculpted legs, revealed by cutoff shorts he was improbably wearing in the middle of February. On the right, a little potbellied guy, with doll-like arms and stubby legs, an orange hunting cap covering his ears. It took me a long second to realize the little guy was Jaeha. I barely recognized him. For some reason I'd still been expecting the dapper Korean night-club singer he'd once been, not a soiled farmhand in work boots.

"That doesn't look fun," Amy said, watching the van's spinning back wheels raising brown humps in the mud.

"Nope," I said.

"We should probably get out and help, right?"

"I guess so."

"Do you know where my boots are?"

"Way in the back. Under everything."

"Ugh."

We opened the doors and reconvened over the plane of the rooftop. The sun was cold, and the cleanliness of the air came as a small shock to the system. It was nothing like L.A. air. It was arctic air, scrubbed and scentless. I took some deep breaths and waited as the struggle with the van went on. Jaeha and his buddies were continuing their efforts, rocking the van hard, but ultimately making no headway. Soon enough the vehicle was sliding depressingly back into the sludge.

The driver killed the engine. The blond guy straightened, followed by Jaeha and the guy in shorts. They stared at the back wheels, half-sunk and glistening. I was about to say something when Jaeha turned our way, and a tired smile of recognition came over his face.

"There you are," he said, pulling off his horn-rimmed glasses, the last remaining vestige of his former, urban self, and wiped them on his filthy shirt. "About time. I was afraid you'd changed your mind or something." He glanced over at his friends. "Hey, this is Damon and Amy. I've been telling you about them. Damon, Amy, this is Michael and Emilio. And that's Linda in the van."

We waved, and Michael and Emilio nodded back, openly uninterested. An arm extended from the window and retracted. In the mirror I caught a glimpse of a woman's tight jaw and thinned lips.

"The van is stuck," Jaeha said.

"Looks like it," I said.

"The creek is high today," he said. "But it's weird. Usually this spot isn't such a problem."

"Exactly," Emilio said, inspecting the wheels more closely. "It's never been a problem. It's looked way worse before and I've made it across. I don't know why this time was such a bitch."

"Yeah, yeah," Linda called from the cab. "Everyone else made it across this morning all right."

"That was before it rained again!" Emilio said.

"It rained for ten minutes!"

"Hard, though! You didn't see how hard!"

"Okay. What we need is some gravel or something," Michael, the big guy, said, dragging the group back to practical concerns. His lips almost seemed to hang off his face, and his eyes were permanently sad. "We're not getting any traction here, that's the problem. We could keep pushing forever and it wouldn't matter if we don't get traction."

"We should use some plywood," Emilio said. "There's a whole stack behind the toolshed, I'm pretty sure. Someone just has to go up there."

"Or how about a winch?" came Linda's disembodied voice. "We'll be out in three minutes that way."

"If you guys need any help," Amy offered, "we can lend a hand, no problem."

"You'll just get all wet," Jaeha said.

"We're happy to do it," she insisted. "Really."

Jaeha looked over at Michael and Emilio, and inasmuch as

they'd been listening, they seemed amenable to the offer. He turned back and gave a shrug. "All right. If you're up for it. Come on over. We'll give it one more try."

Amy was pleased her offer had been accepted so quickly. She liked making a good first impression. To keep it rolling she stepped boldly into the mud, as if she did this kind of thing every day. I figured I didn't have any choice but to follow her lead, even if I seriously doubted we'd make any difference in the van's movement.

The mud was cold, and immediately soaked into the deepest fibers of my socks, adding about five pounds to each foot. I trudged over to the bumper and took a place next to Michael, near the corner, and Amy went over by Jaeha and Emilio. We placed our hands on the metal skin, and as soon as everyone was ready, the engine started. Linda shifted into gear, and we pressed our weight toward the hill.

The van edged forward a foot or so, the wheels slowly grinding. I could feel the tread digging at the earth, straining for grip, but unable to mount some invisible obstacle. Water kicked up onto my arms and the side of my face. And soon, after a final burst of angry spinning, the wheels once again slid back into their ruts.

"Stop! Stop!" Jaeha yelled, and Linda cut the engine. No one bothered thanking us, but instead went straight back to their previous debate as if we weren't there.

"We need gravel," Michael said. "That's it."

"Or a piece of plywood," Emilio said. "I've used plywood before. It works."

"Or a winch!" called Linda.

"Okay, okay," Jaeha said. "It doesn't really matter what we use, does it? Someone just has to go up there and take a look."

A long moment of group contemplation elapsed, during which the sun beamed through the branches and distant water trickled over rocks. I almost volunteered to go up myself, hating the tension, but eventually Emilio accepted responsibility. "All right, all right," he said, and without further discussion sloshed his way to the edge of the mud field and stalked up the hill, the mud sucking at his feet as he climbed.

"He shouldn't even be allowed to drive," Linda said, stepping out of the cab and perching on the van's running board. She was a stocky woman with close-cropped hair and restless energy, wearing a shapeless lavender sweater and knee-high boots. "I mean, look at this shit. If he'd just stuck to the middle he would've been fine."

"He said the sun was in his eyes," Jaeha said.

"Give me a break."

"A little culvert down here and this wouldn't be a problem," Michael said, sitting down on the bumper. "I say it every year. No one listens."

"I thought this was a county road," Linda said.

"I don't see them doing anything, though."

"We'd need permits. That's the hang-up."

"This is a hang-up, too."

"Anyway," Linda said, losing interest in Michael and wheeling her eyes onto Amy. "So you guys are here from California? Is that what Jaeha says?"

"That's right," Amy said.

"What part?" Linda said.

"Echo Park?"

"I know that area," Linda said, squatting and resting an elbow on a knee. "I used to live there. I had a neighbor who listened to

Elvis Costello every goddamn night. All night long. Loud. For two years. Drove me absolutely fucking insane."

"That's funny," Amy said. "I had a neighbor like that for a while, too."

"This guy ended up getting hit by a car," Linda said.

"So did mine," Amy said.

The two shared a moment of surprised, tentative recognition.

"The shoe in the tree?" Linda said.

"Yes. Horrible. And that kid with the napkins. Awful."

"Where did you live, exactly?"

"Thirty-four Logan. Those apartments with the pebbled siding?"

"I was right across the street."

They stared at each other longer, chuckling, searching their memory banks for any lost impressions. Linda came to something first, but shook her head, changing her mind. But then she changed her mind again. "Did you wear a yellow dress sometimes?"

"Yeah."

"And did you look at magazines at the Rite Aid?"

"Embarrassingly often."

"I remember you!"

"Get out of here!"

The rest of us stood around listening as they patched together mutual memories. It turned out they'd been neighbors for seven months back in 2003. They knew some of the same baristas and shopped at the same consignment shops. They remembered the same slummy barbeque shack. I wasn't sure whether the coincidence qualified as a good sign or not, but for the moment anyway, Amy seemed pleased by the connection, even after the initial flush of enthusiasm wore off and she and Linda seemed to get a little shy.

It almost came as a relief when the conversation was cut off by the return of Emilio, carrying a sack of cat litter under one arm and bringing an additional recruit: a slightly older fellow, mid-fifties, maybe, with a burly build and curls of reddish hair boiling up on the sides of his prominent bald head. He moved smoothly, like a former athlete, keeping a low center of gravity, and as he got closer, picking his way down the hill, I could see his lively blue eyes taking in the scene with an air of command.

"That's Peter Hawk," Jaeha said, as if that name meant something.

"Okay," I said.

"The founder of Rain Dragon," he added.

"Ah."

I'd heard of Peter Hawk, but that was all. Maybe Amy had talked to me about him, but if so, I'd forgotten what she'd said. In any case, he didn't seem at all interested in me, entering the problem area and heading straight to the rear tires, crouching down to inspect the depth and viscosity of the mud. He rose, rubbing his chin, and muttered, "Jesus."

"I had no idea it was this deep," Emilio explained. "I wouldn't have tried to get across if I'd known."

"Is the van full?" Peter said, expecting the worst.

"It's empty," Emilio said. So at least that was a relief.

"All right. Well. Let's give this a try."

The addition of one more body didn't seem like it was going to make a major difference, but dutifully everyone returned to the bumper and took their positions. Emilio poured the cat litter into the sludge near the tires where it was swallowed almost as quickly as it went down. Meanwhile, Linda climbed back into the cab and got the engine going. Peter slotted in next to me, rolling up his sleeves to reveal bulging, veiny forearms, and still no introductions were attempted. It was too late for that anyway— Jaeha was already calling out that we were ready and Linda was giving the engine some gas, and sure enough the wheels proceeded to turn and, sure enough, to slip just like before.

But inch by inch, the van edged a tiny bit forward. Muddy water seeped between my toes and I repositioned my feet, wondering if the ground was any better beyond this patch, or if we were just pushing from one impasse to another. We teetered for what seemed like a full minute, going nowhere, until for no apparent reason Amy slipped and fell, drenching herself along the right side. The van lost a little ground in the confusion, but she quickly bounced to her feet, resolute, and retook her place. I was proud of her.

Amy's fall seemed to focus the group's energy, and for the next few moments we all pushed extra hard. The wheels rocked upward and caught on something, and then, without warning, the van jumped. The change came so quickly that Linda wasn't ready, letting the vehicle jet off-course toward the shoulder, and for a sickening second it looked as if she was going to plow into the woods. But thankfully she managed to swerve and bank into a mossy tree trunk. The branches overhead shook, sending a cascade of fat raindrops pinging onto the roof, and a second later Linda sprang out pumping her arms and laughing, and everyone cheered, laughing along with her.

We walked up to the mansion as members of the party, reliving the victory from every angle, and at the parking area we received many backslaps and heartfelt promises to help us out in whatever way possible. The group dispersed, and Jaeha led us over to a spigot where we washed our hands, the pinkness shining in the cold, and even though we were still soaking wet, he suggested we take the grand tour immediately, as the weather was probably going to turn anytime.

"It's so balmy, though," Amy said, looking at the sky, which was indeed highly blue.

"False spring," he said. "It changes fast this time of year."

He spoke with authority. And he was already walking, so we followed him along the side of the mansion, admiring the fine masonry, the bank of arched windows, the lovely cupola, listening to a history lesson about how it had all come to be.

"The mansion used to be the regional poor farm," Jaeha told us, "built by debtors back in 1911. They raised vegetables here, took in laundry, canned fruit, slaughtered hogs, and then in about 1927 the state reclassified poverty as a mental disease and shipped them all off to the nut house in Salem."

"Bummer," I said.

"Yeah," he said. "Since then it's been a sanitarium, a reform school, and a huge teenage party pad. Until Peter Hawk found it, and the land became fruitful again."

"How many acres?" Amy wondered aloud.

"About a hundred," Jaeha said. "There's a national forest to the east, so it feels bigger. We never have to worry about neighbors in that direction, which is nice."

"And how many people?" I said.

"Thirteen staffers," he said. "About that many interns. It changes all the time."

Turning a corner, we entered the back gardens, a bushy, beaded wonderland of rhododendron, camellia, jasmine, and currant, carved with gravel pathways, dotted with funky sculptural installations. We passed alongside herbal gardens, vegetable gardens, grape arbors, teased by scents of rosemary and mint, and soon ended up on a bluff overlooking the entire property. The main creamery was down below—three Quonset huts staggered on the banks of a tumbling stream—and beyond that a thin band of woods. Beyond the woods rolled gentle pastureland, and beyond the pastures rose grassy hills and steeper, forested hills. Beyond the hills loomed Mount Hood itself, a hunk of white papier-mâché vibrating against the diamond-blue sky, a dark smudge of rain fluxing off to one side.

"Wow," Amy said. "Quite a spread."

"Just wait until summer," Jaeha said. "That's when this place really gets nice. You won't want to leave."

"I don't want to leave already," she said, to my surprise, though maybe, too, she was just being polite.

"Well. Come on then. Lots more to see."

He took us to the round barn, a postcard-perfect structure in the pasture where cows and goats loitered; the beehives, a small city of chapped wooden boxes in a clearing of plum trees; the tortilla factory, a dank shed with a single tortilla machine. Along the way he introduced us to the various staffers and interns that crossed our path, all of whom were young and busy-seeming, and numerous of whom felt the need to comment on the depravity of our former home, Los Angeles. Yes, we always agreed, L.A. was venal and shallow. The air was terrible. The culture was plastic. The traffic was even worse than everyone said. And in return for confirming their prejudices, the workers of Rain

Dragon congratulated us on getting out when we did, and assured us we were going to fit in just fine.

"I didn't know there was so much going on here," Amy said, standing in front of the domed brick kiln, its mouth glowing pale orange with embers. "We only get the yogurt down in L.A."

"The yogurt is the main thing," Jaeha said. "But we're always trying new things. You kind of have to in this business. You have to be nimble if you want to survive. So these days the granola and the honey are both doing pretty well. Emilio wants to brew beer. It's hard to say what we'll end up doing. It all depends on who's here. Depends on what the world wants."

"So there isn't any long-term plan?" Amy said.

"Oh, it's all interconnected, if that's what you mean," Jaeha said. "The honey goes into the honey granola and the honey soap. The honey granola supplies the granola bars and gets packaged with the yogurt. The yogurt supplies a local ice cream maker. So the system is always feeding itself that way. The growth of each part helps push the growth of the whole, ideally."

"Vertical integration," I said.

"Ha," Jaeha said. "Horizontal, at best. We're just trying to keep as many doors open as possible."

We toured the ground floor of the mansion, decorated like a San Francisco bordello circa 1849, and the inside of the yogurt factory, a city of silver vats and pipes, loud with the rattling conveyor belt commandeered from an abandoned ice-cream factory. We paused at the badminton court, but fled when the clouds suddenly massed overhead and began spitting down nuggets of hail.

At the kitchen garden, after the sky cleared, we bumped into

Peter Hawk again, picking parsnips, and this time he greeted us like old friends, raising a dirty palm, his bald head shining with rain water. His eyes followed us merrily. "Jaeha showing you the sights?"

"You've got quite a place, Mr. Hawk," Amy said.

"We like it all right," he said, brushing a muddy parsnip against his thigh. "An experiment-in-progress."

"The experiment looks to be working," she said.

"So I guess Jaeha hasn't shown you the ugly stuff yet," he said. "That's good."

"Soon," Jaeha said.

"Or maybe just skip the mass graves this time," Peter said, laughing. "Let's not scare these two off too fast, all right? I have a good feeling about them. I think they're here for some kind of reason."

By late morning we found ourselves in a greenhouse, inspecting Jaeha's peonies. It turned out he'd gotten into flowers since coming north—news to us—and presided over a whole floral side business at Rain Dragon. Standing in the muggy tent, the panes of plastic brightening and dimming with the changing sunlight, we talked more intimately about his Rain Dragon experience thus far, probing for gossip about the staffers we'd met, and not turning up anything that sounded too salacious or scary.

Michael Byles was a true genius, Jaeha said. An amazing engineer plotting to bring the farm into total energy independence. Linda Hutchins was kind of a genius, too, the farm's COO and main beekeeper, not to mention a mean slide guitarist and a scholar of classics. Emilio Spank could also maybe be considered a genius in a way, able to fix anything in the realms of plumbing, electricity, or carpentry. And try to find a place on the map he hasn't been. It was impossible.

We talked about Peter Hawk, too, whom Jaeha claimed was truly a remarkable man, responsible for not only the success of Rain Dragon but the very existence of the whole organic food distribution network as it currently existed on the West Coast. It was largely through his efforts decades earlier that the market had evolved from a handful of health food stores along the I-5 corridor to the ubiquitous cultural movement it was today. It was no surprise that he spent much of his time lecturing all over the world lately, sharing his theories about food and civilization with high-level business and state leaders. And yet he still somehow managed to keep a firm hand on the levers of the farm. It took a special guy to pull that off.

"So you really like it?" Amy said. "You're happy?" Alone in the greenhouse, she seemed to think we could expect his fullest candor.

"I do," he said, without hesitating. "I am. Totally."

"No regrets? Really?"

"None that I can think of."

"You don't ever miss L.A.?"

Jaeha fingered a tiny green shoot, pressing the soil around the stem with his thumb, pondering. He furrowed his brow, doing her the honor of taking her questions seriously.

"It wasn't working for me down there," he said, moving to the next shoot and peering at it carefully. "When I got here, though, I felt like something finally clicked. I miss the music scene, I guess. But whatever. I still play my music. And now I also raise these peonies. I built this greenhouse myself. I ordered all the seeds. I tend the shoots every day. Now I'm selling flowers from

Ashland to Seattle. I never would have been able to do any of this down there."

He leaned over, squinting at a leaf, touching its edges.

" 'Do what you love and the money will come,' " he said. "That's what Peter always says. Just do what brings you happiness, and the details work themselves out. I've come to think that's true. I don't feel like I'm missing anything here, no."

"I'm glad," Amy said.

We exited the greenhouse and looped back onto the gravel path toward the gardens. I was sore from the morning's labor and my clothes were still damp, but I felt invigorated. Breathing the mountain air, I harbored almost no doubts about our decision. The land was gorgeous. The people were cool. The products were wholesome. And I could tell by the pressure of Amy's hand against my back that she felt the same way. After months of planning, weeks of driving, we'd finally landed someplace we might want to be.

"When would we start?" I said, returning to the bluff's ledge we'd visited hours before. "I mean, theoretically. If that's what we end up wanting to do?"

"Whenever," Jaeha said. "Now is a good time."

"And where would we live?" Amy said. "We haven't really thought about that."

"You could stay with me for a while," Jaeha offered. "Rent's not as cheap as it used to be around here, but it still beats L.A. You'll find something."

"And how about the whole pay situation?" Amy said. In all our phone calls over the fall, the topic of money had never explicitly come up. It had always seemed a far distant concern compared to other issues we were facing. And besides, we didn't need much. Just enough to cover our rent and groceries for the time being. We'd worry about savings at some future date. But ambling along the bluff, the mountain rising into the broken clouds on one side, the mansion on the other, it seemed like an appropriate moment to broach the subject.

"For volunteers," Jaeha said, "there's no pay, unfortunately. We give everyone free breakfast and lunch. And lots of free produce in the summertime. But that's about it."

"And how long does the volunteer period last?" Amy pressed.

"Depends," Jaeha said. "Sometimes not very long. Sometimes a while."

"But generally how long?"

"Well, it's really hard to say. We've had to cut back on hiring lately. But you never know. Something always might happen."

"So there's nothing available right now? Is that what you're saying?"

"Nothing right now, no."

"But something might come up," I said.

"Definitely. Eventually."

"Is that how people usually do this?" I said. "They come and volunteer for a while? And then they get hired on?"

"By and large."

"How long did it take for you to get hired?" Amy said.

"Mmm. Three years? Thereabouts."

Amy was silent. A crow landed on the creamery roof and began beating a nut against the metal. Three years was not the time frame she'd been hoping to hear. Three years, I was pretty sure, sounded like an eternity in her mind. Three years ago she had just been starting at the SEIU. Three years ago I was still working at the bookstore. To think back that far was like a journey to the moon. Three years from now, who knew where we'd want to be? The whole point of coming north was to get something going now, not just take a seat in a new waiting room. Flickeringly, the shadow of the owl seemed to flash on the ground at our feet.

Jaeha checked his watch, oblivious to the tectonic shift going on in front of his face. He had a meeting to get to, he said, and he suggested we meet up later for lunch. In the meantime we should keep wandering around, talking to people, see what we thought. And before we could say anything, he was gone, walking down the gravel path, leaving a thick, invisible wall between us and Rain Dragon in his wake.

We watched the empty path bending out of sight, listened to the diminishing sounds of his footsteps. The sun peeked out, returned to the clouds. Our breath wisped in the cold air.

"Three years," Amy said, still staring at the path. "Huh."

"Could be shorter," I said.

"We have enough money to last three months, tops," she said.

"I'd say six."

She kept staring. Voices and muffled laughter drifted from the kiln area nearby, taunting us, and the tiny yellow birds darting among the barren lilac branches taunted us, too. In her mind, Amy was hastily putting things together, making the case for staying versus going, contemplating the day's signs, weighing the day's facts, teetering back and forth dangerously on the brink of faith and doubt.

"He said things happen," I hurried to say. "We just have to be a little bit patient. See what develops."

She didn't say anything, but only stared at the kohlrabi and squash pushing through the dirt at our feet. Not far away, the legs of the wooden water tower rose to the tank splashed with the Rain Dragon logo, a half-dissolved dragon shape encircled by crude, calligraphic hand lettering. Maybe I needed to push her a little harder, I thought. This was what we'd come here to find, after all. It was what we said we wanted. We should take the risk and find a way to make it happen, shouldn't we?

She kept her eyes on the ground. I couldn't figure out exactly what to say. How many times could I give her the same advice? I wondered. We'd been together for six years, and we couldn't ply each other with this kind of wisdom anymore. No, the best thing was to stand quietly and hope she came around to the brave, confident conclusion by herself.

A cloud's shadow crawled up the mountainside. If only she wasn't so worn down by the search, I thought. If only the earlier stops hadn't planted such grave questions. If only we could assume something would meet us on the other side.

The cloud shadow reached the mountaintop and disappeared. The wind picked up, and the sound of falling droplets ticked from every direction like hidden clocks.

"So?" I said. "What are you thinking?"

"Huh? Oh. I think we should stay," she said. "Definitely. I mean, of course. Don't you?"

"Oh. Yeah." I was a little shocked by the determination in her voice. "Really?"

"Come on," she said. "Look at this place. I feel like we practically know half these people already. There's so much we can learn. We'll just make ourselves indispensable. How hard can it be? Don't you think?"

"Uh, absolutely."

"You look surprised. You didn't think I'd say this?"

"No, of course I did," I said. "Maybe just not so fast." I stepped over and wrapped my arms around her and buried my lips in her neck.

"Cold hands!" she said, laughing, and pushed my fingers out of her shirt.

The lunch bell began tolling, three clear gongs in the brisk air. We parted and began our way back through the gardens, walking hand in hand past the camellia bushes studded with tiny minarets, the crowns of the first daffodils. As we walked, the sun came out again, and seven perfect spiderwebs appeared in the boughs of a Japanese maple, as nine crows lifted from the kitchen garden and flopped from view over the trees.

For a second, watching the mansion's shingles steaming, I had the distinct feeling that we'd made the right decision. The lightning rod on the roof's highest peak seemed oddly familiar, as did the stately portico and pilasters.

The landscape surrounding us felt strangely, happily coherent. It was only midway to the back deck, when a pale rainbow appeared, that I realized why. Of course this place was familiar: We'd been visiting it for years, in the form of the crude, hand-drawn picture on the liter yogurt tub. For years this building had been showing up in our refrigerator. I'd scooped breakfast from its roof, reused its walls for our compost bins and leftovers boxes. And now, at last, here we were, inside it.

THREE

THAT NIGHT WE SLEPT AT Jaeha's warehouse in Portland's inner east side. We were exhausted by the time we got in,
thick-headed from the days of driving and the hours of drinking
that had followed quitting time, and the interior registered as a
pleasingly decrepit blur. I caught glimpses of arching windows
along one wall, crumbling patches on the ceiling, an antique bou-
doir, a brass bed, a warm quilt. We didn't get a much better view
in the morning, either, as Jaeha woke us before dawn with steaming coffee in hand and hustled us out the door and into the car.
Before we knew it we were back on the road for the commute to
work.

On the way, the still-sleeping city drifting by the windows,
we talked a little more about what the coming days and weeks
had in store. We could expect a somewhat protracted initiation
process, Jaeha reiterated, and one thing we needed to know up
front, and which we'd probably already figured out: nothing at
Rain Dragon happened in a very straightforward manner. There
was no ladder to climb per se, no bases to touch. Many people
came and went, and the ones with real staying power were the
ones who forged their own paths. The ultimate goal, he said, was
the establishment of a special niche in the organization, in the

way Jaeha oversaw the flower-growing activities, or Linda, the bees, special roles in addition to the shared duties of general farm maintenance.

"The best way to get a niche," he said, "is to do some leg-work. You want to explore the whole organization if you can, and figure out the whole range of possibilities. You'll either end up attaching to a niche that already exists, or, even better, figure out a new one. You want to see what's missing from the big picture, and make it."

"What do you mean?" I said. "What kinds of niches are you talking about, exactly?"

"I don't know, fire-baked bread?" he said. "Artisanal jellies and jams? It could be anything, really. Whatever you think the world needs."

"Crystal meth," Amy said.

"Internet porn," I said.

"As long as it's all certified organic, yes, that's great."

Breakfast was served in a many-windowed dining hall lined with beams of old-growth timber. Emilio Spank, Linda Hutchins, and Michael Byles were all there, along with about a dozen other staffers and interns, talking in low morning voices. We joined the buffet line, filling our trays from a pine table crowded with steel-cut oatmeal, buttermilk biscuits, homemade granola, strong coffee, and, of course, fresh yogurt. By the time we were collecting our silverware, Jaeha had us matched with partners for the day.

"Amy, you'll be spending the morning with Linda, tending the bees, all right?" he said. "And Damon, you'll go with Emilio. He's got a project and could use your help. If you need me, just give me a call. But you're in good hands. You're going to learn a lot."

And so, as the sun rose over Rain Dragon, the crows squawking and the squirrels chittering, I found myself hacking through the forest in the wake of Emilio Spank, en route to an outbuilding that would one day serve as a storage unit for Rain Dragon's nonperishable inventory. From what I gathered, we would be tiling the floor today, and the fact I had no experience in tiling was no big deal whatsoever. I would learn by doing, and within a few hours I'd be an expert in the activity. It wasn't exactly the job I'd expected, but then again, I wasn't sure what I'd expected, having never really pictured anything about our new life beyond the day of our triumphant arrival. It was only now, passing under the wet trees, listening to Emilio talk about his most recent trip to a Hindu monastery in Poona, India, that a mild dismay began to take hold. We'd made it to Rain Dragon. And already I was wishing that some minor accident would keep the workday from coming.

A taut cobweb broke on my face. My fingers burned from the weight of the buckets loaded with bags of adhesive powder we'd picked up from the toolshed. Emilio moved so nimbly along the narrow path, I kept losing him and having to race to keep up.

Down in L.A., I thought, I'd still have been in bed. In another hour I'd have stumbled into the kitchen for my toast and coffee, and from there into the car for the commute along the Santa Monica Freeway. The next hour would have been spent creeping down the pipeline of asphalt, looking for my favorite commuters—the beautiful lady in the green Mercedes, the beefy guy with the wild orange mustache—barely noticing the graffiti and sagging cyclone fences and faded exit signs greeting me along the way. At the end of the journey I'd have come to rest in a padded office chair overlooking the gray palms of Venice Beach. And with the thought of my desk, the smell of the office supplies in my top drawer, a sudden pang of loss bloomed in my stomach. Now that my former life was so definitively behind me, I could see it for all its wonderful comfort and ease.

"Here we are," Emilio said, coming to a stop. Up ahead, a big brick cube had appeared among the trees, the roof coated in moss, the remnants of a wooden porch hanging from the front wall. The walls were threaded with ivy and the windows filmed with opaque yellow grit. Judging from the masonry, the building dated from about the same era as the main mansion. I could hear the creek rushing somewhere, and up above, the boughs of the fir trees blotted out the whitening sky.

"Our future storage facility," Emilio presented, with a sweep of the arm.

"Fantastic," I said, though I wasn't sure what kind of exclamation was in order. The prospect of more storage space didn't seem to merit all that much enthusiasm, and I couldn't tell if the state of the building was a cause for excitement or dismay.

"I don't know if you can tell," Emilio said, climbing the rickety steps, "but we're only about a hundred yards from the yogurt factory right here. A little pathway alongside the creek, and it'll be a four-minute walk. Once we get this guy watertight, we can quit schlepping everything down from the mansion."

"Great," I said. "Awesome."

The door of the building was just a piece of wood propped against the jamb. Emilio moved it aside, and we crossed from the darkness of the forest into the darker darkness of the indoors, a single large room capped by a ceiling barely visible through cobwebbed crossbeams. The floor was immaculate, though, a wide expanse of fresh, golden particleboard awaiting our tiling efforts, exhaling a sweet, woody odor that almost covered the scent of the building's deep-body mildew.

"You should have seen this place a month ago," Emilio said, dropping his buckets. "Old carpets, canning jars, rocking chairs, piled up six feet high. I found some bones in here that might have been a pterodactyl."

"Huh," I said.

"I cleaned it for about a month," he said. "Pulled out all the floorboards and put down this new subflooring. Now we're ready for the vinyl." He clapped his hands and pointed at a pile of cardboard boxes in the corner, one of which was open to reveal a slivered stack of black plastic squares. "They've been acclimatizing to the room for a couple days now. Should be ready to go."

The first task, he said, was making a snap line. I didn't know what a snap line was, but I found out when he pulled a ball of twine from his bag and stretched two strands across the room so they crossed perpendicularly. The snap line secure, he went about laying out dry runs of tile, getting the alignments right, adjusting the squares until the borders of the room were uniformly a quarter-tile wide. I stood around, waiting for orders, and every once in a while asking if there was anything I could do. Eventually Emilio said I could go ahead and move the last remaining floorboards outside, which I did—there were only about four—and then I came back and continued my hovering. My primary duty seemed to be listening to an endless anecdote about an encounter he was planning with the spirit of Saint Germain, an ascended master on Mount Shasta whose last body had manifested in the seventeenth century. According to Emilio, Saint Germain offered select visitors a drink from the cup of omnipotent life itself, and the year before had taken his friend Sierra on an astral flight to all her past incarnations.

Eventually, I got restless and asked for more physical work to do. Emilio looked around and suggested I mix the adhesive, as we were just about ready to start gluing.

"There's a faucet in the back there," he said, nodding at the back of the room. "Directions should be on the bag."

I lugged a bag of dried powder over to a grimy sink in the back, but of course when I got there I couldn't find any directions.

"I don't see any directions," I called out.

"No?" he said. "Well, just mix the stuff with water, that's the thing."

"Do you know the ratio?" I said.

"It doesn't say?" he said.

"Uh-uh."

"I'd just eyeball it."

"How thick is it supposed to be?"

"As thick as . . . I don't know . . . just hold on."

Emilio got up and lumbered over and inspected the bags. He concurred that the directions were not to be found, and decided they must have been on a piece of paper that had gotten lost along the way. He ended up making the adhesive himself, pouring the thinset powder into a bucket with an acrylic additive, mixing in the water, and emptying half the substance into a second bucket, which I understood to be mine.

"We'll work in quadrants," he said, heaving his bucket back to the middle of the room. "I'll start over on this side of the line and you do that side, all right? You just go tile by tile."

"Okay," I said. "Is that it? Any other instructions?"

"Don't slide the tiles in. Just kind of drop them. You don't get so much oozing up that way."

"Okay."

I didn't really understand what he was talking about, so I took my time getting into position. I watched Emilio crouch down near the axis of the snap lines, and I crouched near the axis, too. I watched him dip his brush and spread the adhesive on the floor, and I dipped my brush and gooped it onto the floor, too. Then I watched him gently lay the tile in place and scoot over to lay the next tile. I did the same.

I kept watching him for a few more tiles, sticking to his example as closely as possible. I dipped the brush, scraped off the excess, spread the glue, then gently dropped the tile into place. I patted it, and moved on. It turned out tiling wasn't that hard. In fact, it was easy, even automatically boring in a way. It was an okay boring, though. The kind of boring that demanded so little thought I could easily fall into my own pattern of thinking without any danger of messing up. I got to thinking about Amy for a while, what she was doing, how she was faring, and then for some reason the Raiders came into my mind. I wondered how their season would go, and whatever happened to Al Davis, the old, hard-assed owner. Was he alive? From there I drifted to the idea of Astroturf, and real sod, and then to the way flowers devoured sunlight and turned it into photosynthetic energy. How did that work?

Whenever I started to think about how boring and repetitive the job was, I just reminded myself that this was in fact important work I was doing. To the untrained observer, it might have looked like I was just laying tile in some moldering brick hut in the middle of a rain forest in the western foothills of the Cascades, but in fact I was doing a lot more: I was building a new world here. I was contributing my part to an alternative society based on principles of sustainability and justice, counteracting all the self-destructive drives that humanity had blindly adopted since the industrial era and the onset of the consumer society.

I checked my watch. It was 7:23 a.m. I would have been somewhere around Exit 34 by now, sipping my coffee, catching the second round of the morning news on public radio.

My sense of noble purpose lasted almost an hour. It was around then that my back started to ache and my knees began to hurt. I lifted my head to see how we were doing, and I was surprised by the enormity of the floor still surrounding me. The tundra of raw wood spread in every direction. Multiplying the hour or so we'd already worked by the remaining uncovered surface, I calculated we had at least three more hours of tiling to go, and I'd already run out of major thoughts to think. Outside, the sun was shining onto a world of birds and grass and interesting human interactions, none of which I was able to see from where I was crouched.

Emilio seemed to be enjoying himself, though. His hands flew from tile to tile, filling the floor space almost twice as quickly as me and making me feel guilty.

I put my head down and kept going, fitting the edge of a square to the edge of the square before. Soon I'd fallen back into a trance.

Hours passed. I barely noticed when Emilio finished his section of floor and rose, taking the measure of what he'd accomplished. I assumed he would take a short break, but instead he set right to work cutting border tiles and laying them along the edges of the room. He worked his way around the entire perimeter and then worked his way around again, the second time forcing air bubbles from under the tiles with a rolling pin. By the time he finished I was getting close to finishing my patch, though I still had another fifteen or twenty minutes to go. I was sure he'd take a break now, but without pausing he washed his bucket and went outside with a crowbar and began ripping at a windowsill on a small outlying shed.

Around eleven o'clock I finally finished my area. I rinsed my bucket and wandered outside to find Emilio still prying at the windowsill. He didn't say anything when I sidled up. I had the feeling he wasn't hugely impressed by my labor thus far. But then again, what did he expect? This was my first time tiling. Of course I'd be slow. I stood there while he brushed off the last clinging splinters and took out a measuring tape, stretching the flimsy strip vertically and horizontally.

"Anything I can do now?" I said.

"You're done?" he said, which I took as a little jab.

"I think so," I said.

"Well, you could cut two three-foot pieces out of a two-by-six if you wanted," he said, still without looking at me. "That's what we'll need for the top and bottom of this new sill."

"Two pieces, three feet long," I repeated.

"Yeah," he said. "The circular saw is under the eaves over there. Next to the generator. And if you want to get fancy with it, you can round off the edges on one side so it slips in better."

"Right."

I didn't know how to work a circular saw, but the thought of asking any questions seemed galling. So even though I only partly understood my orders, I wandered off to find the two-by-sixes. I figured the first step was locating the right wood. Once I had that in hand I'd ask for further clarification. The problem was, I couldn't even find the wood. I saw a pile of two-by-fours, but I knew that wasn't right. I also saw some old quarter rounds. I walked back inside the building, thinking the two-by-sixes might be in there, but they weren't, and then, not wanting to show Emilio that I couldn't accomplish this ridiculously simple task, I walked outside again and circled the building. I walked around three times, getting distracted on the last circuit by a batch of spotted mushrooms at the base of a fir tree, and as I turned the far corner I heard the growl of a gas generator and the squeal of a saw blade cutting into wood.

When I came up on Emilio he was standing next to a pile of freshly cut two-by-sixes, fitting a length into the space on the window he'd cleared.

"I couldn't find the wood," I said, as the sweet smell of freshly cut boards mixed with gasoline scolded me.

"Yeah, don't worry about it," he said. "I got it."

"Where was the wood?" I said.

"Right there," he said, nodding at the pile of boards I'd taken for two-by-fours.

I hovered nearby for the next five minutes, awaiting further instructions. The sun barely made it through the thick boughs of the trees. The creek sounded like a million bugs cleaning their mandibles. At last Emilio got tired of my lurking and gave me a chore that would carry me out of his line of sight.

"Here's something you could do," he said, handing me an old pickle jar filled with rusted nails. "You can sort these. Bent ones in this can. Straight ones in the jar. And if you're feeling really ambitious, you can sort them by size."

★ ★ ★

We didn't take a break until one, by which time I was starving. It was another fifteen minutes before the mansion returned to view, and by then I was almost dizzy. I was used to a punctual noon lunch break. The lunch line was a slow-moving affair, too, what with all the other workers drifting in from their morning labors, emerging from the brush in trios and pairs. At least the buffet table had been replenished since breakfast with trays of enchiladas, multiple red and green salsas, hot peppers, Spanish rice, and refried beans. A feast.

I found Amy out on the back steps of the deck, already nearly finished with her lunch. Her elbows were propped on the step behind her, and her dress was bunched in her lap to let the weak sun onto her beautiful legs. I dropped down next to her and began shoveling in my food. Kindly, she looked the other way, sipping from her glass of carrot juice until my eating pace had slowed to the degree it was worth asking me how my morning had gone.

"I'm not exactly indispensable yet," I said, snapping a band of melted cheese with my fingers. "In fact, I might even be worse than dispensable. I might be actively hurtful."

"I'm sure you weren't that bad," she said.

"I was pretty bad," I said, and recapped my morning's tiling adventure. I tried to spin my incompetence as somehow charming—a comedy of manners—and thankfully she went along with this routine, smiling ruefully, laughing out loud when I got to the wood pile, shaking her head at my ultimate, degrading chore of sorting nails. In the end, though, she stuck with her upbeat argument that I could have done a lot worse.

"I could have burned something down," I agreed.

"First day," she said, patting my foot. "Whatever."

I concentrated on trapping the last few pieces of rice in the tines of my fork. The sound of a basketball game—the scuff of the ball on pavement, the whang of the loose rim—drifted from somewhere nearby. An intern walked near the railing with a pile of clean dishes.

"But what about you?" I said, cleaning the last bits from my plate. "How was your morning?"

"Good," she said, her eyes closed to the sun.

"Really?" I said. "Good?"

"Yeah," she said, "It was good. Really good, actually."

"What was so good about it?" I said.

"It was just good," she said. "It was weird."

"What did you do?"

"We got new bees."

"New bees?"

She hummed affirmatively, resting the glass on the wood stair. She arched her back and rearranged her skirt. And then, lightly, almost like the topic wasn't worth talking about at all, she proceeded to describe the great triumph of her first morning's work at Rain Dragon.

"We drove out to this old logging town," she said. "At the end of this gorgeous road up into the mountain, almost at the timberline. I don't know where we were, exactly, but the town was a real shit hole—just a couple blocks of old storefronts and some RVs around the edge. The only thing open was this Chinese restaurant. We walk in and it's filled with taxidermied animals. I'm serious. Huge grizzly bears and antelope and cougars in these giant vitrines. Animals from all over the world. From Africa, Asia, everywhere. Turns out the guy who opened the restaurant was a big-game hunter. All his spoils are still in there. And now it's this shitty Chinese place. Anyway. We go in and ask for the line cook, and this old Chinese guy with about five teeth and a hook for a hand comes out of the kitchen. He hugs Linda like she's his daughter or something and takes us back to his truck. He goes to the bed and pulls out four little crates. They're filled with bees. They're like these vibrating shoeboxes, these little bricks of energy or something. It was amazing. It was like a drug deal. Linda says this guy's bees are the best in the country."

Bees, she went on, were fascinating creatures. They'd been around for thirty million years already. Their wings stroked 11,400 times per minute. They visited between fifty and a hundred flowers on a given pollen-collecting mission.

They also happened to represent a real growth sector at Rain Dragon. From what Linda was telling her, the raw honey was gaining customers every quarter, and the beeswax lip balm and honey bath soap were coming on strong, too. If demand continued building at its current rate, she was definitely going to need more hives soon, which meant at least one full-time assistant. And somehow Amy was already on the top of the list.

"Shit," I said. "Do you already have a niche?"

"We'll see," she said, closing her eyes again, a smile tugging at her mouth. "It might not work out. You never know."

"I told you something would happen."

"We'll see. But I don't care. They're just so cool, the bees. When we got back we sprayed them down with sugar water to get them out of the box. They eat the sugar off their little legs and they become like mud. They just ooze out onto the mesh."

"You did that?" I said.

"I oozed the bees," she said. "Yes."

By the time the bell chimed, signaling that work was to resume, Amy had gone in search of Linda, and whatever new batch of chores she had waiting. I bussed my plate and went looking for Emilio. I found him waiting for me at the head of the stairs. He greeted me with a terse nod, and I followed him down the path back to the brick house where the unfinished windows awaited. The other workers wandered off into the cradle of the land, too, disappearing down the pathways and into the aisles of trees to whatever tasks they'd left undone. Some drifted into the offices and some filed into the Quonset huts. Some stayed in the dining room for what looked like a book club meeting. The birds had quit singing for the day. The slow hours of late afternoon stretched ahead. I couldn't say I was exactly looking forward to whatever was in store, but knowing Amy was happy made everything a little better. If she was happy, I figured, then I must be happy, too.

FOUR

DO WHAT YOU LOVE, and the money will come. It sounded
like an excellent principle, in theory, and for the next few weeks
I honestly took the sentiment to heart. I tagged along with whoever would let me and tried my hand at whatever they told me to
do. I worked the conveyor belt, I loaded boxes, I stacked boxes,
I loaded boxes onto palettes, I weeded the lettuce beds, I made
deliveries, I watched Michael solder together a new fruit-peeling
machine, I watched Simon, the bookkeeper, installing new
software.

My guides were all sweet, enthusiastic, generous people, with
many insights to share into the workings of Rain Dragon, not to
mention the geology and climate of the region in general. They
had interesting hobbies and opinions about contemporary culture and politics to discuss. They had peculiar fashion styles to
decipher, accents to parse. And all had fascinating stories about
how they'd ended up at Rain Dragon.

Michael had once been an aerospace engineer. He'd worked
on drone control panel technology down in San Diego, a job he'd
taken mostly for its proximity to excellent surfing. Engineering
had always come easily to him, and some of his clearest ideas
tended to arrive out on the ocean. He'd solved algorithms out

there, envisioned ingenius electrical bypass systems. Then one day he'd had a moral insight. He'd realized his daily work, as abstract and challenging as it was, existed solely to dismember and maim other people who might like to surf. At that moment, he decided he couldn't clock in for the war machine anymore, and he fled to Oregon to apply his brainpower to something more positive. He missed the surfing, he said, but otherwise didn't regret the move whatsoever.

Linda was an eastern girl. She'd moved West to escape her blue-blood family and had found more opportunities than she'd ever imagined. She'd become a Jane-of-all-trades, teaching classics at a community college, playing slide guitar in a country/western band, leading cancer-survivor support groups for women without health insurance. The secret to thriving here, she asserted, was never admitting lack of expertise. Out here, unlike Massachusetts, no one worried about credentials. You were who you said you were. You could even be incredibly mediocre at something, and no one seemed to notice or care.

Her beekeeping was something that had come about during her search for a cure for her breast cancer, and she had fallen in love with her swarm. She was in remission now, whether due to Western science or Eastern mysticism, she wasn't sure. But one thing she knew: she was sticking with her bees just in case.

Simon was the child of Mennonites. He devoted his free time to giving hospice care to immigrant communities. Michelle, the secretary, was a drug dealer, full of stories about louche parties in the penthouses of Portland, and desirous of little more than to be left alone during certain hours to negotiate her deals. Mr. Lam, the creamery manager, was a Laotian immigrant, and nothing at Rain Dragon ever seemed to bother him in the least.

They were all lovely, adventurous people from wildly different points on the map, and all of them had found exactly what they were looking for at Rain Dragon. For some, it was a vehicle of social change. For others, a refuge. For others, an arbiter of distinction and good taste. Interestingly, though, no one could seem to agree on what the name Rain Dragon meant.

"It's a weather thing. Like an El Niño," Linda said, cleaning her honeycomb. "I don't know the exact conditions. Probably some kind of freezing fog or something."

"I think it's a drug reference," Emilio said, practicing his judo near the creek. "I'm pretty sure it means a group hallucination. And if it doesn't, it should."

"I think the words just sound good together," Michael said, greasing the conveyor belt with his natural WD-40 substitute. "They have a nice ring."

But as pleasant as everyone was, as helpful and supportive, the opportunities for new positions on the farm turned out to be pretty scant. Everyone already had their own routines in place, their own little fiefdoms to protect, and they didn't seem to relish the idea of anyone else knowing exactly what they did all day, how much or how little they got away with out of sight. If anything, I found, the farm was already greatly overstaffed.

It didn't help that I had so little to offer. I'd grown up in the suburbs, far from any tractors or livestock, and my father—in some revolt against his own midwestern upbringing's dull practicalities—had never bothered teaching me the basics of the masculine arts. I hadn't learned about carpentry or auto repair as a kid, or been indoctrinated into the joys of cordless tool maintenance. It was only in adulthood that I'd started to see his disinterest for what it was—a kind of prejudice against his own dad—and by that time it was too late. I was no longer inclined to install shelves, or extend branch circuits, or figure out how best to pack some box. Like my dad, I was more comfortable in the realms of the wholly abstract. So long as a given activity held no practical use value whatsoever, I was intrigued. As soon as any sensible realities kicked in, I tended to drift. It became evident to everyone quickly that I was basically dead weight, demanding more effort to order around than to just let be.

I kept trying, though, hoping this new place and these new people would magically bring out some new, more capable part of me. I spent a whole day building a rock wall alongside the kitchen garden, only to come back the next day and find it rebuilt, more sturdily. I dug some postholes, unevenly spaced. I helped paint the round barn, but arrived on the scene too late to feel like a real member of the team. One day I even assisted in the unbuttoning of a cow, which involved plunging an arm into the cow's birth canal and blindly unfastening the remains of the placenta from the womb, but I only made it to my elbow before I had to excuse myself and get some fresh air.

I probably would have given up and gone off to find a job at a bookstore or coffee shop if not for the fact that Amy was responding to the farm life so passionately. Every day she came home to our little makeshift corner of Jaeha's warehouse bursting with new bee-related arcana to share. Honeybees were not native to North America, she said, but had been brought to the continent by early European settlers. Worker bees lived only six weeks in the busy summer months, and literally worked themselves to death. Bees were the linchpin of all life on earth, and without them the whole chain of being would probably crumble. In the summer she and Linda were planning to take the pollinating bees on the road, renting the swarm out to apple and pear orchards in eastern Washington. In the fall, they would attend a conference in Yakima.

"You've already got your whole year planned," I said, moping.

"You'll find something soon," she said. "Be patient."

"I've tried everything. More than once."

"Seriously. Just give it a chance. You're doing great. Everyone loves you here. They tell me all the time."

"Now you're just making me feel pathetic."

"You're trying. Something will open up."

Out of love for Amy, if nothing else, I kept pushing. I swept, I chopped vegetables, I cleaned gutters, and in the late afternoons I got into the habit of hiking over to the northeastern corner of the property, the site of the future methane digester, a contraption Michael said would someday channel the gas of the farm's fermenting cow manure into usable electricity. The patch of ground wasn't much to look at yet—a bald hilltop scored with half-dug trenches and grids of string—but once the turbine was purchased and shipped from Germany, it would supposedly be transformed. In the meantime, occasional preparatory digging efforts continued as anyone had the time or wherewithal. I liked the solitude the work offered, and even though I didn't get much out of the shoveling, it was at least something I could manage to do unsupervised.

Usually, after carting a few wheelbarrows of dirt to the piles growing on the far edge of the hilltop, I took a little break to watch the afternoon light shift on Rain Dragon's grounds. From my perch on the hill, I could take in the patchwork gardens surrounding the mansion's rear deck, the ribbed metal rooftop of the Quonset huts shining in the sun, the water tower casting its long shadow, the clusters of sheep, goats, and cows in the pulsing grass. I could even keep an eye on the Rain Dragon workers, their slow, unsynchronized movements along the trails, identifying each one by clothing and gait, just far enough away that no one suspected they were being watched.

Do what you love. The thought itched at me. If I knew what I loved, I thought, I might be able to get somewhere. You weeded a bed, and the weeds just came up again, though. You watered a plant, it needed water soon enough. What was the point?

Do what you love. I contemplated the notion from many sides. But what if you loved doing nothing at all? What if you'd been raised nominally Buddhist, under the conviction that worldly desire was the great enemy of enlightenment? What if you'd been taught reality was just a transitory illusion, and most human exertion a fundamental waste of time? Part of the reason I'd become a CPA in the first place was for the daily humbling it offered, the daily extinguishing of want. It was a job that reliably kept every unattainable aspiration—the root of all suffering—at bay.

Amy and I were running low on money, and still I couldn't seem to make myself act. The desperation wasn't strong enough yet. The pain wasn't pointed enough. I felt like I was locked in a game of chicken with the future, and I didn't want to swerve until absolutely necessary. So I just sat, waiting, wondering what would happen, half expecting God to come and shake me out of my torpor, and hoping, if he ever did, that he didn't shake me too hard.

It took a few weeks for my waiting to end. Early in May, I was on the rock I'd come to think of as my own, watching the wind riffle the aspens, when the butterfly bushes behind me rasped and footsteps sounded on the dirt not too far away. I assumed it was Jaeha, my only regular guest, and I didn't bother turning around as the steps drew closer and stopped a few paces off to the right. I just kept staring at the land, letting my visitor sink into the view alongside me, and it was only after a full minute of shared watching that I bothered to offer a hello. The voice that came back wasn't Jaeha's, though, but that of the CEO, Peter Hawk.

"Howdy," he said, a wry bite to his tone. "Nice view, huh."

"Oh," I said. I was caught. "Yeah, for sure. Amazing."

"One of my favorite spots," he said. "I don't come up here too often anymore. I oughta check in more."

At that moment, I probably should have jumped up and started looking busy. I should have grabbed the shovel and tossed some dirt into the wheelbarrow just for show. But for some reason, I couldn't seem to make myself do it. I'd been sitting there too long. Inertia had taken hold, and it had become more powerful than shame. And anyway, who was I going to fool? I'd come there to avoid work. It would have been absurd to pretend otherwise. The most dignified thing to do, in my mind, was to stay still, keep staring, and try my best to act like everything was perfectly normal.

Neither of us said anything for a while. We kept our eyes on the world down below, marking the movements of a tiny Emilio mending a fence post, a tiny Linda pruning a hedge. I hadn't seen much of Peter of late. He'd been out of town a lot, flying to Europe and Japan to deliver his lectures on how best to fix the broken circle of food production and consumption that had overtaken the modern world. When he was home, he generally stayed in his third-floor office, working on his papers, descending only occasionally to lend a hand, solve a problem, or offer some inspirational talk, and then quickly going back to the consulting realm he mostly inhabited.

Still, if I expected to land a spot at Rain Dragon, I probably needed to make some kind of decent impression.

The breeze stiffened, relaxed. I stole a glance at Peter's profile, hoping for some clue as to how to proceed. His nose looked strong in the splash of the raw sun, suggesting intelligence and refinement, his brow especially severe, suggesting resolve.

"So, uh, how's it going?" I managed.

"Good," he said. "Beautiful day, right?"

"Totally," I said. And again we lapsed into silence. I wanted to keep it in check, though, so I added, "So, you were gone for a while? Is that right?"

"Just got home," he said. "Yep."

"And you were where?" I said.

"Big Sur this time."

"Oh. Beautiful down there."

"Sure is."

The conversation faltered, but thankfully this time Peter took up the yoke.

"Looking real good up here," he said, glancing at the partly dug pits. "Making real progress."

"Slowly but surely," I said, with what I hoped sounded like resolve. Thankfully Peter rarely visited the hilltop, and the gradual movement of dirt looked more impressive than it was.

"The digester will be pretty amazing someday," he said. "All that anaerobic energy. Just waiting to come out."

"Michael says the turbine is pretty expensive."

"We'll get it. We have to. Shit into energy. That's the dream."

Somebody's dog romped on the grass near the mansion's deck and snuffled its way into the underbrush. A flock of birds spread and contracted and lit in a gum tree. Finally, as if I'd only been taking a short break this whole time, I pulled myself upright and went back to my shoveling, assuming Peter would take off pretty quickly. Surely he had other obligations to attend to.

But instead he stayed, picking at the bunchgrass, taking a piss on a patch of forget-me-nots, and finally returning to his original spot, where he stood with his legs widely planted and arms folded, scrutinizing the mansion's stately roofline. I filled a wheelbarrow and dumped the dirt on the edge of the hill, and was about halfway through my second load when he called over, his eyes still on the view below.

"Hey, Damon," he said.

"Uh-huh?"

"I wonder if you got a few minutes?"

"Right now?" I said, as if my digging duties were incredibly urgent and I hated the thought of leaving my post.

"Yeah. I thought you might want to hit the milking barn with me for a little while."

"Yeah, okay, sure," I said. I would have preferred staying at my rock, but what choice did I have? He was the boss, even if I wasn't yet getting paid.

I stowed my shovel and joined Peter at the head of the trail. As we started down to the round barn we talked about nothing much. John Boehner, the congressman from wherever, was a terrible person, we agreed, psychologically damaged in some profound way. The Blazers would never win another championship thanks to the Indian curse Bill Walton had almost certainly placed on the franchise in the late 1970s. The weather was unseasonably warm, but still had the chance to turn chilly. By the time we got to the pasture, we were engaged in a reasonably animated back-and-forth about Peter's long-standing fascination with the writings of Krishnamurti.

I was getting the distinct feeling, though, that his interest in my company was not entirely innocent. Most likely, the griping among the other staffers had finally reached him. Word was out that I was having motivational problems, that I was failing to contribute my share, that I didn't seem to be embracing the workload, some variation on that theme. I probably should have already bowed out and saved us the embarrassment of this forced intervention long ago.

"I thought you might want to do some milking with me," he said. "This is one of my favorite things in the world. A real, simple pleasure. I wish I got to do this all day long, I really do."

"Great," I said, and more than ever I knew I was being tested.

We entered the wide barn door into the smell of dry straw and packed earth, and ambled along the circle of stalls, passing black cows and white cows until Peter finally stopped in front of a mangy brown cow he called McQuillen. She was an aging, sag-backed animal, her hide blotchy, her feet caked in shit, but Peter didn't seem to mind any of that. He parked himself on a three-legged stool in front of the pink, veined udder and set to milking.

"You ever done this before?" he asked.

"Nope," I said.

"Old-timers say a wet tit helps their grip," he said, rubbing his hands on his knees. "They like to spit on their hands to get things going. But we only use the dry grip here. Wet's unsanitary." He reached out and grabbed two teats and began pulling on them in rhythm, spurting milk into the gauze-covered bucket until the hard streams rang on the metal walls.

"You start with the top," he said, "and you pull down. Then you let up and relax your grip and the udder fills with milk again. And while you're eased up over here, you're pulling down over here, with your other hand. She likes it. So don't worry about that. You're relieving the pressure in there."

The bucket sang, and like a picture in some children's book, two mewling cats materialized from the shadows. Peter showed off by shooting streams of milk directly into their mouths, a few times hitting the pink targets of their tongues.

After a few minutes we switched positions. I sat on the stool and took the teats. They felt like warm, spongy carrots. I didn't want to look too fussy, and tried my best to match his enthusiasm for the job, but for me the milk only drizzled into the bucket. I attempted a few different grips and tempos, but nothing caught. I had trouble concentrating knowing someone was watching me. Plus, I knew this was mostly ceremonial labor. The vast majority of the milk came to Rain Dragon from other dairy farms, and most of our own milking was done by machines. I resented the fact I was being asked to submit to this theater. When the cow eventually wandered off, bell dinking on its neck, I called it quits, looking expectantly at Peter for my next challenge.

He'd gone over to another stall and was tossing some feed in a trough. It appeared our disciplinary conversation was going to have the pretense of casualness.

"Good stuff, right?" he said, as I loitered nearby.

"Very satisfying," I said.

"You've been here a few weeks now, is that right?" Peter said, returning the bag of feed to its hook.

"More like a few months."

"You're liking it all right?"

"Oh, yeah. It's great. Amazing. We're just so glad to be a part of the team."

"And what were you doing before you got here? I don't know if I ever got that story."

I hesitated, not sure what to say. To admit I was an accountant was always such a disappointment to people, and I dreaded the look of mild pity that would most likely come into his eyes. At the same time, the advertising industry where I'd done the accounting was an object of great scorn at Rain Dragon, a major part of the rapacious industrial combine everyone was explicitly against. On both fronts, I was slightly embarrassed. I considered scrolling back and framing my past in a different way entirely, highlighting my volunteer work, my spotty creative endeavors. But what was the point? Most likely I'd be out of there in a few days anyway. I went ahead and cast myself in the worst possible light.

"The last couple years I was in advertising," I said.

"Oh?" he said, with less opprobrium than I might have expected. "Where at?"

"Meier and Hamburg," I said.

"Yeah, I've heard of it," he said, surprising me again. "Big place. They've got some major clients, don't they?"

"Mennen," I said. "Pennzoil. Pepsi was there awhile."

"Do anything I'd have seen?"

I rattled off some of the firm's prouder accomplishments: the logo for a sweatshirt company—a knotted rainbow—and the tagline for a celebrity perfume, "You smell like love." I also mentioned the campaigns for running shoes and sesame crackers, iced tea and deodorant. I'd kept the books on all those accounts, but the nature of advertorial authorship, I'd learned, was such that whoever was doing the talking claimed the credit. When it came to the manipulation of clichés in the interest of capital, who could really claim authorship, anyway?

"I liked that iced tea ad," Peter said. "That was funny. You're good."

I shrugged, hoping to wrap up the conversation. "It's not that hard," I said. "It's not, you know, farming."

"So what made you want to leave?" he said.

"Amy wanted to get out of L.A.," I said. "I wanted to go where she went."

"And you didn't want to find something in that line of work up here?"

"It just kind of ran its course."

"I see," Peter said, wandering out of the barn into the gentle springtime sun. High above, giant white clouds were passing like migrating whales, and the dogwood trees were teeming with buds. From the way Peter stared intently at the flattened patches of grass, I could tell that his interest was alert to something. As much as people made a show of hating advertising, they also inevitably felt some fascination toward the industry. "Sounds like you had the knack," he said. "That's interesting."

"This is much better," I said. "Amy's a lot happier now. We both are."

"Your friend Amy is really helping Linda out," he said. "She's a real catch."

"Yeah," I said, though whether he meant as an employee or something more, I wasn't sure. Maybe he was even leveling some kind of backhanded insult: she was a catch, and by extension,

I wasn't a catch. She was more of a catch than I deserved. In any case, I agreed with him enthusiastically. "She's fantastic."

"So anyway, now you're here," he said.

"That's right," I said. "We're here to stay. I hope."

"You've had a chance to poke around now. Is anything calling out so far?"

"No real calls thus far, no."

"What about sales? We're always looking for people who want to hustle up more shelf space out there."

"I'm not much of a salesman."

"We need carpenters, too."

"No experience, sadly."

"Deliveries?"

"Seems like most of that work's taken."

"How about day care?" he suggested. "People have talked about starting a day-care center here for years. There are farm families all around these parts that could use something like that. I know it could work if someone put their mind to it."

"Hmmm. Yeah," I said. Watching children wasn't exactly what I had in mind for my next few years.

Peter pulled on his lower lip, comprehending that we had reached an impasse. I appreciated his effort—I knew he had better things to do—but sadly I couldn't see doing any of the things he'd suggested thus far. I'd dug myself deep into a hole, and I was having trouble seeing myself doing anything, period. He wiped his hands on his jeans and looked me over with a new level of scrutiny, examining my unshaven face, my loose, lanky arms, my long, knob-kneed legs. Was it worth the effort? Apparently so. By the time he'd snapped back up to my soft eyes, he had seemingly jumped ahead to the next thought.

"You got a few more minutes?" he said.

"Sure," I said.

"Then come on," he said. "I want to show you something. It might be something you'll like."

Before I could respond, Peter was already marching off, his legs pumping, his arms swinging, leaving the round barn behind. I hurried to keep up, and as we angled onto the path to the mansion he explained his new line of thinking.

"You know, I should have talked to you about this a long time ago," he said. "I've just been gone so much lately, it's hard to keep up with everything. The fact you've got this media experience is really interesting to me. It's one of the last things anyone wants to think about around here. Everyone's into the making, but not the marketing, you know? And I don't have the time for it these days, either. We have a monthly promotions meeting, but I doubt we've generated a decent idea in two years. The meeting's going on right now, as it happens. So what do you say we get up there and sit in? Maybe you'll have some new ideas for us."

"Don't count on it," I said, embarrassment already seeping into my stomach region. My little prevaricating was already on the verge of being exposed. If he expected me to toss off some incredible PR ideas on the spot, he was about to be sadly disappointed.

"That's the spirit," he said. "Modesty. I like it."

We hurried through the trees, over the creek, up the stairs to the deck, as I racked my brain for some reason to peel away. I had a doctor appointment? I was picking up someone at the airport? I couldn't think of anything fast enough. Within moments we were entering the back door to find the PR meeting underway.

As it turned out, the whole of Rain Dragon's PR team was

Jaeha and Linda. They sat together in the Meditation Room, a high-ceilinged multipurpose meeting area just off the main deck, surrounded by Persian carpets, fringed throw pillows, and a gigantic rice paper lampshade hanging from the rafters. Not far away stood a lone dry-erase board filled with words and phrases connected by furious arrows—PURPOSE? WHY? WHAT IS THE VISION? THE VISION OF THE VISION?—the product of a brainstorming session that had trailed off long ago into unresolution.

"Mind if we join in?" Peter said, already lowering himself onto the floor and making himself comfortable. "We were in the neighborhood. I want Damon to see some of this."

"Not at all," Jaeha said. "We were kind of hoping you'd come by. We've got something to show you."

"Great," he said. "Let's see it."

Peter gestured for me to take a place beside him on the floor, and although I felt like something of an intruder, I sat down.

The day's agenda, it turned out, consisted of a single item—the finalizing of a new package design for the liter low-fat yogurt tub, Rain Dragon's biggest seller. It was the first in a series of design changes Jaeha and Linda were planning to institute in the interest of broadening the brand's public appeal.

"Without a bigger distribution network opening up anytime soon," Linda elaborated, largely for my benefit, "we're having to think more creatively about expanding our market share. How can Rain Dragon reach out beyond its base clientele of friends and hardcore organic food lovers? How can our products stand out on the shelves? The old carton design with the landscape and the sun rising and everything is fine, and has its place, but it's way too earthy for most people's taste. The new design we're thinking about is meant to attract more mainstream consumers."

"Just show us what you've got," Peter said, testily. "We get the idea."

"You want to know a little bit about how we got here?" Linda said. "We've been working on this—"

"Nah, nah, we know the drill. Just show us."

They looked at other blankly. They would have preferred to give the whole story of their creative process, and properly frame their ideas, but Peter wasn't interested and there was no point arguing. Without ceremony, Jaeha reached into a cardboard box and pulled out the fruits of their labor, a gleaming new plastic tub printed with a fresh graphical identity.

"Here it is," he said. "The product of all our research and development."

"We're really happy with it," Linda said, mildly.

Peter took the bucket from Jaeha, looked at it briefly, and handed it to me. I looked it over with sober decorum. The new design was simple enough. The lettering was clean and thin, and the colors—lemon and blueberry—were soothingly wan. In the background floated vaguely jazzy geometrical shapes, mostly triangles and rectangles with fuzzy edges. The majority of the remaining surface was white. I could see what they were going for. They wanted something reassuring and hygienic, with a light kick of harmless whimsy on the side to appeal to the children. It was a bucket that could have slipped easily into the refrigerators of Safeway beside anything from Dannon or Yoplait.

"People think the old label looked too grubby," Linda said. "Too weird. We wanted the new label to feel really reassuring to people. And clean. And fun."

"We hired a friend of Simon's," Jaeha said. "He's very good."

"What do you think?" Peter said, as I inspected the tub.

"Yeah," I said, turning the cylinder over in my hands. "Yeah. It's all right."

"Come on," he pushed. "Tell us what you think. You're a professional, right? Educate us."

"You're a professional?" Jaeha said. This was news to him.

"Sure," I said. "I buy things."

I turned the bucket a few more times, wondering how much effort Jaeha and Linda had spent on this redesign. I knew these graphics assignments generally looked a lot easier than they were. I'd heard enough designers grousing about the reception of their work to understand that everything took painstaking effort. "Just move this line here." "Just change that color there." None of it happened by itself. But on the other hand, I didn't see any reason to lie about what I saw here, either. I'd probably be out the door by the end of the week. I could afford honesty.

"You know, I don't think it looks much like Rain Dragon," I said, gently setting the plastic container in the middle of the circle. I was almost surprised by the conviction in my voice, but there it was: I'd always kind of liked Rain Dragon's packaging. It had always struck me as genuine and relaxed—those cruddy, hand-drawn lines, those amateur attempts at mountains and clouds. "There's no real character here," I added. "You guys, I mean, we, have a great personality to share, a great story to tell. The history of the property, the mission of organic food production. I don't see any of that reflected in this packaging. It seems . . . I don't know . . . sterile."

Peter nodded, wanting more. I'd forgotten the power of a contrary opinion in this kind of setting, the authority that ac-crued to anyone who expressed negativity with some level of certainty. I hadn't realized I missed listening in on these concepting sessions. And after weeks of failure out in the fields, the sense of some competence came as a giant relief.

"Who drew this?" I said, batting at the old tub with its scrawled graphics.

"Michelle," Jaeha said. "One of the secretaries."

"See, that's a story right there," I said. "Rain Dragon is so down-to-earth the secretary designs the label. That's grassroots. That's powerful to people. In a mass-market economy, people want that kind of authenticity. You want that story on your Web site. I understand you want to relaunch the brand in some way. You want to reach more people. But you don't want to start from scratch, either. You don't want to lose the people you have."

"So what would you do?" Linda asked.

"For the package? Off the top of my head? I'd stick with the old drawing. Add some spot color, maybe. But keep this basic look. This is your voice. Work with what you have. There are other ways of getting attention. Lots of ways."

"Enlighten us," Peter said.

"Okay," I said, and scanned through the standard industry list of attention-grabbing PR ideas in my head. "How about a music festival? The farm is an amazing venue. Get a few bands, build a stage. You get three hundred people out here, hand out free samples, and those three hundred people become your sales force. You want to influence the people who influence other people, is the thing. That's one way. Or sponsor a team. Or choose some kind of charity. The way this works is not one big statement. It's lots of little connected statements adding together."

"We should maybe write some of this down," Peter said, prodding Linda to captain the whiteboard.

"Publicity stunts are outdated," I continued, settling in to my own pleasing authority on the topic, "but I have a soft spot for them anyway. I like biplanes pulling banners over beaches. I like skywriting. You could sponsor scavenger hunts. You remember *Charlie and the Chocolate Factory*? How about a golden ticket inside a few cartons, and whoever finds them gets a vacation? Eh. That's a corny idea. But you see what I mean. There are a lot of ways to get attention. I wouldn't throw away the whole identity just yet."

"This isn't what I thought you were going to say," Linda said, racing to catch up with the pen.

"I thought you'd like the new design," said Jaeha. "It's slick."

"Sure. And slick has its place. But it's about being true to who you actually are. And standing out for the right reasons." Almost unconsciously, I was echoing the words of my former boss, Dan Hamburg, a high-minded adman who never saw any contradiction between his own lofty ideals and the art of selling things. I'd heard him use this line of argument on dozens of clients before, assuring them they were essentially good and upstanding citizens of the world, and that a few simple, clearly enunciated acts of speech could inform the public of such. Watching him, I'd learned that one of the main fallacies of advertising was the notion that it was about communicating anything to the consumer at large; in fact, the advertiser's job was primarily to tell the client what they wanted to hear in ever new and more invigorating ways.

"This makes sense to me," Peter said. "If we can't be ourselves, I don't see the point."

"Exactly," I said. "This is about being yourself in the biggest way possible."

"So it's really just a matter of figuring out who we are."

"Exactly!"

From there we turned to logistical matters: event coordination, the art of the press release, the mystery of buying media. We discussed the importance of names: Rain Dragon versus Rain Dragon Organics, and the utility of keeping uniform nomenclature across the spectrum of products. In the end we came up with a sizable list of potential directions to pursue, more than anyone would likely accomplish in the next six months, if not a year.

Peter rubbed his callused hands together. "This is good," he said, standing. "This is really good. This is the kind of session we've been needing to have for a long time now. I think we got more accomplished in the last half hour than we have in the last year and a half. Let's move forward on these suggestions, all right? I'm excited. Damon, you want to take charge of these initiatives? What do you think? Is this something that'd be up your alley?"

"Me?" I said. I was still staring at the whiteboard, trying to sort the clouds of words into useful categories. "Take charge?"

"I've heard all I need to hear," Peter said. "Jaeha? Linda? You have any objections?"

"God, no," Jaeha said.

"Take over," Linda said. "Please."

"Excellent," Peter declared. "Meet our new publicity director. Or marketing guerilla. Or whatever you want to call yourself. I don't care. Tell Simon. He'll do the paperwork. Very exciting stuff here, Damon. I'm really pleased we talked today. Go ahead and get started however you see fit. All right? I'll check in next week and see how things are going."

And with that he departed, leaving me with Linda and Jaeha under the floating rice paper globe.

"Nice job," Linda said, hurrying to collect her papers and get out of the room before Peter changed his mind and redeposited the PR chores on her table. "Lots of good ideas. You're going to have a lot of fun, I can tell."

"Yeah," Jaeha said, punching my arm. "You pro. I think you just wrote yourself a niche."

Usually I could count on finding Amy at the beehives in the afternoon, so after descending the back steps into the blossoming gardens I headed over to give her the good news. Sure enough, I found her swaddled in her veil and canvas jumpsuit, lumbering among the hives with her smoker, a metal cone packed with smoldering burlap. From behind a wild rhododendron I watched her lift the lids on the boxes and gust in the smoke to calm the brood, then pull out the honeycombs and count the bees on each slat of wood. When her rounds were finally over, she went back to the shed and stripped off her helmet, at which point I couldn't wait any longer. I leaped like a cougar from behind a tree trunk and pretended to maul her.

"You fucking idiot!" she said. "You scared me!"

I wrestled to keep her in my arms, and landed a kiss on her forehead, another on her chin, before her elbows came up and wedged against my ribs.

"Guess what," I said.

"You ate something you liked."

"No."

"You watched something on TV."

"No," I said. "Try harder."

"I have no idea."

"Actually, it's kind of hard to explain. I'm not really sure what happened myself."

I proceeded to give her an account of the day's events the best

I could. Peter's appearance, our visit to the round barn and the Meditation Room, my new title. Her reaction was confusion at first—I'd been where? Doing what?—but eventually she came around, and her second reaction was more like gratifying pride and relief. With two paychecks we could finally move out of Jae-ha's place. We could finally unpack the boxes we had in storage. We could finally really start living.

"You're going to love it," she said. "I know you are."

"Might be a huge mistake," I said.

"Of course it's not," Amy said. "Peter knows what he's doing."

"If you say so."

We decided a celebratory hike was in order. It was a beautiful afternoon, and in the last month everything at Rain Dragon had erupted into green fire. It had started quietly enough, with a single maple shoot filtering the sun through fresh, starry leaves, and spread quickly, jumping to the plum tree speckled with fine bright green points, and scattering onto the grass, which had grown to knee length in a week. Sparks of yellow Scotch broom had sprayed from the road shoulder and the dogwood trees had ignited into pink, in turn igniting the anemone and ladyslipper cracking through the moist beds. The fire had followed a rope of grape winding its way over the arbor and snuck onto the magnolia tree, popping open its trembling buds like firecrackers. Branch to branch, hill to hill, the fire had grown, until the whole countryside was burning green. The green poplars and green oregano. The green camellia and the green euphorbia. One green being with one green mind.

We took our regular route through a stand of fir trees, past a small waterfall, to the edge of a clear cut mounded with honeysuckle and mountain heather. Amy sat near a rain-softened stump and I sat down behind her, and together we watched three planes slowly crossing the sky, their white contrails fattening in the long spaces behind them. I massaged her shoulders as a shining, oblique triangle briefly hung overhead, and then gradually the sky healed. The white scars faded. The blue skin returned to perfect smoothness.

For the next hour, as the sun sank, the meadow was our bedroom. The fresh grass was our mattress. The pinkening sky was our wallpaper. The milky stars our enormous, domed roof.

SUMMER

FIVE

"HOW LONG HAVE YOU BEEN at Rain Dragon?" asked the stone-faced Japanese electronics executive, the lenses of his sunglasses like two black voids in the summer light.

"About five months," I said. "Give or take."

"And what do you do here on the farm, exactly?" asked the biofuel venture capitalist from Marin, a fatless man in a mock turtleneck and shoes that fit his toes like gloves.

"Lead booster," I said. "Head cheerleader. 'Public Relations' is what my card says."

"What does that mean, more precisely?" asked one of the VC's two underlings, also in a mock turtleneck.

"My duties are still coming into focus," I said. "Basically, I write Rain Dragon's press releases, I design advertisements, I do outreach. And then there are special projects I take on, too."

"Tell them about the rock concert," Peter said, standing just outside the half circle of visitors in the vegetable garden. He was doing his best to stay out of the conversation and allow a clear channel of communication to open between myself, Rain Dragon's employee, and the day's tour group of Japanese executives, California entrepreneurs, and a single reporter from the

Oregon Business Journal, but as usual, he was finding it hard to avoid inserting himself.

"I organized a rock show," I told the group. "It was down in the pasture, just last weekend. It went all day long. It was free to anyone who wanted to drive out. We were expecting about fifty people. We had almost five hundred."

"And how did it go?" Peter prodded.

"Well. They were all incredibly well-behaved guests. They even cleaned up after themselves."

"And we've been hearing about Rain Dragon T-shirts showing up all over town ever since," Peter said. "We can't make them fast enough. And tell them about the balloons, too."

"I hired some hot-air balloons," I explained. "In San Francisco, Portland, and Seattle. They landed in public parks and handed out samples of the new boysenberry frozen yogurt popsicle. It was pretty popular."

"I saw one," said a guy from the Marin contingent. "My kid was floored. He talked about it for a week."

"We landed the front page in the *Seattle Times*," Peter said. "Above the fold. 'Rain Dragon Organics,' bigger than the biggest ad you could buy. Sales jumped ten percent that week. And they've been climbing ever since. This guy is a master. In fact, I shouldn't even be letting you talk to him. You'll steal his ideas. Or worse, you'll steal him."

I shrugged modestly. I was glad Peter was happy, though I knew, and everyone on the farm knew, a compliment from him was about on par with a compliment from one's mother, his enthusiasm overflowed so easily.

"So what's the secret?" asked the bug-eyed, unshaven newspaper reporter. "What's the secret of Rain Dragon?" From the perspective of the PR department?

"There's a secret?" I said. "Shit. No one told me."

The group laughed, a little louder than necessary. They were a friendly bunch, and already duly impressed by Rain Dragon's organizational innovations and self-evident good vibes. They'd toured the creamery and gone through the lunch line; soon they'd be wrapping up their day with a visit to the library on the mansion's second floor. I'd been answering their questions for almost twenty minutes now, and it seemed an opportune moment to usher them along. If not for the reporter who kept pushing for a more complete answer.

"Seriously," he said, clicking his ballpoint pen, "What makes Rain Dragon tick? In your own words. As someone on the inside."

"Yogurt," I said, blandly. "That's the main thing. A quality product. People can taste that we care about what we're doing."

"That's it?" he said. "Really? Come on, man. Some of these guys have come a long way to hear about how this company works. The world wants to know more about Rain Dragon. Give us a little more, from your perspective."

I glanced at Peter, who remained expressionless. Usually he fielded the questions on these junkets, but in this case he seemed pleased to let me step in. I'd heard his rap enough by then that I had some idea of the major talking points.

"Rain Dragon stands for something," I said. "It means something to people. It's an idea. And people like that."

"And what's the idea?" asked the Marin guy, taking up the interrogation. Again, I glanced at Peter, seeking permission, and he just arched his eyebrows, urging me onward. It seemed he wanted to hear what I had to say today, too.

"The idea of Rain Dragon is about a new kind of organization," I said, channeling Peter's past words the best I could. "Most companies out there still think of themselves as machines, you know? For the last four hundred years, that's been the case. Companies see their employees as interchangeable cogs. You stick them in, wear them out, replace them when they die. It's made sense, in a way. But it's had its costs, too. When you think of the organization as a machine, you end up with a certain set of values. Efficiency, profitability, speed, power. Machine values. Machine thinking. All of which have their place, to be sure. Nothing against machines. But we're trying to get beyond that here."

I was starting to list away from Peter's normal rhetoric, drifting into more improvisational terrain. I hoped I'd catch up with myself along the way.

"But you think of an organization from a different angle," I said, "say, as a living body, the way Rain Dragon does—you get a different set of values, don't you? Health, balance, flexibility, pleasure. Those are body values. And they call a lot of those old hierarchies into question. What's more important in the body, the heart or the lungs? What about the brain or the lungs? The brain or the heart? None of the above, right? No one part of the body is more important than another part. The brain controls the heart, but without the blood from the heart the brain would stop working. You start looking at an organization as an organism—organ, organization, organism—not a machine, and the priorities, the possibilities, suddenly become a lot different. To me, that's what Rain Dragon is about. It's a space for human creativity to happen. Human exploration, human invention. And along the way, we happen to make prize-winning yogurt and honey."

I realized I'd been staring at the reporter's shoes—wingtips with specks of glitter on the toe—and glanced up to find him jotting feverishly on his pad of paper. The rest of the group was nodding and murmuring appreciatively, too. Peter also looked quite impressed.

The interview finally drew to a close with cheerful handshakes and smiles all around, and Peter shepherded the group off to their next stop, giving me a thumbs-up sign as the jasmine bushes closed behind him.

Alone again, I returned to my Adirondack chair next to a low stone wall draped in nasturtiums, where I'd been working on label copy for the new line of boysenberry kefir before the interruption. My day's materials—a yellow legal pad, a glass of iced tea, a ballpoint pen—were scattered on the ground, and I collected them back into my lap. I was just pulling my thoughts together, pondering alternatives to the tired word *organic*, hoping I could come up with something that passed Peter's muster, when my concentration was interrupted yet again, this time by Amy wandering into the garden, looking lovely in her regular farm uniform of beat-up clogs, old blue jeans, and loose peasant blouse. She didn't see me at first—her face was partly blocked by the addition of a wide-brimmed sombrero—and I leaned back to watch her picking her way through the rows of chard.

The farm life was treating her well, I thought. Her arms were tanned and her face was freckled. Her hips were looking supple and trim. Over the last month, she and Linda had been having some trouble with the bees, I knew, failing to raise the money for the expansion they wanted to implement, but with the sun filtering through the leaves, the gardens in full bloom, that problem seemed far from pressing today. Amy was radiant. Like an Impressionist painting come to life. A rosy, fragrant vision of womanhood among the dappled greenery.

She was halfway across the garden before feeling the pressure of my gaze on her cheek, and turned to find me watching her. "Ah. There you are."

"Here I am," I said.

"I was trying to find you earlier," she said. "You weren't in your office."

"Yeah, I was out here."

"Yeah, I see that."

She stepped over the collards, through the carrot tufts, and came to her destination, the beefsteak tomato bushes, where she knelt down with her basket to check the week's harvest.

I gave up on writing anything to watch her. I hadn't seen her much lately, and enjoyed the view from this middle distance. Gently, she pushed back the leaves and reached deep into the plant, rifling through the inner vines. The sound of the shifting dirt scrunched under her knees, and she leaned in further still. She didn't find what she was looking for, though, and shifted over a few feet and reached in again, but again came up empty-handed. Now noises of strangulated anger were coming from her throat. She rolled back onto her heels, staring at the bush. Our eyes met briefly, and she turned back to glare at the plant.

"Unbelievable," she said, her face netted with sombrero shadow.

The tomato plants exhaled their tomatoey smell, and the hammering on the roof, which had paused, restarted lazily.

"What?" I said.

"No tomatoes," she said, and batted once more at the plant. "Look at this. Someone took all the fucking tomatoes already."

"Oh. Well. There'll be more soon, won't there?"

"Yeah, well, I needed them today. I was making lasagna this week. I guess you forgot."

In the distance a screen door slammed. On the edge of the garden, a pendulous fig tree rustled and shrugged. It took me a second to realize that she was leveling some kind of accusation. Was I to blame for something? Was someone else to blame? Were the tomatoes themselves to blame? I wasn't sure. Our schedules had become so packed lately that I'd fallen out of touch with her daily moods.

"Uh, so, how was the meeting?" I said, remembering she and Linda had had an appointment that morning, the most recent in a series of meetings about potential investors outside the company. I imagined it hadn't gone too well, and that was the real source of her aggravation, not tomatoes.

"Not so hot," she said.

"Oh? No?" I said.

"They weren't interested."

"How come?"

"They don't have any money," she said. "They were looking for money, too. No one's got any money."

"Bummer."

"Yeah."

She stared at the tomatoes. A hummingbird zipped into the air between us, a tiny green brooch pinned to the world, then zipped away.

"Maybe you should talk to Peter," I suggested. "He might

have some ideas." I assumed she knew it already, but the normal route for finding seed money at Rain Dragon generally involved presenting a business plan to Peter and then, with his help, building it into something to share with the whole staff. Every quarter the staff voted on which projects deserved funding, and allocated available monies as such. It was one of the examples of innovative organizational techniques that the tour groups found so fascinating: an in-house microfinancing program, responsible for the tortilla machine, the peony greenhouse, and numerous lesser accomplishments along the way.

"He's the one who said we should look for outside partners," she said. "We need too much."

"Oh. Well. I'm sure you'll find one then."

"Yeah, we'll see."

"You will."

"I wish you had any idea what you were talking about."

"I do. I know things."

"Uh-huh."

"I do."

"How do you know? Can you see the future?"

"I know, because everything always works out fine in the end."

"Bah."

The lethargic tinkle of wind chimes collected in the air. A dragonfly rose, revolved, and sank from view. Amy abandoned the tomatoes and shifted her attention to the chard, ripping off leaves and stacking them in her basket.

"So how's your day going?" she said, with only the mildest of interest.

"All right," I said. "Getting some things done."

"Did you pay the rent yet?"

"Yep." We'd lately moved into a bungalow in North Portland, a big place with wild poppies scattered in front and seven
shades of pink on the inside walls, and paying rent had become
my responsibility. I assumed she'd be pleased that I'd remembered, but as it turned out, that wasn't the case. Immediately, she
was looking for another problem to lob my way, scanning for
another potential conflict.

"I can't believe how much we've spent on rent in our lives,"
she said, casting a wide net. "It's ridiculous."

"Yeah," I said.

"It's just a joke," she said. "How much longer? I'd like to know."

"Yeah. Hard to say."

"I can't see how we're ever going to get a down payment together."

I didn't respond. I didn't know exactly where this was going,
but clearly it wasn't going anywhere pleasant. The topic of down
payments could lead to any number of dark areas. For whatever
reason, it seemed a black cloud had entered her mind and was
now spreading out, seething, in search of some object to engulf.
I could tell it was only a matter of time before it found me.

I wished I had some kind of good news to share. A compliment to pass on. An opportunity to discuss. Then I might have
been able to disperse the cloud before it gathered more strength.
But I didn't have anything, and therefore my best option was to
lay low.

On the rock wall, two ladybugs were mating. The abdomen of
the male was distended toward the female's, and flecks of pollen
stuck to their elytra. I watched the male ladybug grip the female
with little serrated claws, admiring their patient, immobile, tantric
lovemaking.

"We need to paint that bathroom, you know," she said, laying further land mines.

"I thought that was low on our list."

"Well. It's on the list."

"Are you saying you want me to do it?"

"Forget it. I'll do it myself."

"No, no," I said. "I'll do it. If you want me to. I'm just making sure you want that."

"Don't do me any favors. Forget I asked."

I doodled a face on my paper. Another few exchanges like this and we'd be in the middle of an all-out fight. And what for? I still didn't really know. By most rational standards, things were going fine lately. We had the jobs we'd wanted. We had a decent house. We had interesting new friends. The negative turn of mind seemed not only groundless but almost perverse in my book, an exercise in making problems where they didn't exist.

"I'll paint the bathroom this weekend," I offered.

"If you say so."

"I will."

"Okay. Great."

She ripped more chard and set it in the basket. Already, I was becoming resigned to whatever was coming my way, and hoping we could just get through it quickly. A brief flare-up. Angry words. Remorse. Maybe we could get it all done before dinner. But I wasn't sorry when our conversation was cut off by the arrival of Peter onto the scene, his voice booming at us from across the berms.

"Hey, what's going on over there?" he said, scaring the ladybugs into the air. His head poked from a jasmine bush, and the red fringes of his hair, backed by the spiky glare of the setting sun, caught the light like a fiery halo. "You guys doing anything? I kind of need someone to help me out." Without waiting for an answer, he started barking orders: "Damon, if you could pick me some plums, that would be great. I need about fifteen or so, all about the same size. All right? And Amy, maybe you could help me set up the chairs. It's almost six. Time to get rolling, kids."

And so, mercifully, whatever turbulence we'd encountered was settled for the time being. Amy got up and walked away, and I got up a few seconds after, heading in the opposite direction.

Every Wednesday the workers of Rain Dragon assembled in the Meditation Room or, weather permitting, on the back deck, for our weekly staff meeting. The regular attendees were always Michael, Linda, Emilio, and Jaeha, as well as whatever interns, part-timers, and guests felt like sitting in, forming themselves into an oblong, unhierarchical oval, the center of which was always unquestionably Peter.

Amy complained the meetings were a waste of time, and that was probably true, but it was a waste I found relaxing. We talked expansively about new product lines, civic politics, guiding principles, and whatever conceptual provocations Peter had cooked up lately. One week we might discuss the shift from agrarian to industrialized civilization and the current third wave of digital development, and what that meant in terms of emerging human consciousness; another week we might ruminate on harnessing the physical activity of little children into a renewable energy source, turning their bouncing balls and teeter-totters into rechargeable batteries. Sometimes we'd spend the whole meeting dissecting a poem.

On this day, the meeting was jolly and unhurried, accompanied by the sound of the crickets scratching out their nighttime song. Peter opened by telling us we were having a good summer so far—the numbers were up—and congratulating Jaeha on his photography show at the Blue Sky art collective downtown. From there, he led us in a quick thought experiment involving the plums I'd gathered, the gist being something about the infinite varieties of difference visible inside the seemingly identical, and offered a preview of the new artisanal goat cheese. Afterward, the group broke apart and re-formed on the rear deck for chips, homemade guacamole, and a keg of homebrewed lager. Plans were made. The gossip of the week was tendered and confirmed. A guitar came out, and Dylan was channeled.

I assumed Amy wanted to get going, but when I came around to collect her she couldn't be budged. The meeting had leavened her mood a little, and she was now caught up in a conversation with Linda about the electrostatic charges carried by honeybees.

Fine, I thought. Maybe the subject of down payments and bathroom paint was finished. Maybe we'd said all we needed to say and were ready to move on, without any gratuitous analysis of our future arrangements or intentions whatsoever. I could dream, anyway.

I poured myself a beer and parked myself on the deck's far corner, enjoying the view of the half-moon's dark perimeter against the purple cosmos. I was about midway through my cup when Peter sidled over and placed his elbows on the railing beside me, nudging my shoulder by way of hello. Together we observed the moon's soft powder falling over the night leaves, lost in the squares of electric light glaring from the mansion's windows. Eventually, when it was clear he wasn't going anywhere, I cleared my throat and acknowledged his presence.

"Seemed like a good tour today," I said.

"For sure. Interesting folks," he said. "You gave a great talk, by the way. Really appreciated that. As always."

"No problem at all."

"And also, great job on that flash animation for the Web site. I've been meaning to tell you that for a while. I can't believe we had that crummy site up for so long."

"It wasn't hard."

"And those popsicles in the park. Still can't get over that. I swear to God."

"Aw shucks," I said, and I could tell by his expression of approval that I had said the right, humble thing.

We sipped our drinks. The moon continued to burn whitely, illuminating a distant shell of ice crystals in the upper atmosphere. The mountain glowed along the ridges of its seams.

"I really appreciate all you've been doing here so far," he said, gazing into the darkness. "It makes a big difference, having you around. Having a real writer in the house for once."

"I'm just glad to be here."

He took another drink and squinted at the night sky. The moon was making him philosophical, and I girded myself for one of his regular, rambling disquisitions on whatever article he'd just read, or moral problem was currently plaguing his mind. We were all used to the conversations, or rather the one long conversation.

"The thing is," he said, "most people out there—I mean out in the world in general—they still don't really understand what we're doing here."

"You don't think so?"

He shook his head. "We still haven't been able to get that message out. They see Rain Dragon as a health food company, and that's about it. They think of the yogurt, the cheese, maybe the tortillas. That's only natural. People are literal-minded that way. But I've always thought of Rain Dragon as a lot more than that. Like you were saying today. On a certain level, food is just the side effect, the medium, of what we're doing here. I loved what you said about Rain Dragon being an idea."

"I think I've heard you say the same thing before."

"Well. Never that clearly. You have a very clear way of talking, Damon. Having you around is making me see a lot of things in new ways. You've got a way of putting things. You know that, right?"

"Well . . . I don't know about that . . ."

"No, no, don't deny it," he said. "You have something. You do."

"If you say so."

"You have a gift for metaphors," he said, decisively, as if it was a question he'd pondered at length. "And that's a big deal, man. I don't need to tell you, the metaphors we use are incredibly important. They dictate the reality we see. They can mean whole new ways of being in the world. I've thought about this a lot. In the seminars I teach, that's what I'm always trying to get people to understand. I'm trying to get them to reexamine their old metaphors. To accept new metaphors. To create their own metaphors. And you know what?"

"What."

"By and large, they're happy to try. Most people are hungry to change their ways of thinking. You know what I'm saying? Am I making sense here?"

"Yeah," I said. "I'm pretty sure, anyway."

"I heard what you said to that group today. All that stuff about organs in the body. That's a fucking great metaphor, Damon. It's something people can hold on to, something they can use. It's a serious idea. You've got the knack, man, believe me. Not everyone does. I've been waiting a long time for someone like you to show up here. Someone who gets what we're doing on the idea level. Someone who thinks on that wavelength."

"I think everyone—" But he cut off my next humble disavowal of specialness.

"You know, for the last couple years I've been trying to pull together some of my thoughts into something people could use in their day-to-day lives. I've got a lot of pages piling up. I still don't know quite what it is, but I'm thinking I'm ready to put it all together into something. It might be a book. I don't know. I don't want to put any definitions on it yet. What I'm saying is, I like your way with words, Damon. I would love your help on this."

The ragged clouds ringing the mountain sucked up the moonlight. The guitar was playing a song I didn't know. I wasn't sure what Peter was asking for, but I didn't have to think twice. My job, more than anything else, was to be available.

"Yeah, totally," I said. "Whatever you want."

"Yeah?" he said.

"Yeah. Of course."

"I don't know what it's going to be. You'll have to be flexible."

"Oh, I'm flexible."

"It might take a while. And it might not come to anything."

"I'm just excited to see where it goes."

"That's the spirit," Peter gripped my shoulder and kneaded it like a doctor. "I knew I could count on you, man. I really think this thing could go somewhere. I wouldn't bring it up otherwise. These ideas, this language, it could be a place where Rain Dragon has a real impact. Companies are dying for new ways of understanding how to get ahead in this economy. If we can give them the tools, we could end up helping a lot of people. We could end up with more work than we know what to do with."

An hour or so later Amy and I found each other and decided to head home. We said our good-byes, walked to the parking lot, and plunged into the dark tunnel of trees leading back to Highway 26. Soon we were cruising past now-familiar landmarks: Giant Burger, Hair Force One, the rows of tractors at the John Deere rental agency. Only minutes earlier, at the party, she'd been gabbing happily with Jaeha and Linda about Claus von Bülow and the Green River Killer, but now, alone with me, she was gloomy again.

Hot, summery air funneled through the windows into our sleeves. I tried to cheer her up with the news of Peter's proposal, but the details were too hazy to make it seem exciting. Without him, it all sounded so vaporous as to not exist. A book? A Web page? I couldn't say. I'd hoped it would answer whatever worries she'd been feeling, but that wasn't the case.

"He thinks the project might really go somewhere," I said, lamely.

"Great," she said, and reached outside the window, cupping the wind.

Already, our earlier conversation was coming back around, a black sun peeking over the horizon. We eased to a stop at a red light on 122nd Avenue. The car beside us shook with a plodding bass line that rattled the windows in the doors. Amy stared blankly at the road shoulder, breathing in the day's trapped heat.

"So, what are you thinking about?" I said. I figured I might as well take the lead. I didn't want anyone to accuse me of shirking any duties tonight.

"What am I thinking?" she said. She rested her head on her palm. "I don't know, Damon." The bass kept booming. She sighed. "I just don't know."

"Come on," I said.

The stoplight beamed red through the windshield. The bass line kept coming, centerless, rhythmless, just rumbling sound pouring into itself.

"Oh, this is hard, Damon," she said. "What I'm thinking is, I need some space. I think we need to take a break."

SIX

I SHOULD HAVE KNOWN. I should have seen it coming the second Amy walked into the vegetable garden. I should have seen it a lot earlier than that, even. I should have seen it the day she cut her finger chopping the parsnips and hurled the knife into the basement, knowing how careless she got when she was frustrated and needing some life change. I should have sensed it in the days of morose TV watching, the moment of near violence over the lack of a decent dress to wear to a croquet party, the argument over the kitchen sponges and which one cleaned what. All of them were hints, fair warning that something more major was massing on the horizon.

At first I didn't really believe she was serious about leaving. The conversation in the car petered out, and for a day or two we gave the whole topic a rest. We followed our routines and kept talk to a minimum. We were extra polite. But sure enough, the conversation picked up again two days later, and nothing had changed. She still wanted a break, she said. She still needed her space. And she still couldn't exactly say what the problem was. Why now? I wanted to know. What was the issue? She had trouble answering. But then, she didn't need any stated reason per se. There may have been no reason at all. It was just a feeling she had. Whenever life became too comfortable, too settled, whenever we edged within sight of stable happiness, she had this tendency to throw things into disarray.

The first time we'd gone through this was only two months into our time together. She'd sat me down and told me she'd enjoyed knowing me, but she had other options she needed to explore, and she'd headed off to an adobe ranch in New Mexico, the headquarters of the southwest regional clean water movement. She'd come back a few months later, contrite, and we'd had a lovely interlude until, in the lead-up to moving in together, she'd left again, this time to spend a few weeks organizing farm workers and investigate the possibility that she might be in love with a woman named Julia. She'd come back and left yet again to live in our friend Jay's guesthouse. She even took the cat that time, and it had been unclear if and when she would ever return, but at some point we woke up and she had.

In this way, we split up to some degree every nine months or so, with many smaller, less serious rifts in between. It had gotten to the point where the break-up was just one peculiar phase of our intimacy, a staging ground for whatever the next level of commitment was going to be. I'd come to accept the pattern, and appreciated its power. In order to ascend to a new level, we sometimes had to back up and get a good running start, and while the aftermath always brought a special period of security, a rededication to our love, the critical component of a good breakup was the genuine fear that it might actually be permanent. Only then did it provide the proper momentum, the proper illusion that a choice was being made, without which Amy doubted she was truly alive.

And so, in early August, a few weeks after my talk with Peter, she moved out of the house and relocated about three miles across town to Linda's ramshackle Victorian off Division. We were well practiced in this routine, and went through the whole range of scenes the parting implied—scenes of sadness, misunderstanding, pathetic comedy, halting conversations full of pauses, outbursts of crying, tortured rephrasings, questions upon questions responding to questions. It was almost liturgical in nature. We doubled back, repeated ourselves, advanced by small degrees.

Her mantra this time was that she needed her space, she needed to think and to collect herself. My stock response was that she could have all the space she wanted, right here at home, but apparently that wasn't the kind of space she was after. She said she wanted her own space, where she could think and receive clear signals as to how to proceed. She wanted a clean, private zone of contemplation.

"You want God to sit you down and do career counseling," I said. "That's what you want. A burning bush."

"Fuck you," she said.

"A talking lion," I said. "A pillar of smoke. I don't see what else is going to satisfy here."

"I just need to work on myself for a while," she said. "All right? I need some privacy is all."

"I thought we had a plan," I said. I was lying on the bed, watching her pack her financial papers into a beat-up Dole pineapple box. Handful by handful, the dog-eared bills and envelopes were being swallowed by the maw. A chopstick precariously held her hair out of her face.

"We did," she said, refusing to look at me. "We do. The plan is to see what happens. And that's what we're doing. We're seeing." She dropped a final rubber-banded bundle into the box and closed the flaps, struggling to make the folds come together properly. Once the seal was closed, she took the box downstairs, and I followed a few paces behind. "I don't know how else to explain it," she said. "I need to feel like I'm doing things for the right reason."

"So how is this all going to work?" I said.

"What do you mean?"

"I mean, I'll see you every day at the farm."

"So?"

"It seems weird."

"What's weird? There are weirder things."

"Yeah, but—"

"People do all kinds of things, Damon," she said, and turned to face me, then changed her mind and turned away. "It's not weird. This is part of what I'm talking about. You have these ideas . . ." She tapered off without finishing the accusation. Even she knew she was reaching here. One label she couldn't put on me was judgmental.

I lurked behind her as she crossed the foyer. "I can give you all the space you want right here," I repeated for the thousandth time. "You don't have to go anywhere for the space. I can join a gym or something. Fix up the basement. I can get out of here whenever you want."

"I can't do what I need to do here, Damon," she said. "It doesn't work that way. Please don't make this any harder, all right?"

She deposited the box at the front door and we drifted through the living room, already partly disassembled in preparation for her departure.

"Did I do something wrong?" I said, more to bother her than to elicit any real information.

"No," she said. "It's nothing like that. It's nothing you did."

"Did I not do something?" I said.

"It's not about you, Damon," she said. "It's about me." She made an effort to make this sound like new information, though it had been said many times before. "I have to figure some things out. That's it. That's all."

We arrived in the kitchen, where the smell of overripe bananas was almost overpowering. Not for the first time an ugly light came on in my head, and I found myself pushing into a new, more masochistic line of questioning: "Is there someone else?" I said. "You can tell me if there is."

"No."

"Would you tell me if there was?"

"Would you want to know?"

"No."

"Then there's your answer. But there's no one."

Amy washed a fork and decided against washing anything else. Instead she continued out onto the back steps. A sparrow was cleaning itself in the birdbath in the middle of the yard. The sky was colorless and the wind had died, leaving the bushes and trees inert. The flapping of the sparrow's wings was the only motion to be seen.

"I thought we were doing this together," I said glumly.

"We are," she said. "Together, but separately for a while."

"Separate but equal. Apartheid. Great."

The sparrow dug at its breast and wings, jerking its head with its tiny black eyes back and forth. The branches of the elm tree were losing detail against the twilight. The wind came and got tangled in the trees, and then, soon after, Amy was gone.

★ ★ ★

I predicted she would be back in a week or two, at least if past experience were any guide. That was how long the initial flush of freedom usually lasted, at which point she usually started to forget why she'd wanted her freedom and started wanting her comfort again. But I could never be sure this would be the case.

A nice, clean separation would have been better. Ideally, we would have stayed apart for a while, contemplated our lives from a distance, and then, eventually, started over again with a renewed sense of mutual appreciation. We should have kept out of each other's sight long enough to reimagine each other. But in this circumstance we weren't given that chance. We saw each other at breakfast the very morning of Amy's departure, and then on the bridge over the creek, and on the rear porch at the end of the day when the staff congregated for beer and homemade pretzels. We were civil, knowing our gossip-hungry coworkers were eagerly watching, but there was a low-grade fakeness we couldn't shake.

I was glad Peter's project came along when it did. It could have been anything, really. I would have shined everyone's shoes if that would have kept me busy.

It was only a few days after Amy's move that Peter plucked me from the lunch line and took me upstairs to his tiny writing room on the third floor. At first I didn't understand why we needed to go there—it was just a manuscript we were talking about, after all, something he could theoretically hand to me in a box or in a binder and which I could take anywhere to read. But I found out soon enough the manuscript we'd been talking about wasn't a manuscript at all, in the sense of typed or even handwritten pages stacked together in some discrete order. Rather, the document Peter wanted me to look at existed as a mass of disorganized scrap paper packed haphazardly into two four-drawer filing cabinets.

"Kind of a mess, I know," he said, a little sheepishly, as we surveyed the chipped drawers in the suffocatingly hot room. The blinds were drawn and piles of manila envelopes covered every flat surface, forming a series of striated plateaus. "I don't know where to tell you to start," he said. "I guess you'll just have to sift for a while. Get your bearings."

"Yeah," I said, peering at the towers. "Okay."

"I could show you a few things if you wanted," he offered. "Get you started . . ."

"No, no," I said. "It's all right. Just let me take a look. If I have questions, I'll ask."

"You're sure?" he said.

"Oh, yeah," I said. "This will be, like, interesting."

For the next hour I just sat there, sinking into the hush of the almost totally unpopulated wing. On the wall hung a poster of a monastery in Tibet, a beautiful temple clinging to sheer Himalayan rock walls. The lone chair was a molded plastic tulip from Denmark. The window offered a clear view of the herb garden and whatever the cloud cover decided to unveil in the distance. The glass was speckled with pollen.

Eventually I got up and rolled open the drawers to see exactly what we were dealing with here, and immediately I sat down again. It was a mess. He'd made the project sound like some kind of grand collaboration between us, a mutual wrangling with ideas, but in fact it was looking more like clerical work. Sorting, culling, bringing order to chaos. Peter had obviously been stuffing scraps into the cabinets for the last ten years, assuming some dumb sucker like myself would eventually come along and do cleanup. But the longer I sat there, the more I became almost pleased by the assignment. The more isolated and time-consuming, the better, I figured. My vacation from Amy had been granted.

I took my time doing inventory. Starting the next day, I pulled out everything and made piles on the floor and partway into the hall. Out came an enormous, hand-drawn flow chart labeled "The Flowering Organization," representing the biological growth pattern of a healthy institution over time. Out came a diagrammatic pyramid detailing the three universal levels of energy—Maintenance, Management, and Transcendent—which coincided with the upward progression from vulgar self-interest to enlightened selflessness. Out came a grid of incredibly morbid affirmations: "I am thankful I am not a soldier in a trench being bombarded with mustard gas"; "I am thankful my toes have not been amputated due to severe frostbite"; "I am thankful my spouse is not physically abusive." There were also many mystical aphorisms, multiple-choice questions, 3-D diagrams, visualization exercises, personality wheels, quotations from medieval scholars, and assorted, uncategorizable doodles.

The goal of all the material, Peter told me during one of his frequent visits, was to give Groups a tool kit for achieving their highest potential. Because the whole history of human development, he was fond of saying, was one of Groups at work. Groups motivated by some shared mission. Groups attempting to live out some shared fantasy of the good life and do battle with what they viewed as the bad.

"Jesus and his disciples, the Masons, the Spanish armada, the Surrealists, every rock-and-roll band in history—all just a few guys pushing each other to new levels," he said. "Right?"

"That's quite a list," I said.

"What they have in common is, they know exactly what they're trying to achieve. They have a clear vision of where they're going, and why. And when you have that vision, the way forward becomes easier. That's true in anything."

"Pol Pot had a vision."

"An incoherent vision. A crazy vision. If anyone had been able to sit down with him without worrying he was going to kill them, that would've been clear. You can't have real vision corrupted by that much fear."

It was Peter's aim to help these people, wherever they were, in making their life maps. If they could only articulate what really mattered to them, and figure out what they really wanted to create, so much more could be accomplished, and so much wasted effort, even destructive behavior, could be avoided. Clarity was the goal, he believed. Clarity led only to the good.

The project remained fuzzy to me until one day when he dragged me along to one of his introductory seminars. The client was a small bread company called Hallelujah Breadworks, located in the industrial part of northwest Portland, and the owner was an old friend of his. The session took place on the main factory floor among the droning ovens and air conditioners, in a simple circle of folding chairs. Peter sat with the employees in the yeasty air, much like he did with us every Wednesday at Rain Dragon, and led them through a handful of his exercises.

He started by offering a little background on himself, recounting his entrepreneurial bona fides, establishing his storyline, and telling a few self-deprecating jokes. He then asked the group to introduce themselves. And from there, in good Socratic fashion, he began asking questions. There was nothing tricky about it. Just a gentle, persistent interrogation starting with easy stuff—names and hometowns, hobbies and favorite movies—and gradually, organically, shifting into more challenging terrain. What is Good Work? he asked the group. What is a worthwhile use of a person's time on earth? What is the Purpose of your own work as you currently see it? What would you like the Purpose to be?

It was more or less the same line he pursued at Rain Dragon most days, homing in on the big, existential topics no one ever bothered discussing out loud, and in that way forcing people to examine the basic assumptions and unarticulated hopes upon which their lives rested. As it turned out, his curiosity drew these people out just as it did his own staff.

From my perch off to the side, I watched the morning session unfold. It was hard to say exactly how it happened, or where the pivot points were, but over a few hours the spell of Peter's attention had a profound and galvanizing effect. His centered gravity and cool, continuous eye contact held the group together, and almost without their knowing it they began to embrace his language. Hallelujah was not only a bread company, they concurred, but an Idea, too, a shared Vision, and if that was the case then a whole new set of possibilities became imaginable. The workplace was not a fixed set of protocols and rules as it sometimes seemed, but rather something more malleable, more alive. It was a social construct, a fiction under their power to redefine and to improve. Together, the employees formed the very substance of Hallelujah. Their shared time was the institution's soul.

"What is the Purpose of Hallelujah Breadworks?" Peter asked, and the answers spilled from around the circle.

"To make bread," said the beady-eyed janitor.

"To nourish people," said a matronly sales associate.

"To give people energy to allow them to do what they want

to do," said a pert college girl, eliciting general hums of agreement all around.

To give energy, the group decided, echoing Peter's suggestion. And if that was the true Purpose, then what were some of the ways Hallelujah could better live up to its Purpose? How could it do more? How could it do better? Almost effortlessly, the circle began to generate ideas about new products, improved efficiency measures, streamlined production chains, better quality control, enhanced communication. And as the ideas spilled forth, they were recorded on huge tablets of graph paper for easy recall and future implementation.

A week later I watched the same process unfold at Lotus Tempeh, and then at Tao Tea. Peter had a simple, sturdy procedure in place, presented with an unflappable, optimistic demeanor, and as such, on any given afternoon, he was capable of refashioning a roomful of people into a machine of deep group exploration. He turned the workplace into a Quaker meeting, a Catholic confessional, and a Native American sweat lodge all rolled into one—a secular, thoroughly Americanized assembly line of insight.

Back at the mansion, up in my office, I continued sorting his papers, arranging his human potential technologies, making minuscule improvements in phrasing and structure along the way. I was starting to get the basic concept he was chasing—more of a how-to manual than a manuscript, proper—and I began to make better progress in my editing. Maybe it wasn't even such a mess after all, I decided. I brought a laptop and printer upstairs, salvaged some paper from the recycling bins, and began shaping the materials into a document of normal eight-and-a-half-by-eleven proportions. I gave each technology a page, each batch of technologies a chapter. I wrote introductory paragraphs, footnotes.

I inserted a cross-referencing tool and an explanatory preface. I entitled the whole thing *Infinite Energy,* which Peter loved.

We spent long hours talking it all through, joking about corporate jargon, telling stories from our respective childhoods. It turned out we liked each other, which made the work easy.

During my breaks I went often to the window and stared down at the gardens below. Sometimes I caught sight of Amy down there, talking to Peter near the rosemary bushes, or to Jaeha near a lattice of climbing peas. I was too far away to hear anything, only the peaks of her laughter, the flat tone of her hollers, but I'd stand there until the conversation ended, and everyone hugged, and usually I'd wait around a little longer until she wandered off into the ocean of trees, disappearing into the coursing green shadows.

I watched the shadows long after she'd gone, coiling and crossing on the ground, a restless, two-dimensional beast. If she wanted more time, I would give her more time. And I'd turn around and get back to work.

SEVEN

LATE IN AUGUST was Dragon Days, Rain Dragon's annual shareholders' meeting, a three-day party bringing together the company's friends and family and former employees from up and down the coast. Officially, it was a time of financial reports, strategy meetings, and renewed vision statements, but even more so it was a time of music, food, and general debauchery, and from what everyone said, an excellent opportunity for reuniting with an estranged loved one.

The days leading up to the party were hectic with added chores. We raked the paths, built stages in the barns, hung paper lanterns from the limbs of the cherry trees, and carted in copious amounts of alcohol for the bars scattered throughout the property. Amy and I kept our distance from each other, staggering our lunchtimes and breaks, and if communication was absolutely necessary, resorting to the old playground triangulation technique, with Jaeha as our main go-between. It was silly, but we avoided conflict that way, and also, in my mind, began the subtle process of positioning ourselves for our inevitable reunion.

Already the signs were moving us in that direction: a stray glance during the Wednesday-night meeting, a significant pause in the kitchen doorway, a comical stagger-step on the deck stairs. And then, only days before the party, a book by Peter Drucker on management theory appeared on my desk, with a short note and her initials. She was most definitely coming around, I thought, smelling the pages. As the summer tapered to a close, we were entering the first phases of our reconciliation.

I tried to keep my expectations low. Quite possibly, we wouldn't do more than talk at the party. At the most, we'd probably kiss. But by the night of the big event I was indulging more elaborate fantasies, too, mostly involving tearful confessions and torrid makeup sex in the second-floor bathroom. I made sure to wear clean underwear just in case.

The night of the party was gentle and warm, the air scented with the first vinegary fumes of apples rotting on the baked earth. My first Amy sighting came early on, near the buffet table in the herb garden. She had a new haircut, I noticed, and possibly a new sundress, too. On closer inspection, I saw she was wearing the orange leather sandals that I'd once referred to as my favorites, possibly a personal message of some kind. It was hard to say.

I considered strolling straight over and saying hello, getting the first pinched greeting out of the way, but in the end I decided against it. Better to bide my time, I thought. Better to let things simmer a while. We still had hours this evening. For the moment, I'd just hang around the buffet table, taking it easy, picking at the cheese plate, flaunting my general happiness and composure.

I couldn't help glancing over sometimes, though, just to make sure she was still around. She was. Talking to Linda for a while. Talking to Simon. Totally oblivious to my presence across the garden. It was on my fourth or fifth glance that I finally caught the edge of her gaze zipping away, and could reassure myself she wasn't oblivious, just quick.

I turned back to the table, testing the barley salad, the kale salad, and the beet salad with chevre and crushed walnuts, which was delicious.

I was on my third plate when Michael came lumbering into the garden and struck up a conversation with Amy. They warmed up with what looked like little comic jabs, a staccato of self-deprecation and false inanity, and then he settled into some long story about something. I couldn't hear anything he said, but from the way she listened rapturously to every detail, with huge, helpless smiles breaking over her face, it looked pretty fascinating. She touched his arm, her eyes sparkling, and he added a few more flourishes that she found hilarious. I was just edging closer, hoping to catch some of the content, when the whole scene was extinguished by a powerful burst of white light.

"Cheese!" Jaeha said.

The dancing spots faded, and I found Jaeha standing there, holding the hefty antique camera he trotted out for special occasions. He squeezed off one more shot before bowing his head and compressing the accordian lens.

"Finish that food," he said, snapping the latch. "We're going to explore."

"Okay." I said, still blinking off the bulb's tracers. "Lead the way." Amy and Michael were breaking apart, and from what I could tell, she was heading toward the pastures. It seemed like a good time to begin testing the many bars across the land.

Beers in hand, Jaeha and I wandered through the gathering crowd, taking in the braided beards, batik sundresses, and children in long T-shirts and no pants. The scene was still gaining strength, the energy still middling, ascendant, with fresh clusters of partygoers entering the gate at ever more frequent intervals. The freshly raked pathways remained uncrowded and the sheltered tents and lean-tos to house the families in from Eugene and Seattle were still going up.

As we wandered, Jaeha clued me in on the scene, and pointed out the many feuding parties and unfinished romances that had converged. The Choad family, from Linnton, evicted from Rain Dragon years before due to an episode involving an exploding meth lab in the mansion's mudroom, but who remained on friendly terms with Peter nonetheless. The two Mrs. Kennedys, the former and current wives of Butch Kennedy, the first Rain Dragon utility man, who had since moved on to Tektronix. Boyd Crawford, the inventor of the Rain Dragon pureeing machine, now a software programmer in Palo Alto, and rumored to moonlight for Lockheed.

It was at the cow pasture that my second sighting of Amy came. She was walking near the fence, and again I held myself back. Let the tides of the party wash us together, I thought. Let the meeting carry all the proper force of serendipity and magic it deserved. She paused to talk to Emilio, and her gaze drifted in my direction, but before we could establish anything she turned away. She turned so abruptly, in fact, it was possible she was telling me something, anticipating the scene of her inevitable, groveling return.

Eventually Jaeha peeled off for the bathroom, and I decamped on the deck stairs, where the bulk of the partygoers had decided to congregate, eavesdropping on a group of women discussing the significance of the gas giants in astrological charts, and two grave little boys debating the threat of unguarded nuclear materials in Uzbekistan.

"Nixon, Westmoreland, Reagan, Cheney!" Michael was ranting near the keg. When he got drunk the shyness sloughed off and his politics became borderline violent. "It's all the same fucking guys. They're the same guys as Goebbels and fucking Rommel. They won. They won that fucking war. They just changed costumes in the end."

"You haven't been to Chichen Itza?" I heard Emilio scold a buxom teenage girl in combat boots. "Such an incredible culture. You know the Aztecs used to wear the flayed skin of their enemies until it rotted off their backs."

I waved to Simon, traded a joke with a llama farmer from Troutdale, and somehow, without trying, entered the party's slipstream. I moved from conversation to conversation, biding my time until all the other obligations were done and Amy and I could truly connect.

The hours passed, and the fat harvest moon tightened into an ever smaller circle, the aureole burned out, its ridges and mountains clearly branded on its smooth skin. At some point I found myself at a fire pit, staring into the twisting flames, the waves of crowd noise breaking overhead. I'd gotten more drunk than I'd meant to, and for some reason my pants were stained. Mostly, I was thinking about where to take my next piss. Before I could make any moves, though, a burly arm clamped my shoulders and a familiar voice was growling in my ear.

"You're having a good time? You're getting everything you need?"

Peter's face bobbed nearby, sweaty and reddish, and the hairs on his chest poked out of his shirt collar. His strong teeth flashed in the firelight. As the hub of this whole constellation he was obliged to talk to everyone, and it seemed it was finally time to say hello to me.

"We're just getting started," he said, releasing me at last. "So hey. What are you doing right now anyway?"

"Dunno. Why?"

"I got some news."

The fire washed us with orange heat. On the other side of the flames, Amy suddenly materialized beside a hulking blond man in distressed leather pants, and through the heat-warped bodies our eyes almost met. Once again, I had the pleasant, almost groinal sensation that she was keeping tabs on me.

"News?" I said.

"News," he said. "Come on. Let's go. Take a break. I could use a break, myself."

"Right now?" I said.

"Sure, why not?"

Amy glanced in my direction, laughing at something the leather-wearing man said. She was so close, I hated to leave, but it also occurred to me that maybe removing myself from circulation for a little while wouldn't be such a bad idea. I'd been making myself all too available thus far. I'd come across as almost desperate. It was time to create a little market scarcity.

"Lead the way," I said. And we headed from the garden, past Michael plucking his banjo and a little girl pushing a yoga ball, picking up new beers from a laundry tub on the way.

The door to Peter's office swung open into heavy blackness. He stepped inside and began flicking on lights. The first revealed a swath of Persian carpet and a wall of bookshelves. The next,

Peter's desk, an L-shaped fortress constructed from scavenged doors and sawhorses, surrounding an ancient leather executive chair. He hit one more and the wall opposite the bookshelves appeared, covered in musical instruments collected from garage sales and flea markets around the world—a lyre from Africa, an autoharp from Austria, maybe, and numerous objects that looked like dried gourds. Behind the desk, a huge picture window framed the party from above, and at the same time reflected us near the door.

I gravitated toward the bookshelves, the rows of sturdy, multicolored spines, an almost geologic progression of a certain West Coast intellectual tradition, braiding streams of sustainable agricultural technology, self-actualization, and Eastern religious discourses, anchored by names like Gurdjieff, Stewart Brand, and Alan Watts.

"Borrow whatever you want," he said, cracking his beer and taking his chair. "Kind of a lending library in here. Just bring them back when you're done. And have a seat. My God, make yourself comfortable."

I drifted over to the bay window, where I hoped Amy might catch sight of me from down below. I could count four bonfires across the property. On the movie screen a film featuring macramé owls and lemmings battling each other in a papier-mâché Arctic was playing.

"Good to get out of there for a while," Peter said, watching the scene. "It wears me out. All that glad-handing."

"You're a good host," I said, cracking my own beer.

"Yeah, yeah." He waved off the compliment. "I start to feel like some kind of politician out there. Kissing everyone's baby.

Don't get me wrong. It's good to see everyone. But, man oh man . . ."

"It's a job," I said.

Peter grunted his agreement and flicked his bottle cap at an ashtray, missing by a few feet.

"So we got some news this week," he said. "It could be nothing. Could be something interesting. Figured you might want to hear, as it'd affect you."

"Yeah?"

"You remember Jake Redden?" he said. "The reporter from the *Business Journal*? He came out in the group of San Rafael guys?"

"The sweaty one," I said. "With the wingtips. And kind of pushy."

"That's the one. He covers the whole food industry for the paper these days. He's made a nice little beat for himself over there. He writes about potatoes in Idaho, pinot noir in the Willamette Valley. Anything that involves buying and selling of agriculture. He's covered us a few times now. He was also at the Hallelujah seminar the other week. That first one you came to."

"I remember," I said.

"He was doing a follow-up piece," Peter explained. "It's funny. You just never know what's going to happen with these things. You never know what jack'll jump out of what box."

Peter pulled on his beer, watching something down below, letting his thoughts deplete, then pick up: "He watched the seminar. He saw the new technologies we've been working on. Wrote it up. The *Journal* needed to fill some more space, so he beefed up his little thing into a full feature. By the time the copy went on to the designer, they needed something on the front page, and all of a sudden Jake's little piece got bumped into the prime real estate."

"Good for him," I said, not seeing how any of this affected me and not really caring. A group of fire dancers had emerged into the garden, followed by some men on stilts dressed like Uncle Sam and Santa Claus, eliciting a mild roar.

"So last week," Peter went on, "four thousand copies of the *Business Journal* rolled off the presses, with this article about our consulting gig right up front. Went out to magazine stores and tobacco shops all around the state." He revolved in his chair and pulled open a drawer in his file cabinet and tossed an issue of the *Oregon Business Journal* onto his desktop within my reach. "Check that out."

Sure enough, page one held the article in question, under a headline reading "Encounters with New Consciousness." I skimmed through the copy. It was a puff piece, detailing Peter's accomplishments in the field of organizational management, with a photograph of Peter sharing a laugh with one of the bakery employees. The pull quote read, "Rain Dragon is about investing in the workforce. It's about providing a space for growth to occur." The article also described Rain Dragon's freewheeling, group-oriented philosophy, and the robust profits it somehow generated.

"Four thousand copies," Peter said, leaning back and clasping his fingers behind his head, leaving steamy palm prints on the desk's glass that shrank into skeletons and disappeared. "Into law offices and advertising studios around the whole region. The distro numbers are small, but it gets to a pretty powerful bunch of folks. How many copies are read—who knows? But I guess it only takes one reader sometimes.

"One issue," he went on, "landed on the desk of a man named Robert Doyle. Who is Bob Doyle, you ask? Bob's an old friend of mine. We went to high school together. We used to swim in the Snake River during the summer. Ran for class office against each other every year. We get together every six months or so and shoot the shit. He also happens to be vice president of human development over at Stanbro Paper. You've heard of Stanbro Paper before, correct?"

"They're . . ."

But Peter didn't want any answers from me. Tonight it was his responsibility to explain and mine solely to listen, and I contented myself watching a little boy carrying a sparkler along the path from the kitchen garden to the kiln, the flower of sparks bobbing, then sputtering out, until he presented the sparkler's burned stem to Linda.

"Stanbro Paper is the leading producer of paper and paper-based products in the continental United States," Peter said. "Five thousand employees. Two kraft-pulp mills. Five bleached paperboard mills. A plywood and ply-veneer plant. A particleboard, containerboard, hardboard, and wood-fiber mill. They make grocery bags and multiwall sacks for pet food, lawn and garden seed bags. They've got lumberyards in Oregon City, Estacada, and Corvallis. They own seven million acres in the United States, the licensing rights for twenty-nine million acres in Canada, and joint operating interests covering major acres in Australia, New Zealand, and Uruguay. They're big."

"Clearly."

"My buddy Bob, he's been working there about seventeen

years now, in the main office, downtown. He's a real solid citizen of the corporation. A real organization man. For as long as I can remember, he's been wringing his hands about the company's long-term competitiveness. For good reason, too. Stanbro's got six tiers of management stacked up between the CEO and the guys on the ground and they're shitting bricks about China. They're reading all the books: *Yellow Tide, The Asian Century, The Last Tiger.* Whatever. They know they're sitting inside a rusty old giant. They can see that the command and control model that built them can't cut it much longer. These guys are not stupid. They know China's going to eat their lunch. And China's only one problem. India, Brazil, Russia, they're all knocking on the door. When these economies get their shit together, man, our little American multinationals are going to be looking pretty meek and mild. They know they have to do something new, become something new, but they don't know what yet. This is a watershed moment. American corporate culture is becoming self-conscious—starting to question its own appetites, its own reasons for being. We're entering a moment when our whole business culture might change how it thinks in a big way. For the better."

Peter took a long slurp of beer without tilting his head. He was rolling.

"So Bob reads the article about Rain Dragon," he said. "He sees the picture of us in there. And it gets him thinking. He calls me up and tells me about a pilot program they're working on. The board's decided they're ready to test some new ideas. Stanbro's ready for help. He wants suggestions. And I say, Well, shit, how about us? There aren't many qualified outfits for this kind of job out there. He calls up Brad at the bakery, and they talk.

Turns out Hallelujah's productivity is up seven percent since we were there. The work force is gelling in a way Brad never figured was possible. Brad says he feels like the workers are finally beginning to get the fact that they share something more than a signature on their goddamn paycheck. Bob hears the same thing from Tao Tea and Modern Dog. He calls me back yesterday and says he wants us to put together a proposal. He thinks Rain Dragon and Stanbro might be a terrific fit."

Peter kicked his feet onto the desk and stared at the ceiling. I could tell this was the first time he'd spoken the whole storyline out loud, and he was still hearing how it sounded to himself. He chewed on his mouth and fondled a paper clip, tinkering out the significance. My own presence in the room seemed almost incidental to the contemplation.

"Success is a weird deal," Peter mused. "Usually more about what it keeps out of your life than what it lets in. You know what I'm saying? You don't notice your stomach if you're not hungry. You don't notice your head if it isn't hurting. Doors open, luck intervenes. You can take it for granted. Some dumb assholes don't even know when opportunity's knocking on their forehead."

"So what do we do?"

"We put together a proposal, I guess," he said, cracking his knuckles. "A budget? Sample technologies? Purpose statement? We assemble a team. We make a bid. It'll be a lot of work—a lot of writing, a lot of time. Could be a total waste. But if things fall together right, it could be pretty huge, too. We could make a serious impact. And the consulting fees at this level are . . . significant."

"What kind of time frame are we talking about?"

"They want the program up and running by the end of the

year. So count backward. I'd say they'd have to award the job by early October at the latest."

"Who else are they talking to?"

"Only one real competitor, by my thinking. Prism Lifesystems. You know them?"

"Prism," I said, with faint, feigned recognition. "Actually, no. Don't know it."

"Human potential outfit," Peter said. "They're based down in Eugene. They've been around for years. They retrained Adidas's upper management last year. They did Citibank awhile back. They're a machine. The founder is a guy named Anthony Cravens. You might have heard of him. Life coach to the last secretary of state. They say he's the one who turned around the Dallas Cowboys in 1998. His books camp out on the best-seller list for months at a time. Pretty remarkable dude."

"Is he the guy who split off from est?" I said. The name floated frustratingly at the edges of my synapses, refusing to attach to anything. "Shows up on commercials at night?"

"Nope," Peter said.

"Is he the one who lost a lot of weight?"

Peter snorted and shook his head. "No. Not that one. You'd remember him, believe me."

"I swear I've heard his name."

"You'd know."

Peter got up and crossed to his bookshelf and scanned the spines until he found a thin volume on the upper shelf. He pulled it down and tossed it over. It was called *Ways of Creating*, and the cover depicted the silhouette of a naked man with rainbows shooting from his hands. I turned it over and checked the back flap copy.

The text was boilerplate, but the author photo was hard to ignore. It showed a lone figure in a shady glade of palm trees, the sun setting in the distance behind sawtooth mountains. The man was wearing a low-slung Panama hat, but if you looked closely you could see that his features were strange. They looked warped and disfigured. His mouth was pulled off to the side, and his cheeks were raked with gouged lines. He looked like the Phantom of the Opera in a white Nehru shirt. Peter was right, I would have remembered him.

"Wow."

"Yep. Burned in Vietnam. It's a compelling story, actually. Came back all fucked up. Did some soul-searching. Started lecturing. One thing led to another. Now he's quite major. People come from all over the world to check him out. But with all due respect, I think his ideas move people in the wrong direction. Very 'I' oriented. I just can't get behind that kind of mind frame."

I flipped through the book, finding mostly inoffensive stuff—affirmative platitudes about finding enchantment in day-to-day living, rendered in an enormous font. A pack of firecrackers exploded dryly down below.

"This doesn't look too intimidating," I said, resting the book on his desk.

"I'm glad you think so," he said. "But the book is only part of the story. Kind of a departure point for his real-time encounter process. That's where he really gets to people, I hear."

"Have you ever seen him do his thing?"

"Nope. You could check it out if you wanted, though. In fact, it seems like a not bad idea, huh? We'd want to know what kind of process he's using, right? What the vocabulary's like. How they structure a two-day session. Could be helpful."

"Sure," I said as another batch of firecrackers exploded.

"They happen every few weeks," he said.

"Great," I said. "I'll sign myself up."

"You might not want to mention where you work."

"Of course not."

Peter grinned, looking through his reflection in the window. "You know, Damon," he said, "I had a feeling when you showed up here, there was some reason. I feel like you know what I'm talking about without all the explaining. I like where we're going with this."

He leaned over and fingered the book. "We just need a fair shake is all, you know what I mean? David knew what Goliath looked like, right? If you're up for it, I think you should go. Let's do it. Let's land this contract, man."

By the time I got back downstairs the crowd had swollen significantly, reinforced by the arrival of a caravan of new guests from Missoula, where a settlement of early Rain Dragon volunteers had retired when they felt things were getting too commercial back in 1989. The vibe was more restless now, seeking toward some culminating event. Laughter frothed from behind the trees. A naked man stumbled through knots of drunken partiers. On the far margins, the younger kids were watching the proceedings with open disgust.

I combed the crowd looking for Amy, but didn't find her anywhere.

She wasn't near the buffet table, nor the kegs, nor in the Meditation Room, and for a second I worried she might have left. But then, to my relief, she appeared in front of the mansion, flushed and gorgeous, laughing at a group of drunken bicyclists riding in woozy circles around a bonfire in the parking lot, one of whom fell face-first on the ground at her feet.

"How are you doing?" I said, smoothly pulling up beside her.

"Great!" she said, yelling over the noise. "How about you?"

"Great!" I said. And without thinking, infected by the secret knowledge of Peter's mission, I decided to be bold. "So, what are you doing later?"

"Huh?" she said, pretending not to hear.

"Later!" I said. "You want to come home with me?"

Her eyes drifted to the bikers, and a forgiving smile passed over her face. She shook her head, touching my elbow lightly. "No, Damon. Sorry. Not tonight."

"Not tonight. So, another night?"

"I don't know."

"But maybe?"

"I said I don't know." She softened a little. "But maybe. Sure. Who knows?"

That was all I needed to hear. Not tonight. I could live with not tonight, so long as that meant maybe some other night. I'd call that a success.

The drums throbbed louder. Through the smoke a dim procession was breaking through the crowd. The drumming intensified again, and soon the procession was right on top of us. It was a group of percussionists dressed in ragged cutoffs and funny high-school band hats, surrounding a long, shaking creature of some kind. The smoke thinned, and the creature sharpened into the shape of a dragon made of wood and papier-mâché. Its skin was scaled in firecrackers, and tall spikes ran down the spinal column. Lurchingly, it wheeled into the parking lot, causing the crowd to erupt into cheers, and then the hide burst into multicolored sparks.

The dragon shimmied in the circle of spectators, shedding yellow comets in all directions. Fiery projectiles bounced off the mansion's walls and ricocheted into the grass. Spinning flowers dropped from its tail. Sparks sprayed from its head. And all the while, the drum corps' chaotic rim shots and clashing cymbals continued, until finally, just as the skin was almost spent, the scales blackened, the dragon's body broke apart, and seven unicyclists launched from inside, a brood of baby dragons, pulling strings of firecrackers, sparklers spinning in their blazing spokes.

Amy was laughing. Peter, not too far away, was slapping Michael on the back. Linda's eyes were white with fear. When the drums boiled up again, Amy glanced my way, still laughing, and shook her head ambiguously. She'd be back, I thought. She'd be back soon enough. If only I could give her something worth coming back to.

FALL

EIGHT

THE DRIVE FROM PORTLAND to Eugene was about two and a half hours long, but in the predawn darkness, with the hops and lettuce rows flanking the highway fluttering like shadowy wings on either side, the distance seemed to race by much faster. The headlights carved a ten-foot swath into the asphalt ahead, and the dinosaurs of the eighteen-wheelers occasionally heaved into view. Before I knew it my coffee was gone, and soon after that the sky was brightening around Salem.

I blew by a Volkswagen poking along in the fast lane and came up on the mudflaps of a laboring Peterbilt. The laser beams of my headlights melted the back tires, and I tossed a few mental grenades in the cab for good measure. Back on the open road I aimed my inner flamethrower at the silhouettes of poplar trees and electrical towers appearing in the growing daylight, incinerating them with the merest thoughts.

I was in a good mood. Two weeks had passed since Dragon Days, and already I was on the road, heading south to observe the Prism seminar and report back on the how and why and what of their process, along with any suggestions I had as to how best to defeat them. This was my job now, though I had no qualifications and the parameters were incredibly vague. But such was Peter's

MO in these matters: move blindly toward the goal, trusting that happy surprises were in store. Use your instincts. Hope for the best. In the meantime, my hotel was paid for and all my meals would be comped.

I was a spy. And as such, the world took on a new luster. Everything was potentially interesting. My own shoes were more interesting—the shoes of a spy. My wallet, with its business cards, photos, and phone numbers, was suddenly an object of great intrigue and danger. My life story, familiar to the point of utter tedium to me, would now have to be jealously guarded, scrubbed of all reference to Rain Dragon or Stanbro. Only yesterday I was a PR hack for a fairly prosperous, shamblingly organized organic food company. Today I was the arrow of Rain Dragon, flying toward the unknowing heart of our competition.

I'd lately begun feeling more confident about our chances of landing the contract, too, after a period of thinking the whole notion was ridiculous. Prism was nationally renowned for its organizational management seminars. Anthony Cravens had bestselling books on his resume. Not only that, he was a decorated war veteran, injured during combat in Vietnam. What were we?

And yet, with Peter's hammering optimism in the back of my head, our prospects had started to seem more plausible. Peter himself had a solid track record of organizational change, didn't he, having consulted with dozens of small- to medium-sized companies over the years? His own company was a model of progressive managerial techniques, coupled with sustainable ecological practices and steady rates of growth and profitability.

Peter admitted we were underdogs. But by his magical way of thinking, our underdog status only contributed to our good chances. It was a classic scenario, he contended: the big, complacent, slow-moving behemoth of Prism versus the hungry, nimble insurgents of Rain Dragon.

"It's always this way. The American colonies versus Great Britain. Castro versus Batista. The Jets versus the Colts. Come on!"

With the element of surprise on our side, he said, and a well-crafted pitch in hand, we had every chance of seizing the day, assuming we could just keep our heads and execute our plan properly.

I was happy to ride his optimism. And it helped that on another front I was feeling optimistic as well. In the last weeks, the signals from Amy had been steadily strengthening. She'd been making herself more available around the mansion, loitering those extra minutes at breakfast, tossing shy glances during meetings, barely evading my work stations whatsoever. Every morning our paths crossed near the Quonset huts, and in the afternoon near the grape arbor, to the degree that it was obvious she was playing a game of some kind, plotting her routes just narrowly to avoid mine. One night she'd even called me with a question about how to fix a toaster oven—as if I knew—and we'd ended up talking for almost an hour about the crap on TV. The next day she'd ignored me, but it didn't matter. She was drifting back into my orbit.

As I drove south, the two optimisms overlapped in my mind, reinforcing each other and building into a kind of euphoria of possibilities. Soon, I thought, Amy and I would be together again, this time in a stronger, more passionate, more irrevocable way. She'd be running her thriving honey business, and I'd have my consulting work, and together we'd live in a comfortable house full of books, art, music, expensive kitchen appliances, and maybe even healthy, inquisitive children. I imagined a cozy little bungalow on Southeast Clinton Street, grape leaves filtering the light, me on the phone organizing some meeting with somebody, her on the couch, surrounded by color swatches for a new honey soap package, maybe changing a diaper.

Yes. Off to the west I burned a field of alfalfa. Nearing Silverton I lopped off the tops of the rolling hills. As the sun peaked over the Cascades I peeled off the freeway, heading west toward the coastal mountain range. I passed a pulp mill pumping clouds of white smoke into the air, a new housing development called River Run II, and a shopping center anchored by TJ Maxx. Rounding a bend, I arrived at the headquarters of Prism Lifesystems, a former junior high school perched on a low hill overlooking an elbow of the Willamette River, fronted by a manicured lawn with a sculpture of brushed steel bent into the shape of a Möbius strip.

I pulled into the parking lot and gathered my papers, and as I made my way to the doorway in the crisp air, I took a final moment to collect my thoughts. Prism's curriculum probably wasn't qualitatively different from our own, I'd come to realize—grounded in visualizations, affirmations, and encounters—and thus, the main thing I wanted to pay attention to was Prism's style. If we had any advantage in this fight, it lay in the fact that Prism was already so well established in the world. The company had a defined profile, a discrete batch of associations, whereas we had nothing of the sort, and thus the chance to define ourselves as need be. I'd learned in the ad world that this kind of self-fashioning really mattered. You took two identical potato chips and gave one the better package, and there was no contest: the better bag won. The trick was figuring out what you wanted to say with your bag. And to do that, it helped to know what your competition's bag was saying. The distinctions you could make were real. Meaningless, perhaps. But real.

At the main doors stood two smiling, white-haired staffers in green polo shirts embroidered with the Prism logo—the silhouette of a naked man trapped inside a diamond—ushering the morning's arrivals into the foyer. The greeters opened the door, and I stepped into the lavender-scented foyer, noting to myself that greeters were a nice touch. We'd have to use that idea. A quick scan of the room suggested the gathered attendees were mostly white, stolidly middle-class people. Men in chino pants and golf shirts. Women shining with foundation and rouge. Exactly the kind of average people we needed to learn how to address.

The clock said 6:30 a.m. The day's events started at seven, so I drifted over to the edge of the lobby to browse the books and pamphlets on display. What I found were mostly transcripts of past group encounters with Anthony Cravens and collected speeches by Prism coordinators, bound in neat folios with plastic coverings and titles like *Insight* and *Breakthrough*. There were also some CDs and calendars and an assortment of board games for sale. Judging from the line at the cash register, people were hungry for the stuff, especially the coffee mugs and key chains.

Rain Dragon could improve on any of these products, I thought. If nothing else, our sense of design was better. I snapped a few photos for later reference. The collateral materials offered a whole revenue stream we hadn't discussed.

I was perusing the liner notes of a Prism-produced musical album when a green-shirted staffer accosted me. I was a little defensive at first, ready to deny any accusations, but as it turned out she only wanted to help. She asked me if I'd checked in yet, and when I said no, she guided me to the intake desk, a folding table manned by a chubby woman with a dimpled chin and a sallow man with mousy brown hair, both of whom greeted me with ghoulish smiles. They checked my name against a computer printout, deposited my money in the cash box, and handed over my receipt and my session materials—a binder filled with vocabulary lists, thought exercises, supplementary texts, and bibliographies; a schedule of the day's activities; and a water bottle, all packed in a simple canvas tote bag silk-screened with the Prism logo.

Tote bags. Everyone loved a tote bag, didn't they? Rain Dragon should most definitely make some tote bags, regardless of whether we retrained Stanbro or not.

I stuck my receipt in my wallet. The employees of Prism were all thus far friendly, well-organized, and neatly groomed people. And while these all seemed like obviously positive attributes, I also wondered if they might be turned against them in some way. Maybe Rain Dragon could present a more freewheeling profile. Maybe our more casual, earthy manners could become a selling point.

I was still pondering this notion when the auditorium doors opened and the crowd began to shuffle inside. I let myself be dragged along with the current, and within seconds I was standing inside a gigantic volume of blackness, a former gymnasium still faintly reeking of wrestling mats. As my eyes got used to the darkness, I made out a field of metal folding chairs, and high above, a grid of gaffing stocked with spotlights and fills and masses of thick, bundled wiring. On the far wall was a low stage backed by velvet curtains, with a podium and a potted palm. The side wall hosted scaffolding for cameras and lighting technicians, and a soundboard bigger than I'd ever seen. The sheer quantity of hardware was intimidating to behold. We had an ancient PA system and a half-broken slide projector back at Rain Dragon.

I took a seat about two-thirds back, between a woman with a platinum bilevel bob and a man with almost no chin, and precisely at 7:10 the doors closed with a light hiss and a click. The crowd did its final resettling, coughing and shifting and rearranging its feet, as along the side walls the Prism staffers struck positions like soldiers at their battlements. We waited another ten minutes in silence. At first the long pause seemed like a fumble on Prism's part, a lapse in planning, but at some point I realized that the dead time was in fact serving a greater aim. The longer we waited, the more our suspense grew, and the further we all settled into a shared state of mind. Throughout the nearly one hundred people in the room, a quiet understanding was gradually circulating and picking up strength. We were on the cusp of a major happening here. We were moving toward a threshold beyond which all was unknown. Across the aisle a gaunt woman accidentally caught my eye and lifted her eyebrows with a sharp look of hope.

Note to Peter: arbitrary rules can foster a feeling of shared anticipation.

Sometime during the waiting period a nearly inaudible tone began to rise from speakers placed discreetly around the room, building gradually into a low, ominous drone. The crowd was breathing in sync now. Our senses were calibrated. The tone got louder by infinitesimal degrees until finally it was unmistakable—a triumphant, choral note of imminent revelation. Sun rising. Birds flying. Clouds streaming. When the note reached an almost operatic level, a single spotlight blinked on, painting a red disk on the far curtains.

The curtain spasmed and disgorged a tall, grave, horse-faced man. He loped to the podium and pulled on the neck of the microphone stand with his ungainly hands, sending a muffled creak into the far corners of the room. The tension was strong enough that every gesture seemed meaningful now. The room itself invested his movements with a vague but weighty significance.

"Welcome," he said, and his deep voice boomed all around the gym. On the curtains tinted lights were coming up—red and magenta and yellow in oblong splashes pulsating in slow, anticipatory throbs. "Welcome to Prism Lifesystems," he said. "I thank you all for coming out to attend our introductory seminar this weekend. I congratulate all of you on a dramatic, life-changing decision."

Around the room the Prism staff began applauding. After a brief hesitation—Was it against the rules? Was this a test?—the crowd began clapping along with them, and the room filled with applause. The curtains parted to reveal a sizable movie screen.

"I wish I could tell you what to expect over the next few hours," he said, "what you're about to experience here together, but I can't. What you're about to do goes beyond words." Above him, overlapping images appeared of a glinting diamond rotating in space, shooting rainbows and stardust, and the word *Prism* assembling from weightless, multicolored letters in the void. Sweeping synthesizer music poured from the speakers and churned through the room.

"I am here to welcome you," the man said. "I would like to welcome you to your coming life journey. It is my great pleasure this morning to introduce your guide for this trip, the author of *Ways of Creating* and *Ways of Creating Sourcebook*, the founder of Prism Lifesystems, Dr. Anthony Cravens!"

The crowd clapped, this time without any hesitation, and some audience members whistled and stomped. The music crescendoed with a cosmic windswell of synthesizer. And from the side of the stage Anthony Cravens bounded joyfully into the circle of light.

I was not prepared for the physical presence of him. His forehead was a pink glob striated with white streams of scarred, hardened tissue. His jowls dripped with reddish pustules, and his nose was almost nonexistent, a slight bump between marbled cheeks. His one arm, the left one, was really just a bright red crook with webbing between his thumb and forefinger. In his crisp white oxford and pressed khaki pants, he took the stage like the consummate showman, seizing the microphone and lurching from one end of the proscenium to the other, squinting into the audience with barely contained delight. At center stage he stopped and raised his hand to urge us to clap louder, which we did, and the screen beamed a closed-circuit image of his actions, zooming in for a close-up on his ruined face. His eyes were pink, wet-looking slits, slick jewels embedded in the scaly folds, and there were deep gouges on his cheeks and jaw. The only unravaged features were his perfect white teeth.

The applause continued. Cravens planted himself at the lip of the stage and lowered the microphone to his mouth.

"Are you grateful?" he said. His voice was deep and a little phlegmy from emotion. The crowd whooped gamely in response.

"I said, Are you grateful?" he asked again, more loudly, and the crowd responded more loudly as well. People began stomping their feet, and soon the whole room was shaking. Cravens's bond with his audience was instantaneous, blowing past the initial horror into fast intimacy.

"We should be grateful every fucking second of the day!" he said. "Look at us. Look at us here." He lowered his center of gravity and spread his stump over the scene. "Here we are living together, sharing our lives on this beautiful planet. We have been collected across oceans of time to find each other and love each other here. Look around you right now." Up above, powerful bulbs in wide silver pans flashed, revealing the assembled crowd to itself in brief, excoriating detail, and just as quickly the lights were extinguished, plunging us back into darkness, the afterimage of our neighbors still blinking on our lids. "Look at these people you are traveling with!" Cravens called. "This is your crew. This is your family. We are speeding through space together on a spinning stone, and we need each other to make it where we're going!"

The audience was well primed for Cravens's message. The first threshold had been crossed. This benign monster was inviting us to follow him on a journey of self-discovery, and we accepted.

"Who are you?" Cravens said. "That's the question I'm asking today. That's the question the world asks you every day, doesn't it? Who are you? What are you made of? What kind of clothes do you wear? What kind of neighborhood do you live in? What kind of cereal do you eat? Every billboard and TV commercial grabs you by the shirt and asks you over and over again: Who are you? Who are you failing to be?

"I'm here to tell you today that 'who' is the wrong question. The question we need to be asking ourselves isn't who. The question is 'if,' 'is,' and 'why.' That's what we're here to talk about this weekend. That's what we're here to figure out. Are you? Is anyone? Do you want to be? Do you have to be?"

Cravens talked for over an hour, delivering a litany of self-deprecating jokes and folksy accounts of men and women letting go of preconceived notions of success, desire, and self-expectation to enjoy true happiness through simple living. His material was solid. He had strong food metaphors. Strong sports metaphors. Strong driving metaphors. He quoted Wittgenstein and Seneca. He spoke slowly, in nested clauses, repeating certain words and phrases in a way that had you guessing which word or phrase would appear next, and pleasurably satisfying or thwarting your expectations along the way. He returned often to the notion of pure, blissful Experience and the way it was papered over, distorted, and misconstrued by language. And how language was also the only way that said Experience could truly be understood. His timing was impeccable. He never paused, but nor did he hurry. The sentences flowed into each other. He strode across the stage wagging his microphone, hopping from aphorisms and koans into well-formed allegorical vignettes. "Feel New," he said. "Suffering is the only teacher." "You are the prisoner and the jailer of yourself." On the screen his quotations appeared and dissolved, interspersed with birds in flight, running cheetahs, time-lapse cityscapes, and clouds passing across the sky. At the center, though, was always Cravens's voice. Tough, flinty, caring, ironic. More than anything else, he asked us to recognize the tremendous choice we held in our hands at any given moment, the choice between fear and love, fear and generosity, fear and joy, and the importance of always choosing joy, love, and generosity over fear. The journey began with merely recognizing the choice. And coming from him, this ravaged wad of flesh, the message actually meant something. If this man could be happy, who couldn't? We all sat in some awe of his gladness.

In the second hour, the lights dimmed and the music stopped.

The screen went blank, and Cravens recounted the story of his time at war. He described the arrival of his draft notice at age eighteen, his sad ignorance of how even to find Vietnam on a map. He guided us through the indignities of basic training, his deployment near Quang Ngai, the boredom of barracks life. He recounted the terror of his first firefight. We were right alongside him by the time he came to the fateful search-and-destroy mission into the jungles around Thien But Mountain. We walked with him under the triple canopy, stood at his shoulder during the shredding ambush in the abandoned village of straw huts. We bore witness to his buddy, Kevin, dancing over a grenade seconds before becoming tinsel in the surrounding trees. We lay with him as the Vietcong emerged from the brush and walked out through the smoking battlefield, tipping carts, kicking corpses, and finally surrounding him, staring down, expressionless as fish.

For the next two years, he told us, he'd lived in a bamboo cage the size of two unfolded newspapers. "Have you ever prayed?" he asked us. "I mean, really prayed? Like, groveled on the ground, rocks in your hands, eating dirt and praying?" He'd prayed like that, he said, daily. Not for himself, but for his mother, who he knew was living through a hell worse than his own back home.

Finally, his story came to the day of his liberation. The morning American voices emerged in the jungle. The burst of hope he felt as the Vietcong raced to abandon their base camp, pouring gasoline on everything in sight. And the sinking horror that came over him when the American grenade rolled into the clearing. The explosion. The sight of his own skin melting like candle wax, his arm fusing to his knee. His mind dissolving as the weight of the universe landed on top of him, destroying his very consciousness. Every speck of being crushed. Breathing fire. The hair in his nose disintegrating into ash.

Anthony Cravens poured himself a fresh glass of water from a sweating pitcher on the table and maneuvered the glass to his lips, one foot tucked under the strut of his stool. There were no flashy images anymore, no homilies or jokes. Just a single spotlight shining down through the darkness onto his reddish skin. He rose and walked to the edge of the stage, passing his patient, gentle gaze over the room.

"I wish I could reach inside every one of you right now," he said. "I wish I could let you know what I felt like in that hospital room, seeing myself for the first time. I wish I could express to you what I feel like even telling you about that time. But I can't. God didn't make things like that. He made them difficult. He put walls between us. He forced us into different bodies and gave us this thing called language to express ourselves with. I can only tell you what I've seen, and hope you can get it in some way. This is it. This is the best we have.

"I lost my Self in Vietnam," he said. "I went there a handsome young patriot, and I came home what you see here. Everything that made me me was taken away. My arm was taken away. My face was taken. My values were taken. I'd been a regular, optimistic kind of kid. But the war took that person. I came home with no dreams anymore. I came home with no me. Here's a question for you: Who are you when everything about you is gone?

"I lost my Self. But over time I came to find I still had something to give. I came to find that only in loss does real peace come. Only in giving up belief is true belief possible. This might sound strange, but it's something we'll be exploring together here. I had no choice in the matter. I had to let go. You may have no choice either. You may be stuck in a Self that is killing you. You may find letting go of your Self is almost impossible. But when the alternative is only more pain, the choice is clear. You let go. Over the next forty-eight hours we will try and let go together. Welcome to Prism, all of you. I can't tell you how glad I am that you're here."

With that, the lights came up and we were released back into the lobby, where Prism's team leaders were waiting to shepherd us to the next installment of the day's itinerary. They lined us up by teams and herded us down the halls to our respective home-rooms. Outside, the dogwoods were like ink seeping upward into the dirty cotton of the sky.

Prism was a well-oiled machine, with a profound, articulate captain at the controls. Anthony Cravens was going to be a tough guy to get around. The competition for the Stanbro contract was going to be stiff.

NINE

WHAT FOLLOWED WAS A long day of processing. We began with mind-clearing meditation, followed by introductions and goal-sharing. From there we broke into dyads for an hour of intensive self-narration exercises, followed by group feedback, art therapy, one-on-one discussion of current events, and pre-lunch calisthenics. Lunch was lentils and brown rice with tahini sauce. Then came tai chi, more dyading, and a group encounter with Cravens himself, during which we were encouraged to tell our life stories in ten sentences or less, and in return got a blast of the full klieg light of his attention.

In each phase of the day we were pushed, prodded, and rigorously kept on schedule, confronted by constant questions, provocative stories, and exhortations to see our Selves in new ways. As citizens of our respective cities and states. As children and grandchildren and distant relatives. As lovers and former lovers. Even as mere bodies sucking air and nutrients. Who are You? we were asked. Who do You want to be? Who did You think you'd be when You were six years old? Seven? Seventeen?

Over the hours my sense of selfhood reshaped many times. I saw myself as a good student, a thoughtless son, a fair-weather sports fan, an excellent parallel parker. Some of the selves were innocuous and others were harrowing, but none of them were taken for granted, with every utterance ransacked for double meanings, and every gesture taken as a clue to some greater, hidden truth. And always, just as some breakthrough seemed on the verge of happening, some glimpse at a holistic truth, a whole new pocket inevitably opened and disgorged more raw psychic material to process.

It was grueling. My one brief moment of quiet came in the bathroom, and even then the lessons didn't stop. I was taking a piss when who but Cravens himself strolled in the door, taking a place at the urinal beside me, and apropos of nothing turned to me and said: "Motherhood is a revolution." And then he zipped up and strode away.

As the day wore on, my optimism around Rain Dragon's competitive chances diminished, and by midafternoon a sense of real discouragement was settling in. Watching my fellow participants giving themselves over to the Prism process—laughing, crying, breaking down on cue—I found it hard to imagine that Rain Dragon could possibly make a genuine bid. Prism's staff was too well trained, too well practiced in the art of human actualization. Their program was almost scientifically efficient. In comparison, Peter's ideas looked haphazard and arbitrary.

The day ended with a simple meal of curried vegetables, after which we were released for a few hours of sleep. I was exhausted, wrung out from so much talk, wanting only a clean pillow and a few minutes of hotel TV. But I knew it was my duty to report my findings to Peter.

Thus, sixteen hours after arriving in Eugene, I ended up outside the Reel M'Inn Tavern, a few blocks from the Red Lion Hotel, walking the streets for decent phone reception. As the signal finally firmed up, I punched in Peter's number and got no response. I left him a message, pocketed the phone, and decided I'd give him at least one beer's worth of time to call back.

Stepping into the Reel M'Inn was like entering the mouth of some Bowery bum, hot with the stench of stale beer and old cigarettes. The rear wall was crowded with neon signs representing practically every American beer company that had ever existed, and yet still the cavelike interior was dim. A decrepit moose head hung over the dartboard, missing an ear, two darts permanently embedded in its once plush snout.

The bartender, a frail man in wide suspenders, floated from his stool to take my order. The only other customer was an old man with a bushy mustache and patched jeans, his head wreathed in cigarette smoke—openly in defiance of state law—that caught the flickers of a football game on the Carter-era TV.

I took a seat a few stools down. The beer arrived watery and cold, and cleared my head a little, which only brought my nagging pessimism into sharper relief.

I could already hear Peter's good cheer ringing in my mind. We can still do it, he'd say. We can still prevail. And maybe he'd be right in that assessment. Maybe I wasn't seeing some obvious opportunity. Maybe Prism's technologies had just rattled me. All those who-are-you, what-are-you-doing questions had gotten me all turned around.

Or had they opened me to a deeper truth? Who was I, after all? What was I doing? What was I failing to do? The flimsy walls of my self-identity showed hairline cracks everywhere. I was very possibly wasting my precious life.

I imagined tomorrow's curriculum was probably going to involve building everyone's sense of self-confidence back up again.

But for the moment, sitting at the bar in the light of the football game, everything was still under serious review.

One thought plaguing me was work. My PR duties at Rain Dragon had dried up lately, and I wasn't sure if they'd be coming back around anytime soon. There was nothing on the calendar as far as new products or media campaigns went, and somehow I still hadn't learned any farming skills. That meant I had no realistic options as to what I might do going forward at Rain Dragon. Assuming no amount of underbidding or surprise endorsements from local business leaders was going to net us this Stanbro contract, I needed to figure something out. I was inclined to head home first thing in the morning and get cracking on a yogurt cookbook, my most plausible entrepreneurial idea to date. At least in the realm of food I had something to work with.

Much worse, though, were the thoughts about Amy. Who was I fooling on that front, anyway? What made me think we still had a chance? Looking back on the past few weeks, I had to admit the signals I'd been telling myself she was sending simply didn't exist. So we'd bumped into each other a few times: big deal. If anything, she'd been sending me negative signals—avoiding me more than usual, finding absurd reasons to slip out of conversations. She'd only called the other night because she was hoping I'd loan her the car.

Sitting in the bar, nursing my beer, I saw with cruel clarity just how finished it was. The break had been a long time coming. We'd been fooling ourselves for years, waiting for some change that was never happening. On my side, I'd been waiting for Amy to give up the scornful, fearful, self-aggrandizing parts of herself and become the loving, upbeat, hilarious person I liked best. She was probably hoping I would tap some unseen vein of ambition and slough off the lazy, mealy-minded habits that made me so intolerable. That wishfulness had always been there between us, that fantasy, and we'd wasted years thinking it would come true. In the worst, bottommost chamber of my thoughts, I wondered if we'd never even loved each other at all.

Seven years of illusion, I thought. Seven years of useless, self-inflicted suffering. What else might have happened in that time? What had I missed?

Still, I was willing to be proven wrong, so I called her, but she didn't pick up. I wasn't so tired anymore—if anything I was getting a little frantic—and I went ahead and ordered another beer, and this time a whiskey, too, hoping to calm down. Assuming I wasn't going back to Prism tomorrow, I figured I could afford to stay out awhile, stewing.

The bartender scratched at a crossword puzzle. Down the bar, the old man was barking at the TV. The Seahawks threw an interception, causing him to growl and look around for commiserators. He couldn't help himself any longer and tipped his beer in my direction. He was in the bar looking for company, and I was it.

"Fucking Seahawks, man," he said out the side of his mustache. "Fucking bums. You call that offense?" He glanced over for some confirmation of his revulsion, his eyes desperate but undangerous.

"No shit," I mumbled. The team's record was unknown to me. I didn't know when the season had started, or who the management had paid to play for them this time around. But I'd faked my way through enough barroom sports conversations over the years to know a few strategic grunts of agreement were usually enough. When in doubt, agree passively.

"That fucking jigaboo Payton," the old man said. "Look at that. A fucking millionaire, and he won't run. They should ax his black ass."

"Yep," I said, without conviction. Sometimes my policy of blanket agreement led me to concur with some unsavory sentiments.

"Nussmeier, there's a QB," he said. "Hawks should draft him. He'd play his heart out. They should clone that kid."

"That's right," I said.

"You see him on Tuesday?" The topic of Nussmeier was apparently one of his favorites. "Jesus H. Christ. What a specimen. He can scramble! That kid should skip college and go pro tomorrow. He's good enough. And they need him."

We were talking on the subject of local prep football, I gathered. Gruntingly, I admitted I hadn't seen the game that week and then it quickly came out that I wasn't from around these parts at all. I was hoping the news might kill the conversation in its cradle, but in fact it only stoked the old man's curiosity.

"But you know Nussmeier?" he said, his suspicion aroused by my previous agreements.

"Everyone knows Nussmeier," I lied. "He makes all the papers."

The old man mumbled something to himself, seemingly satisfied, and turned back to the TV, where women in red, white, and blue bustiers were line-dancing in front of the American flag. Without any effort, we'd somehow become viewers together, bonded by our mutual attention to the screen. And once we were viewers together, we were practically friends.

"Where you from?" he said, lighting an Old Gold off his last.

"Portland," I said. Another policy in small-town bars—don't take noticeable pride in your big-city address.

"Welcome to town," he said, and raised his bottle. "Fuckup capital of the world. If not the state."

"Thanks."

"What're you doing down here?" he said. He couldn't keep from talking now that he knew I was listening. "College?"

"Nope," I said.

"Work?" he said.

"Not exactly."

"Family?"

"Nope," I said. And now I felt like he deserved some tidbit of information for his interest, so I added, "I'm here doing a seminar."

"Seminar?" he said. "What's that mean?"

"It's called Prism," I said. "It's like a human development thing."

Again, I expected this to end the conversation—What did he care? There were no cheerleaders or jockstraps involved—but instead it had the opposite effect. The old man sat up straight for the first time and practically spat into his beer. "Prism," he said hatefully. "Fucking Prism. I know all about Prism. Oh man, do I."

"You know Prism?" I said.

"Do I know Prism? Fucking yuppie assholes. I know Prism all right." I was surprised by the vehemence. But then again, maybe everyone was a yuppie asshole to this old timer, until an introduction occurred and you were proven to be all right.

"Have you done the training?" I asked.

"Hell no," he said. "I work for Prism. I didn't do their goddamn program."

"Must be another Prism," I said. "These guys are more like teachers, consultants." But he was adamant. He worked for Prism.

"They own every goddamn thing in this town," he said.

"The whole west side is Prism. If you live here, you work for Prism. Anthony Cravens. I know all about it. He's buying up the whole town. Who's stopping him?"

The Seahawks made two yards on a handoff down the middle, leading to a long lull in action. The teams huddled, and we drank. I had to admit, I was a little curious about the old man's story. A glimmer of my morning's spy fantasy flickered back to life. Maybe the laws of Peter's universe had rubbed off on me a little. At the end of the road, off in the brush in the wilderness, a new light appeared, guiding the way.

I edged my stool closer and introduced myself. The old man's name was Arnold, he said, which in itself seemed mildly significant. The name of one of Cravens's lost buddies in Vietnam was Arnold. Another small bell to make me pay attention. I tried to play my interest casually, asking some general questions about Arnold's life in Eugene and his family, but it didn't matter. Arnold was so hungry for company I could have been wearing full Gestapo regalia and he would have gladly spilled his tale. Especially as new glasses of beer kept appearing under his nose.

He hadn't always worked for Prism, he said, sucking the foam bubbles off his mustache. He'd worked most of his life for Wakonda Pacific, one of the major logging outfits of the region. He'd spent years up in the coastal mountains, pulling more cord feet off the land than most any man alive. It was good work, bracing work. Made you feel all the way alive. Up until a few years ago, anyway, when Cravens bought the mill and sold it off for scrap.

It was still galling to Arnold. He groaned at the memory, even as the Seahawks gained fifteen yards on a play-action pass. Cravens didn't know dick about logging, he said. He didn't care. He'd just seen a chance to pick up a property and sell it for parts and he didn't mind putting a hundred fifty men out of work to line his pockets.

"The spotted owl means more to people around here than people do," he said. "No one gives a shit."

Again, I made feeble sounds of agreement.

"My benefits ran out a couple years ago," he said, "and I couldn't find shit for work. No jobs around here. I didn't want to up and leave town, though, my sisters are still around, so I ended up applying over at the Green Meadows retirement home as a janitor. Two hundred beds. Guess who owns it? Prism. How's that for your irony? They dismantle the whole mill, send me packing, and now they sign my checks anyway.

"Shittiest job you can think of," he went on, eyes on the screen. "Wiping ass all day. Airing out the old farts. No overtime. No benefits. A quarter the wage I made before. Never put me in one of those homes, man. Time comes, I'll walk into the woods and die by myself. Viking style. There's some dignity in that, at least."

"So it's pretty bad?" I said, trying to guide the listing ship of his attention.

"One nurse for fifty clients," he said. "Watered-down applesauce for dinner. Holes in the ceiling. I could tell you stories."

"Yeah?"

"You don't want to hear," he said. "You're too young. It'll scare you."

"Come on," I pressed.

He wet his lips. The Seahawks were having trouble making it into the end zone on a two-yard push, and we had to wait for time-out to continue.

"Last week, a woman died," Arnold said. "Suffocated in the

harness on the wheelchair. They didn't get her in tight enough. She just slipped down, no one noticed. All through dinner they didn't notice. Only later on, cleaning up, they see she's still there. That's just last week."

"Must be trouble."

"Bah. Nothing happened. They took her to the morgue. That's it."

"But her family . . ."

"These people, no one remembers them. Their families are checked out, man."

"You talked to anyone?"

"I'm talking to you."

"I mean someone official."

Arnold grumbled something about not giving a shit what the government said or did. I bought another round and listened to more of his horror stories. He told me about the rapid turnover among the Green Meadows staff. The lack of training and cutting of corners in all ways imaginable. The broken call buttons. The cold meals. The festering pressure sores. If half the abuses he described were true, the nursing home was a nightmare. If nothing else, it was quite a side business for a company in the lofty trade of higher consciousness.

Back in the hotel, bloated with beer, I called Peter and delivered my day's report, ending with my trip to the Reel M'Inn and Arnold's barroom tale. I told him I was thinking of skipping the second day of the workshop, but maybe staying in Eugene and nosing around a little, getting the details on Arnold's story straight. I was still high on my chance encounter, and for once Peter seemed to be lagging behind.

"You're what now?" he said. "You met who?"

"A guy in a bar," I said. "He works for Prism. It's complicated."

"And you want to do research."

"Basically."

"Whatever you think feels right, inspector. Spy away."

I called Amy, too, but hung up before she could answer. I decided I didn't want to know what she was doing after all. I'd save my spy stories for later, when I had a good ending to tack on. At the moment I would just enjoy my free night in a hotel, pad around the room naked, watch cable spread-eagled on the clean sheets.

In the morning, well rested, I skipped Prism and took my coffee to city hall, where I spent a few hours going through the records in the basement. My luck held. Sure enough, Arnold was entirely correct about Prism's holdings. The portfolio included a downtown restaurant, a discotheque, a car dealership, and a few check-cashing outlets, mostly registered in Cravens's name, but some with more elaborate deeds. There was nothing inherently damning about the holdings, nothing illegal, but with a little imagination it was easy to infer a complex web of interests that Anthony Cravens presided over like a lethal spider.

I made copies of everything—the secretaries were very helpful—and put the pages in my briefcase, a chapped leather number I'd picked up at Goodwill just for the trip. From city hall, just for the hell of it, I drove out to see Green Meadows firsthand.

I found the building out on Wakonda Road, as per Arnold's directions, just past the filbert farms and the collapsing red barn. On first sight it was indeed a depressing place—a flimsy two-story barracks never meant to last as long as it had. The steps were coated in furry moss, the shutters were falling off the second-floor windows, and a black tarp, held in place with broken bricks, covered a major swath of the roof near the chimney. The whole property was shaded by a wall of ragged fir trees that cast a permanent, unpleasant chill.

The lobby was not much better—a dingy, windowless meeting point of grim hallways where a flock of old people sat propped in poses of despair. One pale, papery woman stared blankly into the middle distance, a long stalactite of snot growing from her nostril. Down the hall I could hear the sad keening of someone—someone's grandfather or aunt—unattended in some dank room.

"How old are you?" said a woman with demented eyes, rousing from her trance as I passed by.

"Twenty-eight," I said.

"I'm ninety-two!" she said. "My back is killing me!"

At the front desk a burly woman in a nurse's smock eyed me with suspicion. Before I was halfway across the lobby she asked if she could help me, in a tone that made it plain she doubted she could.

I hadn't given much thought to how far I intended to go with this mission. But standing there, smelling the stink of Green Meadows, looking at the grumpy nurse, the unhappy old folks, I decided maybe I should push a little harder than I'd expected. The nurse's hostility was itself a prod.

She asked again if I needed any help and I told her that I was looking for a place to store my mother for a while, and I wondered if I could take a tour of the facilities.

"Sorry," she said. "You need a reservation for that."

"But I just wanted to look around," I explained. "I don't need anyone to help."

"You need to be on the clearance list," she said. "Or you need to have a relative in the home."

"I'm only in town for a day. I'm thinking about putting her here. Maybe I can just peek around?"

"We need to schedule all tours in advance. Policy." I had the feeling she was inventing the policy on the spot.

"And who would I schedule the tour with?"

"Corporate."

"Could I schedule a tour for today?"

"It takes at least two days."

I looked around the lobby again. A woman dressed in a Victorian bustle shuffled by, her dusty hem dragging. A man hobbled glacially with his walker, the front legs padded with split tennis balls. When I turned back, the secretary had returned to her papers, apparently done with me.

"Thanks for the help," I said, and turned and exited back into the brisk, sunny fall air, all the sweeter after having been inside that moldering home. I figured I might have better luck circumventing the secretary entirely. I was willing to give it a try. This wasn't for my own gain, after all. The facts needed collecting.

I skulked around the side of the building, brushing by the rusting Dumpster and the employees' compact cars, and made my way to the back door, which was wide open. I wandered into what turned out to be the kitchen. The smell of spoiled milk tinged the air, and three cockroaches scrambled on the floor.

The cook, a cherubic Indian woman, emerged from a pantry, ignoring me until I began taking pictures. I wasn't sure what the point of the documentation was, but she seemed to think it was threatening.

"Hey," she said, "who are you?"

"Excuse me?" I said, pretending not to understand the question.

"I said, Who are you?"

"I'm just looking around," I said.

She narrowed her eyes, but already her interest was waning. I wasn't her responsibility. She tossed four pieces of bread in the toaster and let me take a few more pictures of ants carrying boulders of sugar on their backs. Behind her, a door opened and Arnold appeared. He looked at me strangely, dimly remembering our meeting of the night before, and shook his head as if some dream had recurred. He turned and walked away, washing his hands of whoever I was and whatever I was doing.

After documenting the kitchen—expired milk in the refrigerator; flies on the chicken breasts—I snuck into the dining room, snapping shots of the grimy tabletops and battered chairs, and from there I wandered the hallways housing the clients' rooms. I crept around for almost half an hour collecting images of what I imagined to be infractions of code. I got waterbugs near the baseboards on the ground level. I got soiled beds in the east wing. I got the overflowing closet of dirty laundry and bedclothes, the flies buzzing angrily. The peeling wallpaper was mostly cosmetic, but it told the story better than anything else. The water stains on the ceiling were more serious, possible signs of structural damage. The evidence, such as it was, compiled quickly.

At first I made an effort to hide whenever staff people approached, but at some point I realized they didn't care about anything that didn't affect their work directly, and on the rare occasions they inquired, I told them I was visiting my aunt, Mrs. Williams. In a room far at the end of the hall I watched, wincing, as two male nurses forced a patient into a leg brace. I prayed I got hit by a bus at age eighty or so. Anything to avoid this whole excruciating purgatory.

Back in Eugene, I took my camera to the copy shop. After sorting through the pictures, deleting the boring and blurred ones, I printed doubles of the suggestive images and slipped one stack in my briefcase. The other I put into an envelope, along with photocopies of Green Meadows' deed, Arnold's phone number and address, and a Prism pamphlet—all the pieces an intelligent reporter would need to put the puzzle in place. I took the envelope to the post office and stamped it and dropped it in the slot, addressed to Jake Redden, our man at the *Oregon Business Journal*.

TEN

IT WAS NOT EXACTLY an accident when I ran into Amy at the grocery store a few days later. Fresh from my spying mission, still feeling lucky, and having bounced back from the depths of my pessimism, I figured I might as well go ahead and push my fortune a little bit further.

We still bumped into each other most every day at the farm, but I'd gotten to thinking we could use a different kind of run-in if we really wanted to move things along to the next level. What we needed was some magic, something that jump-started our story with a flourish. We needed to feel the hand of fate in our lives. With this in mind, I started frequenting the coffee shops and Laundromats in her neighborhood, hoping to give the hand of fate a little push.

The lurking took a few days to pay dividends. She never came into the coffee shop or the video store during my loitering shifts. Nor the falafel place, nor the park down the street from her house. But one lesson I'd already learned from my trip to Eugene, and from my time with Peter in general: positive thinking maintained its own schedule. You never knew exactly when or how your luck would come, but if you waited long enough, something would surprise you. The trick was stamina. Just sit quietly, don't fret, and eventually the world can't help but throw itself at your feet.

Sure enough, one Tuesday night, I was wheeling my cart down the Safeway aisle, filling the basket with my standard list of corn tortillas, cheddar cheese, and black beans, when I came upon Amy in the canned food section, comparing the ingredients on two brands of minestrone soup. She wasn't expecting to see anyone that night, or so I deduced from her sloppy pigtails and stained sweatpants, but I wasn't passing up the opportunity. I was even kind of pleased to see she wasn't thriving in my absence.

She put the can back on the shelf and picked up another one, which she rotated to read the ingredients. Her eyes squinted cutely as she deciphered the fine print. I rolled my cart in her direction.

"Ahem."

Her eyes stayed fixed on the can, and her foot shoved her cart toward the edge of the aisle. She thought I was some stranger wanting to squeeze by. I ahemed again, and this time her eyes flicked up to mine. The initial look was chilly, but thankfully melted immediately into recognition, and then, if I looked closely enough, even some level of affection, too.

"What are you doing here?" she said, a mixture of warmth and suspicion in her voice. "This isn't your store."

This time, unlike at Green Meadows, I had my answer ready: "I needed some milk," I said.

"There's no milk in your neighborhood?" she said. She knew I wasn't one to deviate from routine, but I had another answer in back of the first one, ready to go.

"I'm taking care of someone's cat."

"Over here?"

"Yeah."

"Ah," she said, dropping her can into her basket. "That's noble. Whose cat?"

"This guy's," I said, vaguely. "Someone I met."

"Uh-huh. Kind of out of your way, though."

"Well. I like to help."

Amy dropped another two cans into her basket, smirking, and
leaned into her cart. I rolled beside her, our two metal cages moving
in tandem, and when she turned left at the pyramid of green beans
I turned left, too. I wasn't feeling any hostile vibrations, so when she
turned into the napkin and paper plate section, I stayed in sync.

"So you're doing all right?" she said.

"Yeah," I said. "I'm pretty good. You?"

"Pretty good. You know."

"I hear your lip balm's really moving," I said, which was true.
Word around Rain Dragon was that she and Linda were enjoy-
ing continuing success with their honey-based facial products,
and were pushing ever harder to bump up the production levels.
There were rumors of expansions, reallocations, consolidations.
But I had yet to hear about any of it from her.

"That's for sure," she said.

We rolled into the produce section as the water system shushed
to life, gilding the cabbage and broccoli with fake dew. Elbow to
elbow, exchanging light gossip about coworkers, we set about
testing the fruit and vegetables.

"Oranges," she said. "And grapes. I thought it was October."

"Everything's in season somewhere," I said, catching a grape
in my mouth. "You just have to ship it halfway around the planet
sometimes."

"Good for the trucking industry, I guess."

I collected a few ears of corn, struggling to open the membrane of the rolled plastic bag, and Amy dug through the squash, wondering how to tell if any were ripe. I told her to bang on it and then caress it and apologize, and she punched me on the arm for my lousy advice.

From the produce section we rolled to the drums of bulk nuts and granolas, past the magazine racks, and alongside the gelid panes of the freezer section, keeping to safe topics—movies, the weather—as all around us our fellow citizens browsed the shelves, weighing their options, participating in the great shared ritual of consumption.

I paused and opened the freezer door, and happily Amy paused to wait.

"Health Mountain pizza," I said. "Excellent."

"Yeah?" she said, selecting a frozen enchilada nearby.

"You should try it," I said.

"Maybe next time."

"Suit yourself," I said, and piled six boxes in my cart.

By the time we arrived at the front of the store the whole bank of cashiers was swamped with rush-hour traffic, every lane backed up at least five carts deep. The dinging, coughing, chugging sound of the registers was almost musical.

We entertained ourselves by making fun of other customers' purchases—the frozen chocolate chip pancakes, the industrial-sized wiener wraps—and telling each other what our grandfathers had e-mailed us lately.

"Mine's been sending porn," I said. "'Here's a picture of some eighteen-year-old Bulgarian, everyone. Just wanted to brighten your day.'"

"Mine's been sending racist cartoons," Amy said. "I don't know if he has any idea how awful they are."

"Do they not understand what's happening? Do they not think the Internet's real?"

"Maybe they're just freer than us. They like naked girls and racist jokes, and they don't care who knows."

"I guess that's freedom. In a way."

I went through the lane first, the register clanging and opening and spitting out a long white receipt like tickertape, and I waited on the other side while Amy paid her bill. On the way out, the electronic doors magically flapping open before us, I asked what she was doing for dinner that night. She said she didn't know, and I asked if she might ever want to come over for one of the delicious pizzas I had.

"What about the cat?" she said.

"The cat?" I said. "Oh, the cat can wait."

"Shouldn't you feed it?"

"The cat's fine," I said. "I'll feed it tomorrow. Come on. Let's go eat frozen pizza."

I had to ply her with a few more offers, but eventually she gave in. She tailed me home in Linda's car, her lights bobbing in my rearview mirror. We pulled up together and I led her inside and what followed was either totally unexpected or utterly predictable. We'd barely stepped over the threshold before our clothes came off. We were like teenagers, craving each other, grappling, going lower, deeper, lapping, grasping, invading new spaces. We ended up in the stairwell, on the floor, then bent over the couch. For a moment her lovely face hovered above me, eyes closed, lips ajar, and then suddenly I was staring at the back of her head pressed into the cushion of the recliner. I wished I'd had a chance to clean the house earlier. At least a little dusting.

Afterward, we lay on the couch, gasping, half wrapped in a

scratchy Pendleton blanket. Her hot skin was stuck to mine. Her hair fell around my neck. It was pleasing to know there was still something between us like that, something animal, or chemical, or vibrational. Because as long as that was there, as long as our bodies still wanted each other that badly, I was sure we could sort everything out. I'd been wrong at the bar in Eugene. We weren't finished after all. We just needed to start fucking again. And otherwise take it easy on ourselves awhile. We needed to go slowly, just breathe, share warmth. We could still get back.

Amy leaned her head on my shoulder. I stroked her hair and rubbed the spot behind her ears that she liked.

I wondered how many more of these sessions we'd have to have before she agreed to move back in. There was no hurry, I supposed. We just needed to let it happen. In fact, secrecy would be a large part of the healing at this stage.

We dozed for a while, my arm going numb, and when we woke up the light was gone from the room. The sound of a far-away plane rippled the sky and headlights crossed the far wall, disappearing as they folded around the corner. Still, neither of us wanted to make the first move out of the blanket.

"The house looks good," she said, her voice throaty and warm from sleep. "Nice vase."

"Garage sale," I said, and resumed massaging the spot behind her ear with my thumb. She cooed.

"So how's Linda's?" I said. "You're still liking it all right?" This was a delicate topic, I knew, but the mellow, postcoital ambiance seemed cozy enough that I could broach it without too much worry.

"I think I bug her," she said. "She's so clean. You wouldn't believe it, how clean she is."

"I'm not surprised."

"And she talks. God, she talks. I thought I'd be getting a little more privacy, but it's just constant blah blah blah . . ."

"Yeah."

We lapsed into pleased silence. Amy was handing me exactly the granules of information I most wanted to hear. Rationing it like candy. She was telling me, in her own way, that the space she'd been wanting so badly was not turning out exactly as hoped. She was admitting that her spasm of decisiveness was once again being followed by disappointment and doubt, to be followed soon enough, one assumed, by return. I breathed in the smell of her hair, relaxing further, wallowing in her discontent.

"I hear you've got a deal going with Linda," I said, giving her a chance to brag about something.

"What'd you hear?" she said. Her head lolled on her shoulders. She seemed almost drugged by the movement of my hands.

"Nothing really," I said.

"Fucking Jaeha," she said, lazily. "He wasn't supposed to say anything."

Outside, the streetlight blinked on. The branches of the maple tree shifted in the breeze, scraping the glass.

"He didn't really say anything," I said.

"We've been talking to some people. Yeah."

"Those cosmetics people?"

"No. A distributor. They think we can go national. The honey soap's doing pretty well in the region. They say they might have something to invest. We'll see. We're talking to Peter about it. He seems amenable."

I hummed supportively. This was classic Rain Dragon thinking, a new line launched from inside the organization, a business within a business. Competition and collaboration, the twin pistons of the system. Whether it was a plausible plan, I had no idea, but I was pleased to hear Amy was securing a strategy for the coming season. She would still be the bee soap magnate; I would still be the organizational management guru. It was all falling into place.

"What would it mean, resource-wise?" I said, with solemn interest.

"More hives, more acreage. A few more employees. An industrial processing machine."

"How much money will it take?"

"Not sure."

"No budget?"

"Not yet."

"What's the competition like?"

"What do you mean?"

"Are there a lot of competitors out there?"

"I don't know. I doubt it. None that we're aware of."

"What about the market history? I mean, has anyone tried this?"

"I don't know that either."

"Hmm," I said, and sensed the slightest edge of testiness enter her body. I assumed it was my imagination, though. I was only making idle conversation, after all. We were just talking shop.

"The advertising could be fun," I offered.

"We're not that far along yet," she said, and this time a note of irritation was definitely discernible. I could feel her muscles stiffening under my fingers.

"Well, when you are," I said, "I'd love to help."

"Yeah," she said. "We'll figure it out."

I stopped asking any questions. I'd only been curious, trying to draw her out, but I could tell the queries were coming across too pointedly. She was getting defensive, and I needed to back off. But sadly I'd already crossed the line. Now even my silence became an indictment.

"God, you know, it's just an idea," she said. "You don't have to start cutting it down before it even starts."

"I was just asking you questions," I said. "I wasn't judging. I was just curious. I mean, I'm sure it's a great idea."

"No, you were shitting on it."

"I wasn't shitting on it."

"Why do you have to shit on it? Now of all times?"

"That's not—"

"Forget it."

And so, whatever brief détente we had achieved, whatever warmth, came undone in an instant. The tissue was pulled apart and cast into the wind.

"You know what," she said, peeling off the blanket, "I should probably get going now. I have some things to do tonight. This was probably a mistake."

"But," I said. "The pizza . . ."

"No. I really should go." She was already searching for her bra on the floor, picking her underwear from the arms of the fern. She crammed on her jeans and fished her keys from under the couch. In a few moments she was dressed and out the door, without so much as a good-bye kiss or a see-you-later. From the window, still wrapped in the blanket, I watched her pull away, unsure whether we'd gone a half step forward or a half step back.

ELEVEN

"HAVE YOU SEEN THIS SHIT?" Peter said, throwing the morning Metro section onto my desk. The paper landed flatly, dislocating a pocket of air near my coffee cup, and presented a headline reading, "Yogurt Time Bomb." I had. The Metro section was the first thing I turned to at breakfast each morning, and whenever I saw the word *yogurt* these days my attention was piqued.

The piece in question was by the paper's regular political columnist. Usually he spent his column inches talking about upcoming ballot initiatives or local zoning regulations, but this day's subject, for some reason, was us. Specifically, an accusation leveled by anonymous sources that Rain Dragon's pasteurization methods were a danger to public safety. According to the columnist, heretofore uninterested in our doings, our pasteurization temperature was too low, and at any moment our much-enjoyed milk and yogurt products had the potential to transform from innocent breakfast accoutrements into teeming pools of germs, vehicles for an epidemic on the level of recent *E. coli* outbreaks in Colorado and California, the ostensible news peg of the piece. It was only a matter of time, he warned, before state regulations forced us to change our production methods, and the sooner the better.

"I did," I said, passing it back. "Pretty interesting."

"It's bullshit," he said. "Misinformation."

"Sure is."

"Who fed him this horseshit?"

"I have one guess."

Calmly, Peter folded the paper and dropped the section in the trashcan. He clasped his hands and gazed out the window. The sun was just peeking into view, pouring onto the yellowing trees and browning pastures, and down below, the workers of Rain Dragon could be seen wandering into the seams of the land, disappearing along the paths and into doorways, accompanied by the thin, far-off rumble of the packing machine in the invisible Quonset huts.

"Hats off," he said. "They're taking it to a new level."

"I'll say."

We remained at our stations, Peter muttering to himself, flexing his knuckles, me sipping my coffee, sneaking glances at the obituaries on the back page. Neither of us felt inclined to say the word *Prism* out loud, although the culprit was no great mystery here. About three weeks had passed since my trip to Eugene, and a week and a half since we'd opened the *Business Journal* to find a major article outlining everything I'd passed on about Cravens's tawdry empire, complete with my own pictures, uncredited, as visual evidence. The story had quoted Arnold, anonymously, and numerous disgruntled graduates of Prism's training workshops, and more or less served up the whole storyline I'd been hoping to get out there. First blood had been drawn.

Happily for us, the story had mushroomed since then. The

evidence of systematic abuse was abundant, and replete with lurid images of sad lives and gross negligence, all of which made for delicious copy. Redden had posted follow-ups on the editorial page, made visits to the talk radio stations, and even landed an appearance on the TV news as an expert on cults. And it hadn't stopped there, either. Within days, the story had jumped to the city weekly, whose editors loved nothing more than this kind of insinuating, sarcastic gotcha piece, and then to the blogs, where the volley of accusations, denials, and grudging remorse had become almost extravagant, and the face of Anthony Cravens had achieved a locally iconic status, a warning to area children about the road of sanctimony and greed. The headlines were sometimes cruel: "Monstrous Conditions." "Meltdown." To a degree, I felt sorry for him.

My plan, inasmuch as it had ever been a plan, had succeeded. The story might or might not end up having any effect on our competition, but even that was part of the plan's vague intention. I'd wanted to aggravate them, expose them as opportunists, not destroy them. I'd only wanted to level the playing field, and shrink Prism's aura of invincibility to the degree that the mere idea of us picking up a sliver of their business became thinkable. And in that, I'd most likely succeeded. We were in the game.

And now came the blowback. I was surprised Prism had zeroed in on us so quickly, but there were numerous possible explanations. Maybe they were just lashing out randomly. Maybe they'd tracked me down through Arnold or Redden. Maybe one of them remembered something from my visit to Eugene. It didn't really matter. The only issue with the article, as far as I could tell, and the thing that got Peter so angry, was the matter of accuracy. The piece in today's paper was not really true. A PR war was all fine and good as long as everyone obeyed the rules and didn't go planting stories with absolutely no basis in fact.

I fingered the paper, rereading a few of the autumn events listings, hoping the tit had been tatted and we could put this phase behind us and move on to the main competition itself.

"We're using shotguns to kill flies here," Peter said, seconding my thoughts. "We're not trying to start a war."

"I think everyone's made their points," I concurred.

"Can you write a letter to the editor?" he said. "Make this go away?"

"There's nothing here," I said. "It's just speculation."

"Well, write the letter anyway," he said, testily. "Set the record straight, and let's just put it behind us."

Peter pressed his palms against the wall and stretched his calf muscles, initiating his calisthenics of thinking. I waited, knowing that his stretching usually produced some kind of idea that needed talking through. Sure enough, as he massaged his patella, he started speaking again, rubbing his way slowly toward a point.

"I was talking to Bob yesterday," he said, his kneecap sliding beneath his flesh. "We were talking about how this whole decision-making process is going down over at Stanbro. Who's in charge and whatnot. From what he says, the budget they're allotting is big enough that an HR director can't approve it himself, but not so big to take to the shareholders. Which means the board of directors are the ones with the final say-so on who gets the job. At the next meeting they're going to have a vote. The choice is down to us and Prism, he says. He's been talking us up as much as he can. But he's a busy guy. He can't do all the work for us."

"Nor should he."

"Nope." Peter moved to the other kneecap, aiming his voice

at the ceiling. "I'm not sorry about Prism's little dustup in the papers," he mused. "A little sunshine never hurt anybody. I still don't know how the hell you pulled that off. But at this point we don't need to convince the whole world we're the better candidate for the job. We only need to convince these nine guys on the board."

"Okay," I said.

"Bob says he already has a couple votes lined up for us. They respect his opinion in these matters. Or maybe they just owe him favors. I'm not sure. Doesn't really matter, I guess.

"He says two of the guys are definitely off our list, though. They're Prism guys, all the way. The COO, Dick Brophy, hit Prism's eighth level last year, and this other guy, Tom Cramer, owes Dick his job. That still leaves a handful of free agents kicking around. No strong loyalties one way or the other. Bob golfs with a few of them. He'll keep the pressure on. But he says one guy, Dale Patton, is the one we really need to bring over. The other board members take their cues from him. He urged me strongly to start working on him now."

"Okay," I said. "How?"

Peter stretched his inner thigh muscles on one side, then the other, bouncing back and forth like a metronome. "That's for you to figure out," he said. "You're the VP of Rain Dragon Energy Management. Go. Convince him. We don't have much time. I have the utmost faith and confidence in your persuasive abilities."

I was glad Peter was so confident. I wasn't. But in one thing he was unquestionably right: I was indeed the vice president of Rain Dragon Energy Management—a recent elevation in title— and as such I had certain responsibilities to fulfill. In exchange for the title, I'd been granted a stake in the new consulting subsidiary, which was to say a portion of any profits or royalties it generated. Which was to say, if Rain Dragon Energy Management were to take off, I would take off with it. And so it behooved me to wrestle the contract to our side by whatever means necessary.

On the way out of Peter's office, pondering my new mission—the various arguments I might try, the various inducements I might offer—I was accosted by Amy. I turned around slowly, unsure where we were at today. In the couple weeks since our little dalliance, our relations had been cool, and she'd more or less avoided me whenever possible. With so much going on I hadn't been able to worry about it much, and hoped my crimes eventually would start looking less horrible in her eyes. It seemed like so many problems resolved themselves if one just left them alone.

"Yeah?" I said.

"What was that place we used to go?" she said, her voice scrubbed of any clues as to what she was really thinking. "You know? The one in Echo Park?"

"The bookstore?" I said.

"No, the restaurant," she said. "You know the one—"

"Marrow's," I said, guessing she meant the Egyptian place we'd discovered early in our time together—the scene of one of our first dates, where she'd wrung a paper napkin until it had disintegrated in her hands, and hours later, slept with me for the first time. It was strange to remember how nervous she'd been in the beginning, how elusive and timid. I took the very mention of the place as a kind of tenderness on her part.

"Why?" I asked.

"Just curious," she said, and swung back into the doorway without clarification. I waited, thinking she might come back and say more, but she didn't, and I turned around and proceeded down the stairs, convinced I'd never really know what went on in her head.

That afternoon I went to the public library, planning to uncover whatever existed about Dale Patton in the public record. The more I knew about my quarry, I figured, the better I could do choosing my weapons, and the better I could do making my ultimate case.

I staked out a carrel in the periodicals section, just outside the smell radius of a bum reading a stack of *Sunset* magazines, and immediately drummed up a few references to Patton in the business press. From there it didn't take long to piece together the general outline of his career. According to the profiles, some of which I read on the scratched pane of the microfiche machine, he'd started out in the textile industry. He'd spent a few years managing a factory in Georgia, learning the ropes, before shifting over to a sportswear company, then swimwear, bringing to each new assignment an aggressive emphasis on metrics and an unflagging devotion to the bottom line. Somewhere along the way, he'd met Don Banger, Stanbro's CEO, and impressed him sufficiently that he'd been invited onto Stanbro's board of directors. The May 2007 *Textiles Monthly* provided a particularly useful piece. It was a long story detailing Patton's whole biographical arc—his childhood in Nebraska, his education back east, his first and second marriages and the four children they'd spawned—and featured a posed photograph of the man himself with a bloody ax in one hand, a calculator in the other, and a butcher's apron covered in gore. That told me about what I wanted to know. He was a hatchet man. His most recent assignment was Jantzen, a local swimwear company, and already a hundred people had been hacked from the rolls.

I still didn't have a real feel for his head, though. The articles were so maddeningly airbrushed they could have been about almost anyone in an executive leadership position. So I called up Jake Redden, who'd written a recent piece on Patton's charity work for the daily's business section, and met him for coffee and a little advice.

"He's very charismatic," Redden said, dumping a third avalanche of sugar into his fourth mug of coffee. We were sitting in a café–cum–thrift store in far north Portland, and Redden was just starting to feel his caffeine, which was to say his opinions were finally snapping into focus. "Smart. Funny. Highly rational," he added. "Hard not to like."

"He's a hatchet man, right?" I said. "He goes in and decimates."

"You could say that," Redden said. "Nice guy, though. Very personable."

"So how would you approach him?" I said. "If you were me? How would you make the case for Rain Dragon?"

"To Patton?" Redden sipped his coffee and stared at the backward writing on the window. A perfectly maintained Model T puttered by on the street. "It has to be nuts and bolts. Rain Dragon is cheaper, hungrier, more effective than the competition. But quite honestly, I doubt he'll bite."

"No?"

"No offense, man, but he's a deeply no-bullshit dude. He wants numbers. And I doubt you guys have numbers."

In this Redden was correct. We had nothing but enthusiasm and good intentions and Peter's driving ambition to offer. But what could I do about that? I had to proceed to the next phase with what I had. Which was nothing.

According to Redden, Patton played basketball every Tuesday at Lloyd Athletic Center, so that week I went and watched the game from behind a thick pane of glass, hoping to glean any final clues to his personality before making my approach. I recognized him on the court right away. He was the hale, beefy guy with the lantern jaw and thinning hair, wearing the baggy sleeveless shirt and beige knee brace. He played the post, and his inside game appeared rough but effective. His passing was supple, his chatter constant, and he groused badly whenever he got called for a foul. He was a real competitor, in other words, the kind of guy you hated on the court, unless he was on your team, in which case you loved him.

Afterward I sat in the lobby waiting for him to emerge from the locker room. I would have preferred to make my contact in a more professional setting, but I'd already been rebuffed five times by his secretary. With the board's vote only three weeks away, I needed to get the conversation rolling, assuming it would take more than one session to bring him around. I could only hope he found my proactivity impressive and not invasive.

The television screens shifted from a beer ad to an insurance ad. Sweating executives and middle managers wandered by, toweling themselves. I'd been sitting there almost half an hour when Patton finally emerged from the mouth of the locker room, his hair damp, his trench coat flapping, and without much thought I got up and intercepted him at the front desk.

"Mr. Patton?" I said, striking a distance a few feet from his shoulder.

"Yeah?" he said, turning to face me. Up close, he was bigger than I'd thought: a full head taller than me. His large, ruddy face was freshly soaped and shining, with the mottled complexion of an aggressive, lifelong drinker. I could see the coarse nose hairs stuffing his nostrils, the razor burn on the underside of his jaw. I cleared my throat and extended my hand.

"I was hoping I could take a minute of your time," I said.

"Have we met?" he said.

"My name is Damon," I said. "Damon Duncan. I'm vice president of Rain Dragon Energy Management. We're hoping to do some business with Stanbro this fall."

"All right," he said.

"I'd like to talk to you about what Rain Dragon has to offer. You know, give you the rundown on our qualifications. Answer any questions you might have. That kind of thing."

Patton's eyes were blank, unreadable. Whether he was annoyed or amused by my sudden arrival, I couldn't tell. He looked slowly both ways, like he was scanning for approaching trucks, and waited for a few of his fellow basketball players to trickle from the locker room into the bar before saying anything further.

"You want to talk now?" he said. "It's almost seven. I was just going home."

"I tried to make an appointment," I said, "but I couldn't get through. And we don't have much time. I think it's important we chat."

He shifted his gym bag on his shoulder, weighing his options. An elderly couple in matching rust-colored sweatsuits hobbled by. He was a naturally sociable fellow, and out of curiosity, if nothing else, he nodded toward the glass doors.

"Walk me to my car," he said.

"Thank you," I said. "I really appreciate your time."

But he was already on the move, pushing through the glass doors into the balmy fall air and turning left toward the Lloyd Center mall a few blocks away. Rush hour was still in progress, and the dusky road was congested with traffic, the swoosh of late commuters passing in waves. Patton wasn't the sort to bother with small talk, I figured, so once we'd fallen into a walking rhythm I launched straight into the topic at hand.

"So I wanted to talk to you about the contract," I said. "I know the board of directors is deliberating right now, and I'd love to tell you a little bit about where we're coming from."

"We have your proposal," he said. "It's all there, isn't it?"

"It is," I said. "I just think face-to-face conversations can be a lot more constructive."

"True enough," he said, though not in a way that made me feel more comfortable. Waiting for the crosswalk, I started my rap. I told him all about Rain Dragon's recent success at Hallelujah, and at the other companies around the region. I told him about Peter's past achievements, his role in the creation of the whole organics infrastructure along the West Coast. I told him about all the talented and committed people we had on staff, eager to take up the job. But as we crossed the street and entered the doorway of the mall en route to the parking lot, I didn't get the sense that any of my talking was getting through.

"If you have any questions, concerns, anything like that," I said, lamely, "I'd love to, you know, try and address them for you."

We came to the ice-skating rink, an oval of filmy whiteness, with tinny Top 40 music blaring from hidden speakers. The smell of popcorn and fake butter floated from somewhere, and down below, four young girls in leotards could be seen making long, overlapping arcs on the ice, defining their territories. Patton paused at the popcorn stand and exchanged a few wrinkled bills for a bag.

"You said your name was Damon?" he said.

"Yes," I said.

"I appreciate the time you're taking, Damon," he said, offering me the popcorn. "I find your group's work pretty fascinating. I do. I understand a lot of companies are getting excellent results with training groups lately. I've used them before myself. Kind of bullshit, for the most part, but some useful stuff comes out, too. Just takes getting you a degree off your sightline, sometimes. I don't doubt you're doing innovative work. But I'll be up front. I don't think Rain Dragon is the right fit for Stanbro at this juncture."

"No?" I said, unhappy for the rebuke, but glad, conversationally, to have some kind of traction at last. Now, if nothing else, I had a place to start. I had some hole to coax him out from.

"I don't think it's necessary," he went on. "I don't think Stanbro is facing a problem of motivation here. I think we're facing a problem of reality. The market is saturated. Japan's been warehousing uncut logs for the last five years at least, and that's pushing down demand all over the world. We've got incredible redundancies in the organization, six layers of management, massive inefficiencies in the supply chain. Environmental regulations are strangling us. You start putting that together, and Stanbro's problems don't seem so mysterious. People want a magic bullet. There ain't any."

"We're not talking about magic bullets," I said. "We're talking about solving these problems from inside the organization, using the best resource you have, your people. We're talking about turning your own workforce into a solution generator. We talking about your human capital—"

"Yeah, yeah," Patton interrupted, "I know the routine. The board wants to throw money away on this training program, that's their prerogative. I've already tried to talk them out of it. As long as we're going down this road, it's purely a question of experience, Damon. Your competitor has a track record."

"We have a track record—"

"Not on this level. Your boss Peter Hawk has experience consulting with small companies. I'm sure he's a talented guy. But this isn't a one-man job."

"But—"

"Look, it's nothing personal," Patton said. "I don't doubt you'll do very well at this someday. But this isn't going to be your training run, all right? And now, if you'll excuse me, I have to get home for dinner."

He strode off, gobbling popcorn. Down on the ice one of the girls executed a wobbly double axel, losing control and skidding on her ass into the wall. Without a pause, she jumped up and brushed herself off and jetted around the perimeter of the rink, skinny legs pumping, adding speed and then gliding it off as she curled to the center, eyes on the ceiling.

"I'm going to keep trying to convince you," I called. "I've still got a couple weeks to go."

"Knock yourself out," Patton said, munching. "You're welcome to try. It'd be a first."

I dawdled the next morning, showing up at Rain Dragon well after noon, and went to Peter's office to deliver the bad news, but he wasn't there. Nor was he in my office. Nor in the kitchen, which he sometimes pillaged for midafternoon snacks. It was in the Meditation Room that I finally stumbled onto him, along with a handful of staffers scattered across the carpet in twos and threes, embroiled in what appeared to be a training session in the unlikely event that we landed the job with Stanbro.

Jaeha was floundering with a giant copy of the flowering organization chart, attempting to pin it to the wall but fighting against the flaps falling on either side. Michael, along with two interns, was pinging away on a xylophone, making a chaotic racket. And Linda and Simon were sitting at the center of a debris circle of butcher paper and felt-tip pens, busily constructing an elaborate diagram of extremely long and narrow proportions. It looked like an adult romper room, a kindergarten for grown-ups, with frequent bursts of laughter rising out of the low turmoil of conversation.

"Behold our seminar coordinators," Peter said, striding out of the scene. "I went ahead and deputized all these guys this morning. Hope you don't mind."

"Yeah, sure," I said, still processing. "A little premature, though, don't you think?"

"Nope," he said. "Not at all. In fact, I'd say we're running kind of late. If we land this thing, we're going to need trainers. We can't do it all by ourselves. I figure we've got to start training the trainers ASAP. There's a shitload of ground to cover."

"Okay," I said, watching Jaeha finally affixing a corner of his paper to the wall. "If you say so."

"We went over the basics this morning," Peter said, either oblivious to my doubts or choosing not to acknowledge them. "We talked about Stanbro's history. The founding principles of the company. The old mission statement. We talked about the overall process we might use. This is the first breakout session you're seeing here. We're really just getting started."

The xylophones jumped in volume, taking a turn for the atonal and off-kilter.

"And so what's everyone doing, exactly?" I said.

"Jaeha's enlarging some diagrams so we can talk them through as a group. Michael's testing an old sound technology. Linda and Simon are making a timeline of Stanbro's corporate history. That was their idea. So far, I'd say everyone's doing pretty well."

"They're enjoying themselves, at least."

"Rome wasn't built in a day," he said, smiling. "They'll get more focused as we go. I mean, these guys haven't even agreed to teach the sessions yet. This is just kind of fooling around."

"They haven't agreed?"

"There are still some issues to resolve."

"What kind?"

"Environmental concerns, labor concerns, what have you. But everyone'll come around. Don't worry."

"You think?"

"Oh, yeah. The opportunity here is just too big. We're talking about reprogramming a major multinational corporation. You don't pass that up. Not to mention the proceeds could have a huge impact on the farm." He slapped me on the back. "Speaking of which, you talked to Patton, right? How went the first contact?"

"Not so great."

I recounted my conversation, the wall I'd already hit, and not surprisingly, Peter remained upbeat.

"You can turn him around," he said. "I know it. You've still got a couple weeks to go. He'll admire your persistence. Believe me."

"He wants numbers," I said. "The only way he's willing to think about us is if we show some empirical proof. And I don't see how that can happen. We'd have to go back in time and land a contract with a company exactly like Stanbro and show him the ledgers. Then maybe he'd start to listen."

"It's always the same bind," Peter said sagely. "No experience, no opportunity. No opportunity, no experience. We have to cut that knot."

"I don't know how."

"I have great confidence in you."

"That's one of us then."

He squeezed my shoulder, digging his thumb into the clavicle. "You are the person who can do this job, Damon. You can't help but do the right thing." With a level gaze he turned and ambled back into the Meditation Room, spinning to deliver his parting words of encouragement. "Just go a little farther, Damon, that's all. A little farther and you'll get there. I know you will."

Michael's xylophone pinged briefly in sequence with the interns' xylophones. A little farther, I thought. Fine. But toward what?

I had no idea what to do. But if Peter wanted me to keep going, he was the boss. So once again I proceeded like he would, as if everything would somehow supernaturally come together in the end.

The first thing I did was write Patton a long letter detailing the manifold reasons our program would make a profound difference in the day-to-day workings of Stanbro. I pulled together what statistical evidence I could find, based on Peter's past efforts, and built them into a handful of graphs and pie charts. They looked kind of bogus, though, so after the letter went out I took to lurking at the coffee shop Patton frequented on his way to work. Waiting in line, over the gurgle and slurp of the espresso machine,

I pestered him with further caveats and explanations and interpretations for his consideration. He was always polite, and possibly even respectful of my diligence, but ever resolute in his refusal to change his mind.

"Nope," he said, paying the cashier for his pumpkin bread. "I see what you're saying, but I'm not buying it."

"I've done the Prism program myself," I said. "I know what you'll be getting, and believe me, we have more to offer—"

"I really have to run."

I phoned him. I sent him books. I worked what few connections we shared—a former Rain Dragon intern he'd hired, a cousin of Linda's who belonged to his church. But he wouldn't budge.

I wrote another, longer letter, taking a more conceptual angle. I explained as simply as possible the fundamental methodological difference between Prism and Rain Dragon. I pointed out that the two companies' technologies might on the surface resemble each other—dyads and group encounter circles and visualization exercises and such—but they in fact stemmed from almost diametrically opposite theories of organizational well-being. Prism's emphasis was all on the individual, the breaking down and reconstituting of the self; Rain Dragon's, in contradistinction, was all about the group, and the belief that only in our relationships with each other did we reach our greatest potential. It was a fundamental dichotomy, I wrote: the individual versus the community. Self-actualization versus group collaboration. The monad versus the institution. I urged him to entertain the idea that Rain Dragon's emphasis would produce significantly better results.

But my point was too abstract. He wasn't interested in such airy, theoretical notions. So said his secretary when I pressed her for details over the phone a few days later. He saw inexperience on one hand and seasoned professionalism on the other, she said. Case closed.

At that point I might well have given up, called it a noble effort, and waited for the verdict to come down. I would have felt all right about it, considering everything I'd done already. It was only when I noticed my coworkers' growing enthusiasm for the project that I felt the need to keep pushing.

Not everyone was enthusiastic, of course. A few of the potential trainers never got over their initial objections to Stanbro, the company's long record of environmental degradation and labor exploitation, in particular. They had all bowed out and returned to their farm duties, even though there wasn't much to do around Rain Dragon during the fallow season. The ones who did stay on, however, were strangely committed. They seemed to relish the idea of exerting some influence on the culture of Stanbro. They liked the idea of contaminating the corporation with their own moral consciousness, and imagined themselves as insurgents of some kind, bringing new concepts to the corporate culture that might well cause it to wither and die, or, alternately, to blossom into something heretofore unseen in the world. Really, who knew what would happen? That was part of the thrill, part of the energizing secret the team shared. Every day they stepped into the Meditation Room and tore down the Stanbro institution, only to rebuild it again as they wished, testing their tools, customizing their game plans, pacing their speech. Even Amy got into the act, swallowing her initial skepticism and letting the mission take over. Watching the trainers, I had to admit they were looking like a formidable bunch. I wanted this experiment to succeed as much as any of them, and I found myself working abnormally hard to do my part.

"What is Stanbro?" Amy asked Emilio one afternoon, locked in a dyad. They sat in facing chairs, knees almost touching, maintaining strict eye contact, staying rigorously on topic. "What's the real unifying purpose of this organization, anyway?"

"It's a collection of people committed to . . . to what? I don't know," Emilio said, faltering.

"Come on," she pushed. "Tell me what you really think. Just think about the lumber divisions. Plywood and particleboard. Why produce that stuff?"

"For shelter? For making people more comfortable?"

"And what's the benefit of that? Why do we want better shelter?"

"More space?"

"And why do we want space?"

"To do what we want to do. To be with the people we want to be with. To share."

"And where does that go? What is Stanbro really selling?"

"Family? Love?"

"Ahh—that's interesting."

In a perfect world, they all understood, they would have ramped up more slowly. They would have tested their skills on some smaller clients and done more background research. But in this case they had no choice. They faced a quantum jump. Evolve or fail. And thankfully, with the shared history of barn raisings, weekly bull sessions, group keggers, grassroots organizing campaigns, and scavenger hunts between them, that evolution was possible.

And when all else failed, Peter constantly advised, we could always just fake it.

"It's all faking it, anyway," he said, standing before us for one of his frequent pep talks. "If you think anyone out there's not imitating their dad, their friends, their president, their movie stars, you're fucking fooling yourselves. You're making yourself feel like shit for no reason. Look inside. You know your ideas and tastes and opinions all come from somewhere else. You know you pick up something here, you steal something there. Just accept it. You have no Self. God knows, I don't. I'm just a bunch of crap I found. I'm pieces of everyone I've ever met stuck together. But what I have is this: I don't give a fuck. I embrace it. I steal from everyone and I pretend it's mine and I sure as hell don't care if anyone steals from me. So let's take the technologies and pretend we know what the hell we're doing. All right? Let's just go for it."

With only three days left before the board's vote, in solidarity with the team, I holed up in a coffee shop in North Portland to write Patton yet one more letter, the ultimate letter, with what I hoped would be the words that would unlock him at last. If I could only figure out what would get to him. What phrases, what images, would set his tumblers in place?

I went with extreme sincerity, grounded in anecdotes drawn from the interviews we'd done with Stanbro's workers throughout the organization. I wrote about the research assistant in the Tigard box factory who couldn't get his data seen by top management. The forklift operator in the Salem lumberyard who wondered why he wasn't given the tools to do his job more effectively. Look at these smart, creative, critically-minded people,

I said, all wanting to give themselves to the Stanbro enterprise, and yet not finding themselves able. It was Stanbro's duty to reach them, and make them part of a larger whole.

I wrote about our team, too, their intelligence and faith, and tried to capture a little bit of their personalities. If we could bring all these people together, who knew what we might accomplish? I'd seen enough of Peter's work to think we had a chance.

The letter was absurdly long, and reeked of desperation. I cut and pasted my clauses back and forth, moved commas, but nothing helped, and in the end I just sat there, staring at the screen. I Googled Cravens, and was surprised to find the news of his disgrace was already gone, buried in subsequent mudslides of information. I toggled back to my letter, but I couldn't concentrate. The exercise was little more than magical thinking on my part, extravagant wishfulness. My words would never exert the effect I hoped they would. I sat there into the night, picking at the sentences, wishing I could think of some way through.

I almost wasn't surprised when Patton himself suddenly walked by the window. It was around ten o'clock, and I was staring out into the street, and there he was, passing right through the frame of the glass, lit in the ambient glow of the background car traffic. I watched him walk down the sidewalk as if the coincidence was perfectly normal. Of course he would show up. I'd been concentrating on him so hard, I'd summoned him.

The surprise hit me a second later. What was he doing here, so far from home? He lived all the way in Alameda, all the way across town. He had church in the morning. The chances that he would just amble past this window at this hour were astronomically small. What cosmic power had guided us both here at this exact time? What was going on?

I had to go say something to him. The stars were obviously aligning. We were meant to have a conversation. I packed up my computer, paid my bill, and stepped into the cool night.

Patton was already well down the street, and before I could call his name, he was turning into the doorway of an old-fashioned steak house named Rose's. I headed after him, wondering if I was perhaps making a mistake, if I should just leave him alone. But no, I thought, this was something worth doing. The synchronicity was simply too weird to ignore.

I'd always wondered what Rose's looked like on the inside. As it turned out, it was gloomy and red. Red curtains cloaked red booths resting on red carpet. The customers were mostly gray-haired, and surprisingly abundant for such a late dinner hour.

I spotted Patton at a plush side banquet, deep in conversation with someone I couldn't see. The person's head was blocked by the booth's high, upholstered backrest. I took a few steps in along the wall, trying to get a better view, and a foursome came in behind me, blocking the way out.

I continued on into the bar and took an empty stool near the serving station. From there the whole restaurant became visible, reversed in the canted mirror above the bottles. I could see Patton's table now, its basket of bread, its water glasses, its flickering, netted candle. And I could see his companion, too: a matronly blond woman with a jolly pink face, a flimsy floral print smock, yellow pumps. I'd seen his wife before, and this wasn't her. She and Patton were talking in low voices, giggling and patting hands. When she kissed his knuckles, I ordered a Scotch on the rocks.

I stayed at the bar all through their dinner, keeping tabs as they ate T-bone steaks and scalloped potatoes and drank three cocktails apiece. I'd never seen Patton quite so at ease before. He laughed boyishly at whatever she told him, took all the teasing she gave. At one point he bent toward her to hear some somber news, and shook his head sadly, and after some shocking kicker they both paused, shared a look, and cackled. Eventually, the plates were cleared and they shared a giant éclair.

When Patton and his date finally got up, I paid my bill, too, and trailed them onto the sidewalk.

They climbed into Patton's town car and headed east on Lombard, and I hurried to my car and followed them. Why not? I'd gone this far, I might as well play the game out. I caught up to them on the bridge over the train tracks, and a few blocks later Patton cut north to Columbia, the most marginal avenue, and turned right again, going east. I followed a few car-lengths behind. They turned into a municipal golf course, moonlight on the trimmed grass, and came out in a neighborhood of airport hotels.

He turned into the Budget Inn parking lot. I turned, too, and watched as the couple climbed from the car and went straight to a room on the ground level without stopping at the lobby. The door closed. The lights never went on.

I sat in my car watching the parking lot. The wall of the hotel was a jaundiced slab of concrete barnacled with air conditioners. An airplane roared overhead, lights flashing on the steel skin of its fuselage.

I wasn't sure what to do. I had a camera back home—maybe I could hurry back and document the tryst in progress. And then what? Surprise Patton in the morning with grainy pictures in a manila envelope? That seemed ridiculous. And besides, I didn't have the nerve for anything like that. I was guilty of plenty of minor moral lapses over the years—white lies, passive-aggressive withholdings, repeated, if largely unnoticeable, chiseling behaviors. But blackmail was beyond the pale. Sitting on the edge of the hotel parking lot, I came to the conclusion that this was a crime I would not commit.

It was mildly reassuring to know I'd landed on some ultimate, bedrock principle of behavior. There were times I worried that I didn't have such a thing, that given the right circumstances, I could be induced to do almost anything. Even worse, I worried I might actually enjoy doing it. But as it turned out, I had limits. Thinking about Rain Dragon, and all the benefits we might derive from the Stanbro gig, and all the men and women that Patton had fired over the years, the vengeance they surely craved, the suffering they'd endured—even then, I couldn't bring myself to cross this bright line.

I was still sitting there when the door of the lovers' room opened and Patton himself stepped back into view. His coat was unbuttoned, his tie loosened, his hair tousled—the classic, slightly ludicrous image of the adulterous executive male. The streetlamps sucked the color from his face, and he pulled a cigarette from his pocket and stood there smoking.

I sat watching him for a while, not saying anything, just staring at the clouds of smoke exiting his mouth. I watched the shadows behind him spread and flutter as occasional cars went by. And about halfway through his cigarette, I cracked my door for some fresh air, easing myself out onto the concrete. I hung there in the wedge of the car's door and body, fixating on Patton and the orange bead of his cigarette.

I didn't make any effort to get his attention. I didn't say anything or make any sudden movements. But eventually, almost lazily, his gaze happened over in my direction. His eyes peered straight through me for a while, scanning the ragged treetops swaying on the opposite side of the road, and finally drew back and focused on my plane of existence. For a moment our eyes almost met. He raised his cigarette to his lips without changing expression, took another two drags, sank the butt into the sandy basin on the top of the garbage can, and then turned and reentered the room. Soon after, I climbed back in my car and drove home.

I found out much later the woman in the hotel was named Aimee Rice. She was an old college friend of Patton's, a state welfare worker with whom he had been conducting an affair for almost a decade. They saw each other only rarely due to the complications of Patton's home life, which he refused to disrupt with a divorce, but which didn't keep him from sending Aimee's son to art school or paying the rent on her small duplex in Southeast.

I never said anything to Patton about that night. It was thoroughly possible he never even saw me. It was dark, and no words were exchanged. There was no reason that I should have been anywhere nearby in the first place. A day later, though, we got his vote.

WINTER

TWELVE

IN MID-OCTOBER Peter signed the papers with Stanbro Paper, committing us to nine two-day training seminars, to be executed over six weeks in November and December. We would wrap up just before the holidays, and if all went well the contract would be renewed for nine additional sessions in the following year, with an eye to training the entirety of the Stanbro workforce—five thousand workers spread over the globe—by the end of year two. The initial participants would come from the Portland metro area, and the initial budget would clock in at about $700,000, covering hotel rentals, catering, transportation, the trainers' $100-per-hour consulting fees, per diems, and a $10,000 signing bonus for both Peter and myself, the main architects of the deal. A fair amount of money would still be left over for Rain Dragon's communal coffers, earmarked for future methane digesters, delivery trucks, honey expansions, or whatever the staff voted was most essential to the farm's upward progress.

The contract was announced at a press conference in Stanbro's main office, in a meeting room overlooking the Willamette River and the purple shelf of the Cascades. It was attended by four reporters, the nine members of the board, Peter, and myself.

The ceremony was quick, with warm, businesslike feelings all around. Peter took the dais with his old friend, Stanbro vice president of human resources Bob Doyle, a flabby, bald Irishman whose coloring matched the smoked salmon on the hors d'oeuvres tray. They were joined presently by Don Banger, the CEO, a short, silver-haired, flinty-eyed man with a bolo tie and three fingers on his left hand, his pinkie and ring finger having been lost years ago to a circular saw in the Salem mill.

By all accounts Banger was the one true locus of power in the company. The fact he deigned to appear at the press conference was seen as some kind of message on his part, the nature of which was not quite clear to anyone. The interpretation of Banger's utterances and gestures was one of the main preoccupations of Stanbro's executive class, the warring factions of which could never seem to agree on the final meaning.

At any rate, there he was, all smiles, in his western suit, shaking Peter's hand and slapping his back under the portrait of the company's founder, Henry Stanbro, the stern, bearded tycoon.

"Always a leader in the paper products industry," Bob Doyle read from the podium, "Stanbro Paper is poised today to enter a new era. With the help of Rain Dragon Energy Management, we move confidently into our second century, building on our legacy as the most pioneering, creative-thinking producer of paper and paper-based products in the world."

Two flashbulbs flashed, and Peter and Banger's shadows flared hugely against the scalloped wallpaper. The face of the founder whitened, and the brass plaque screwed to the frame washed out and reappeared: "This is not for us, nor for our children—but for our grandchildren."

★ ★ ★

The Coho Boardroom looked pretty fine, at least as fine as an executive rental suite in the Crowne Plaza—a corporate convention center/business hotel just off I-5, sharing curb cuts with Appleby's and the Olive Garden—probably could look. The long fake mahogany table surrounded by fake leather captain's chairs was borderline stately, and the smaller section, intended as some kind of reception area with a love seat, a bouquet of fake flowers, and a wall phone over a fake cherrywood banquet, was almost cozy. The easel awaiting a fresh whiteboard was brand-new, and on the brown carpet lay an unopened packet of colored markers and a roll of butcher paper. The window looked onto a view of barren woods. The floor was clean. The temperature was comfortable.

I turned off the light, satisfied, and moved on to the Steelhead Boardroom down the hall, which also looked fine. The same semi-stately boardroom table surrounded by the same comfortable chairs, the same fresh office supplies, and a slightly different view of the naked trees, blurred by runnels of cold rain. Very good.

I turned off the light and stepped into the hallway's recycled hotel air, getting my bearings from the giant oculus in the atrium's ceiling. The sound of falling water drifted up from the lobby's fountain, mixing with world beat music on the hotel stereo system. I could see a Doritos bag stuffed in one of the planter boxes.

The Crowne Plaza was not a pleasant place; there was no point pretending otherwise. The deco interior was crude, made almost ridiculous by the mismatched patio furniture and wrought-iron lamp fixtures, and the outside was even worse: seven stories of brutal modular balconies rising from a plane of asphalt, overlooking a strip of gas stations and chain restaurants, buffeted by the constant noise of the passing freeway traffic on I-5.

But as ugly and depressing as the Crowne Plaza was, it was incredibly convenient for the needs at hand, standing almost exactly midway between Rain Dragon's property line and Stanbro's main mill in Albany. It also boasted all the amenities we might need—moderately sized lecture halls, pocket conference rooms, a restaurant serving buffet lunch and dinner, innumerable little alcoves for private conversing, and a romantic, well-stocked lounge for postseminar winding down. There was a Trader Joe's down the street, too, which might come in handy in case we needed to pick up cheap wine or crudités. Taken together, the pros far outweighed the cons, and I'd booked us in for the entirety of our six-week run.

And now, awaiting the glass elevator to glide into bay, I stood by the decision. We weren't here to enjoy ourselves, after all. We were here to work. And if we had to work in ugly rooms, that was no problem. A part of me could argue there was a kind of grace in the pure functionality of the Crowne Plaza. It was almost like a formation of nature, it was so devoid of beautifying human intent.

The elevator door split open and I stepped into the glass case, plunging downward to the main lobby. Mirrors outlined the entrance to the lounge, a rouge cave lit by flat-screen TVs even at this hour, and the entrance to the swimming pool exhaled chlorine.

I had about half an hour before the other coordinators started to show up, and close to an hour before the participants from Stanbro made their appearance, which gave me just enough time to check our main conference room and make a quick pass through the continental breakfast buffet. I hurried down a narrow hallway to the Plaza Ballroom II, which also seemed to be Plaza Ballroom

III, depending on what door you used, and entered a T-shaped chamber with a small stage decked in flammable curtains and a few folding tables hooded by black fitted skirts, occupancy 250. Quickly, I inspected the chairs, counting them by twos, tapped the podium microphone to make sure it was plugged in properly, and fiddled with the light switch to set the brightness at the proper level.

I checked my watch again. 6:13 a.m.

I was doing fine. Enough so that I could even take a second to go over my mental checklist. Transportation, arranged. Binders, collated. Vegetarian lunches, ordered. Soon enough the men and women of Stanbro would be streaming inside the doors, tote-bagged, name-tagged, primed for Peter's short welcome address, after which they would break into groups of ten and head for the boardrooms upstairs, where the day's outcome entered the coordinators' hands. And from there? There was no telling. We'd all prepared the best we could. The time had come to let our bodies do their jobs.

Still, standing alone in the Plaza Ballroom, feeling the air of the vents on my neck, I couldn't help but experience a prickly bloom of anxiety in my guts. A blushing numbness in my toes; a spurt of acidic juice in my stomach. For all the preparation, so many unknowns remained. What if the participants hated our program? What if our coordinators somehow screwed up their scripts? So many mishaps were still possible, so many hazards, and as much as I tried to push them out of my mind, to downplay their likelihood, my nerves kept on jangling. My body knew a test was coming, even if my mind refused to acknowledge the fact.

Before the creeping anxiety could grow into anything disabling, though, I did what Peter would do, which was a quick thought experiment. I imagined myself standing in the Crowne Plaza parking lot, looking at the islands of barkdust and groomed azaleas. And gradually, gently, I imagined myself rising up into the air. I rose above the cars, over the spreading branches of the trees, watching the outline of the parking lot take shape, like the tarmac of some buried aircraft carrier, getting smaller and smaller, until the curve of the land was falling away toward the residential areas to the south. I saw the commercial zone to the north, bisected by the gray scar of I-5, and I kept rising, past the clouds, through the upper atmosphere, all the way into outer space, the hotel compound shrinking and disappearing into the broader land masses of the region and the globe.

I kept floating until I reached some distant point in the galaxy, and there, at last, I came to rest. Whatever worries I'd been feeling retracted to properly minuscule dimensions. The stakes of this two-day seminar were meaningless in the cosmic scheme, I told myself. In the cosmic scheme, everything was meaningless. Soon enough, this day would be over and I'd be walking away from the hotel with some small new understanding in my mind. At the very least, I'd never again have to wonder about the details of this specific experience again. In a few hours, the doing would have become the already done.

I walked out of the ballroom a little calmer and aimed for the restaurant, spotting Peter hunched on an overstuffed couch, making final edits to his morning speech.

"Hey," I said.

"Hey," he said, not looking up.

"You need anything?" I said.

"Nope."

"You're sure?"

"Uh huh."

I kept going, leaving him to his task. I didn't take his brusqueness personally. I knew there was even a kind of affection in it. Somewhere along the way, we had gone beyond mere politeness, mere friendship, and had traveled into the realm of something more profound: we were business partners now. Unless there was something truly urgent to communicate, it was preferable to give each other a wide berth. Someday, perhaps, we'd talk like normal people again. We'd reminisce about our great victories together. We'd try and piece together all the chaos that had swirled on the battlefield. But until then, we would keep our distance, knowing our collaboration made us more intimate than words could express. I took it as an honor to leave him alone.

I grazed through the buffet, picking up melon slices and an English muffin, and afterward I hurried back into the lobby to find Simon and Jaeha shaking the rain from their coats. I wasn't surprised they were the first coordinators on-site. They were probably our best team—Simon's quiet perfectionism complementing Jaeha's flamboyant perfectionism, leading to a precise routine that made the technologies sing—and after bracing hugs, and some bantering about the inevitable humiliations we faced, we went to prepare the intake tables, draping them with the black tablecloths, laying out the nametags in alphabetical order—all fifty participants, plus our coordinators—and topping it off with a vase of daisies as decoration.

Soon Michael appeared, looking dapper in his new work boots and clean flannel shirt, his hair pulled back in a slick ponytail. Linda showed up in a multicolored wrap and closed-toe shoes, an extravagant gesture on her part. Emilio came in but failed to find us at first, making a meandering circuit of the whole lobby area, touching all the fake hosta plants, before finally spotting us and bounding over. His partner, an intern named Eliza, scurried in half out of breath.

The last coordinator to appear was Amy, my partner. I was just stepping out of the bathroom when I saw her loitering at the front desk, the wind of the revolving door still fluttering in her hair. I was glad to see that she was wearing her most conservative loafers, new charcoal tights, a wool skirt, and a ruffled blouse under a vintage herringbone blazer. One might even think she was looking forward to the day's adventure. It was only seeing her face, etched with mild disgust, that gave me some pause.

"How's it going?" I said.

"All right," she said, watching the window washer scrape the panes with his squeegee.

"You're sure?"

"Why wouldn't it be?"

"I have no idea. I'm just asking."

She remained expressionless, not admitting to anything one way or another. Over the last few days she'd been alternately enthusiastic and distracted, and I'd been too busy to keep track of where she was currently at. From what I gathered she'd been having some belated issues about the whole project, mostly public speaking anxieties, Peter said, and I'd tried to keep my distance. In anyone else I might have had more sympathy, but in her, for some reason, I found the problem bothersome. We didn't have time for that kind of thing now. We had too much to do. Either jump in or don't, I thought. Don't drag everyone else down with your hand-wringing.

"That fountain is really soothing," she said. "Really says 'raised consciousness,' doesn't it?"

"Some people like it."

"You think?"

"Yeah, I do."

We stood silently a moment, watching Peter and Emilio huddle near the ballroom door, discussing some fine point of the day's curriculum. A cart of luggage rolled by, pushed by a teenage valet. I just hoped Amy would turn herself around by the time we were standing in front of our group. That didn't seem like too much to ask.

"The test rats are on their way?" she said.

"Arriving anytime now," I said.

"So I guess this is really happening."

"It better be."

"All right then," she said, and straightened her posture. "Let's get this show on the road." And with that she patted my arm and walked off, grabbing her nametag from the intake table, hugging Emilio, and disappearing into the ballroom to help unfold the metal chairs.

Dry lightning flashed in my nerves. Every relationship had a current of hatred running through the system. Soon this would be over, I thought. Soon we would know something. Soon we would all be safely on the other side.

By nine o'clock, when the first of Stanbro's workers began wandering in the door, we were more or less ready. The nametags were neatly gridded on the main intake table. Our literature was arranged in attractive bundles off to the side. The folding chairs were arrayed in the main conference room. We'd managed to present at least the convincing facade of professionalism. And none too soon, as suddenly two buses arrived and the place was teeming—a mix of executives, floorworkers, secretaries, accountants, and HR coordinators, all sipping coffee, eating Danishes, and chatting about the weather and what the day held.

I made the rounds, shaking hands, giving reassurances, playing the happy host, tamping down the queasy jolts that kept flashing in my nerves. What if these people didn't respond? What if they refused to participate? What if they found the whole proceedings ridiculous?

But always I reeled myself back in. In the worst case, we failed. We were humiliated. And then we forgot all about it. And there was the chance, just maybe, that we wouldn't fail, too. We might do fine, or even extremely well. All these people had dreams, didn't they? They wanted their workplace to become better, more sustainable, more inviting. And they faced a real problem, the rapid dissolution of their industry, their whole way of life. They had to change. Reality dictated as much. They wanted this to work.

At 9:45 Peter mounted the stage and delivered his remarks, talking predictably and at some length about the power of groups to change history, and the deep, untapped energies humans were capable of bringing out of each other given the proper tools. Wisely, he dispensed with the more apocalyptic parts of his normal stump speech, the stuff about humanity sloughing off the command and control model and overturning the ruined institutions of church and state, sticking instead to more uplifting sentiments about turning seeming problems into opportunities, and embracing change in ways big and small. In the end, he exhorted everyone to enter the day's activities with open hearts and minds, and in return the workers offered a polite round of applause. Watching him, I had to admire his reliable charisma. Even after the grueling final days of preparation, he was energized—clean-shaven, hair trimmed, white shirt still creased from the bag. When he'd had the time to pull himself together, I had no idea, but then again, he was the type who thrived on this kind of stress, his cells transmuting anxiety into pure, clean-burning fuel.

The workers poured back into the lobby, giving the coordinators a chance for last-second preparations. Amy and I hurried up to the Coho Boardroom to put the final touches on the space. We laid out binders at each table setting, erected the flip chart, tested our felt-tip pens on a piece of scratch paper. I cracked the window to vent the smell of pineapple disinfectant from the room, and she dimmed the lights a notch, and a notch further.

"Too dark?" she said.

"Too dark," I said.

"You think?" she said. "We don't want it too bright, do we?"

"We're not trying to seduce them."

"Oh? I thought we might be."

I didn't say anything. She edged the light up a few degrees.

A second later, the elevator dinged and our first batch of participants emerged, shuffling their way down the hall. We could hear the murmur of their small talk, the susurration of their feet on the carpet. Within moments they were at the door, nametags bouncing on lanyards, streaming inside.

Much effort had gone into formulating these groups. Many times, we'd mixed and matched the names and job descriptions on a corkboard in the Meditation Room, seeking the best possible balance of gender, seniority, and job title in each subgrouping. We'd rematched the tags based on whatever new information came in, and held prolonged debates as to the best philosophy of sorting. Should we separate the participants who already knew each other, or who worked in close proximity? Or would familiarity breed a faster, easier conversation? Should we separate people with known antagonisms? Or could the tensions help the dynamic?

The debates had gone around, and in the end most of the decisions were pretty arbitrary, by my reckoning. And now, at last, we were able to put the names to faces: here came Nathan Harness, a balding, wall-eyed warehouse supervisor with a half-eaten bear claw on the portable tabletop of his notepad; Melanie Kupchak, an executive secretary with a tightly coiled blond perm, tiny, pug nose, and deep dimples; Rebecca Lane, a mantislike CPA, with long folding legs and a small softball of a head; Eric Bowen, lead foreman in the Tigard pulp mill, an olive-complected, loose-limbed hunk.

The elevator dinged again and another batch wandered down the hall, delivering Amos Wall, Research and Development, a gaunt engineer with a dead front tooth; Rob Pasta, a gangly floor worker breathing through parted lips; Kim Bell, accounting, acned face barely visible under a frizzing, rust-colored mop; and Katherine Dubai, marketing, nearly beautiful, eyes like crystals, mouth smeared with lip gloss, packed into tight designer jeans. Last came Stan McLoughlin and Steve McDoughton, senior executives in matching blue blazers and polished penny loafers, embroiled in talk of the Seattle Mariners. Steve was tall and gleamingly bald, with long eyelashes, and winked at Amy as he entered. Stan was smaller, more compact and hirsute, with a fleshy face, long upper lip, and small eyes that looked like seeds pressed into Play-Doh.

All the while, Amy and I sat quietly, honoring the normal classroom protocol of awkward silence before introductions, not wanting to break the room's nervous spell. Outside, among the naked trees, the glass boxes of new corporate office parks and the spire of a Mormon temple were visible. The clock ticked. A truck's horn bellowed on I-5.

We sat there for a few minutes, letting the group baste in anticipation. We refused to crack any welcoming smiles or offer any hospitable nods of the head. Amy stared at the wall. I kept my eyes on the stack of papers directly in front of me. Above all, we didn't look at each other.

At exactly ten thirty, Amy rose. She jerked her lapels, crossed the room, and shut the door, snuffing the outside world like a match. She returned to her seat, scooting her chair back into place, and under the boardroom table gently touched my knee. The time had come.

I shuffled my papers one more time and stood. Let the show begin. A second later the sound of my voice was vibrating in the bones of my head.

"Thank you for coming out today," I said. "My name is Damon. And this is Amy. We're trainers with Rain Dragon Energy Management, and we're extremely happy to be with you here today. We've been looking forward to meeting you all for a long time now."

The group mumbled, expressing that they, too, were happy to be here. I ignored a sideways glance that passed between Amos and Eric and kept going, just as I'd practiced in the mirror at home:

"We know you're all busy people," I said. "And we want to

thank you in advance for all the time and energy you're going to spend with us here in this room. Over the next two days we're going to be talking a lot. We're going to be talking about the past, the present, and the future of Stanbro. We're going to be talking about management, labor, ourselves, really anything and everything you want to discuss. And most of all, we'll be learning from each other by examining what happens as we talk. We'll be listening, digging deeper. As you know, we have a lot on the line here. We have the power to change this company's destiny this weekend. We have the power to make your workplace what you most want it to be. So with that in mind, we want to get started, all right? In this process, Amy and I will not be your leaders."

The overhead lights buzzed, and the shell of a pen skittered on the tabletop. I sat down and forced myself to fold my hands on the table. Beside me, Amy calmly sipped her glass of water.

The group stared at us. Their expressions were much as we'd predicted in rehearsals. Some were confused, some suspicious, and numerous seemed not to have listened at all. It would have been disconcerting if not for the fact that throughout the hotel, in other rooms exactly like this one, the same scene was taking place. The other coordinators were also rising, also greeting their groups, and also sitting down and abdicating their duties as group leaders. The idea—Peter's idea—was to administer a kind of shock therapy from the very outset. If Stanbro's workers had come here expecting authority, we would begin by robbing them of that expectation. We would begin by forcing them out of the normal hierarchies, the normal patterns, and make them improvise some new way of relating. It was a gamble, to be sure. In a way, it was nothing more than a gimmick. But this was the plan we'd all agreed to, and for our abdication of authority to succeed, we had to execute it with utter authority. Any whiff of uncertainty, and we would be exposed as a joke. Any lapse in confidence, and the spell would be broken.

So we waited, rigid, the vacuum of doubt widening underneath us.

I didn't look at Amy. I could tell from her stillness, her slow breath, that she was maintaining her poise.

"Wait a second," Stan, the fatter of the two executives, said at last. "We're doing what?"

"Whatever you want," I said, making full eye contact. "It's up to you. To us. As a group."

"But . . ." He frowned, looking at the others. "Don't you have a little more to say before we get going? Some instructions or something?"

"Like he said," Amy said, "what we do is all up to you. Collectively."

The sound of a heating duct kicked on deep in the walls. The group continued to stare at us, until eventually, cautiously, they began to glance around at each other, looking for clues. They were disoriented, as we'd hoped. Amy and I remained still, refusing to betray any worry or even really to turn our heads.

"I don't get this," Stan said. "I thought we were here for some reason."

"Yeah," Rebecca said. "We're missing work for this."

"This is crap," Stan said.

"We can discuss that, if you want," Amy said.

"I think what they're saying is, it's up to us to decide what we do," Eric said, watching Amy and me for any response. "I think that's what they mean."

"Is that what you're saying?" Steve, the bald executive, said.

"That's right," I said.

"But what does that mean, though?" Melanie said. "It's 'up to us'? I don't even know what that means."

"Up to us?" Katherine said. "That seems crazy."

"It seems ridiculous, is what it seems," Nathan agreed. "How much is this costing, anyway?"

"Does it, though?" said Steve, sounding a blessedly well-timed note of open-mindedness. "I don't know. I'm not so sure."

"What do you mean?" Eric said.

"I mean, I think we're supposed to start talking to each other, that's all . . ."

And so, hesitantly, we began. Steve's curiosity opened the door a crack, and cautiously, almost fearfully, the group tiptoed to the threshold. They started simply, by discussing the expectations they'd had upon arriving, and why, and the expectations they no longer understood. They posed a few little questions back and forth, debating the process as it had already begun, and wondering out loud whether they had any choice in how to proceed. And soon enough, haltingly, the door opened a little wider. What was their goal here? they asked. What were their hopes?

It was exactly as Peter had promised. Out of nervous energy, the group rushed to fill the void. It took almost nothing. A group was hardwired to come together.

The next hour or so was spent in establishing the parameters of the conversation, and keeping track of every crimp and quake in the process. Every utterance was scrutinized for misunderstandings and possible alternate meanings. Every ambiguity was plumbed to its furthest depths. Almost by instinct the group moved ahead by turning in on itself, communicating an idea, and then communicating about the communication itself. At the hour mark,

Amy and I finally dared to share a sidelong glance. We hadn't said anything in almost ten minutes. How easy was this going to be? How light was this burden?

The group chose Melanie as the scribe for the day, and installed her beside the big pad of graph paper. She had an orange felt-tip pen in hand, with instructions to record everything that was said, and once the recording began, the pace slowed even further.

"Why isn't Rob talking?" Rebecca asked.

"I'd like to share something about what Kim said . . .," said Rob.

"Before that," Katherine said, "could we just go back for a second to what we were talking about before?"

Every once in a while, Amy and I dropped a question into the mix, but by and large it was hardly necessary. When the group laughed at Stan pretending to fall asleep during Rob's rambling description of his first drive across America, we laughed, too. When it coached Melanie on how to speak more assertively, we listened. Almost invisibly, a shared vocabulary was forming, a consciousness was taking shape.

Late in the morning, we took slightly tighter hold of the reins, and Amy introduced the concept of Peter's energy pyramid. Melanie's felt-tip pen flew to collect the group's commentary. How did the different energy levels flow into one another? How did energy escalate? How did energy become focused, intensified? How did it disperse? How was it wasted? We talked abstractly and gradually directed our ideas to the institution of Stanbro itself. How could the company's collective energy best be harnessed? How would the differing parts operate together with the smallest friction? What bound the organization together? What simple principles explained the institution's existence? The pages filled and multiplied and went up on the walls, until the room was plastered with orange text linked by arrows and bubbles, clouds of words bristling with orange connecting lines. The pages spread around the corners like an orange brushfire.

Amy was good. All her skepticism of the morning seemed to slough away, and she became alert and hilarious. I'd forgotten how she rose to this kind of challenge, how she could be counted on in moments of duress. Only in a crisis, even a minor one, did she become grounded in a way that eluded her in the flux of day-to-day life.

At some point we gave ourselves over to the leaping consciousness of the group. When a hand went up, we were there to respond. When a recognition became available, we helped draw the connection. The Coho Boardroom became a universe unto itself, stars being born, dark matter coursing through strange gravitational belts. I crept among the dyads, coaxing, correcting, explaining, encouraging, and when the group came back together I orchestrated its feedback like a musical conductor. If I'd been a participant, I might have gotten annoyed at some of the other members. I might have found them obtuse or frivolous or overly distractible. I might have even hated some of them. But as their leader I didn't have that luxury. I was forced to find all their idiosyncrasies charming. I was forced to shut off the judgmental part of my brain and give everyone the benefit of the doubt. What a pleasure: to anticipate a need, to reveal a new angle of insight, to open a mind a degree, to teach.

In the afternoon, stupefied by the hotel's Chicken Kiev, we hit a slight trough, but we got through it, and in the final hours we made some major gains regarding task cycles and the concept of reciprocal maintenance, siphoning inexorably to the end of the first day.

The day closed with Kim, our shyest member, weeping musically during a period of nondirected sharing. She was in the middle of talking about her father's mental health problem, her own guilt and frustration over what to do with him, when the day's waters suddenly burst. She started with nearly imperceptible sniffs and swallows, and within moments she was a wailing stringed instrument. Tears streamed down her face, and finally Stan rose from his seat and sat down beside her, putting his arm around her shoulders and cradling her against his chest. Eric joined from the other side. Kim kept crying, and one by one, we all went and joined the tight circle.

Finally, deep in the knot of arms, Kim's nose made the sound of a gurgling balloon and she began laughing softly.

"I'm so sorry," she said.

"Don't be sorry," someone said, for all of us.

The group's vision statement coalesced in a matter of moments, woven from the filaments of the day's many conversations. Minutes before the day's session ended, Amy stood beside the flip chart and read the statement out loud to the group.

"A company where employees do their best and consistently exceed the customer's expectations, and in return feel safe and challenged in their jobs, with room to grow."

"Thanks, guys," Amy said, as everyone packed their things. "Great work. You've all done a great job. See you all in the morning. All right. Now we've really got something to talk about."

The participants—giddy, exhausted, mildly dazed by the day's travels—said good-bye and exited the room, joining the other groups exiting the other rooms, and moments later Amy and I were alone, just as we'd started. REACTIVE equals NO THINKING, JUST DOING. The energy we GIVE is equal to the energy we GET. There is no LOSS of ENERGY, only TRANSFERENCE. What is the PURPOSE of the corrugated paper division? The deeper PURPOSE? The DEEPEST PURPOSE?

"Not bad," Amy said, bathed in the pale blue twilight of the rain-speckled window. As she bent over to gather her pens, the gape of her blouse opened and I had a fleeting impulse to pin her against the wall and kiss her on the spot.

"Not bad at all," I said.

Amy tossed a wad of scratch paper into the plastic trashcan. She tapped a sheaf of papers against the desk and put them in her bag, smiling and shaking her head.

"What?" I said, loosening my tie and rolling up my cuffs like a proper white-collar citizen.

She slid her papers into her Rain Dragon/Stanbro Paper tote bag. "You were good today. That's all."

"So were you," I said. "We were good together."

Before leaving the hotel, we debriefed with our fellow coordinators in the lounge, discovering, happily, that everyone else had had equally productive days. The technologies were working, we all agreed. The conversation was under way. We just needed to keep going, full steam ahead.

"You want a ride?" I said, shrugging on my coat.

"Linda brought me," she said.

"We could talk about tomorrow."

"Okay. Sure."

The traffic on I-5 was light, and we sailed around the Terwilliger Curves, scored by a solid block of the Rolling Stones on the classic rock station, the spell of the day's success still floating around us. We recapped the day's high points—the terror of the opening minutes, the free-flowing period just before lunch, the logjam and eventual breakthrough coming out of the afternoon dyads. Nathan was a cool guy, we agreed. His record collection sounded staggering. Kim was amazing, especially considering her childhood in a home of abusive Jehovah's Witnesses and the nearly fatal string of health catastrophes that constituted her young adulthood. All of them were interesting in their own rights. We were lucky, we agreed. We had a good group.

We pulled up to Linda's house, and I turned off the engine. The sliver of a moon hid in the trees, half swallowed by the inky blue sky. I rolled my tie into my pocket, giving Amy a clean opportunity to invite me inside if she so desired, but careful not to push too hard, either. I didn't want to break what we had just started to rebuild.

"What a day," she said, fixing her bag in her lap.

"Yeah," I said. "Long."

"You must be tired," she said. "You were there so early."

"Pretty tired," I said. "Not that tired, though," I added, not wanting to seem unavailable.

"Well . . ."

"Well . . ."

She leaned over and we hugged, the skin of our cheeks, our hair, touching lightly. When she pulled away her eyes wavered for a second, caught somewhere between affection and abstracted regret. The small bouquet of creases at the edges of her eyes became her. The first strokes of age. Death, the artist, slowly working his magic. Love was grief's becoming, I thought. It was sad but true.

She put her hand on my cheek and let it fall away.

"See you tomorrow," she whispered, and retreated from the car. I waited as she walked the path to the porch and climbed the steps and entered the golden door, the walls of Linda's house enclosing her like a shell. The door locked and I waited a little longer, imagining her moving inside the rooms—hanging up her coat in the closet, adjusting the thermostat. A woman and her dog walked by, the tags jingling. A moment later the porch light clicked off, and I had nothing to do but drive home.

THIRTEEN

I DIDN'T KNOW exactly what was going on with Amy and me, or what I was hoping would happen, but I didn't have much time to torture myself about it. Within a matter of hours, the second day of the first session was upon us, and we were back in the classroom with our whiteboard, driving ahead.

We opened the second day with a long-form role-playing game called Regional City, wherein everyone took on the identity of a civic leader in a medium-sized metropolitan area and brokered a budget based on the year's tax revenues. From there we moved to Space Trip, a visualization based on an exploratory space shuttle voyage, followed by Microscope, a visualization in which the listener's body mass was broken down into molecules, atoms, electrons, quarks, gluons, and finally into mere patterns of energy indistinguishable from the energy of all that existed in the cosmos.

We rushed to finish the day's agenda, and in the end the hustle paid off, with exhausted cheers all around. The group was unanimous that they had been through something profound together, and promised each other that the conversations that had begun in the Coho Boardroom would continue in the Stanbro workplace. We didn't have much time to celebrate the victory, though. Hours later, we were already stepping into the room again for the next session, introducing ourselves to a new group, looking toward the third and fourth sessions coming down the pike.

In this way, the next three weeks passed like a dream. Every morning I picked up Amy, and together we drove to the Crowne Plaza under the white winter sky, a garnet haze of naked dogwood bushes flurrying outside the windows. On the way we would discuss the day's strategies, and after sliced melon and massive quantities of weak coffee, we ascended upstairs. As the days went on we improved our technique. We revised the phrasing of the Energy Pyramid, relabeling "Transcendent" "Creative." Anything involving blindfolds was deemed too risky. We pulled those pages.

At the day's end we generally went out for drinks with our fellow coordinators, becoming regulars at Gubanc's Pub, a nearby fern bar, and with our consulting fees already showing up in the mail, we ordered with impunity. We ate focaccia and arbequina olive oil and polenta with white truffles, washed down with Bombay martinis, and compared notes and gossiped. We shared rumors of mutinous petitions circulating among the workers, stories of moronic questions and misstatements, confessions of salacious attractions to the better-looking students, speculation as to what new jobs might be in store. According to Peter, Boeing, Weyerhauser, and United Airlines had all moved into view. They were just biding their time, seeing what we pulled off with Stanbro, and if the results were interesting enough, they would pounce.

After drinks I drove Amy home, and we used that time to sketch the following day's game plan. I dropped her at the front steps, and she never invited me inside.

Overall, we were getting along well. She hadn't lost a certain sliver of contempt for the proceedings, but whatever issues she had seemed thoroughly under control, and were shrinking down by degrees as the days passed. The longer we went, the more fully she embraced the experience.

Someday, I thought, she would let go of all her objections and allow herself the full measure of her happiness. In the meantime, her changing moods were like a crystal turning in space. Depending on the day, the weather, and the angle of light, different facets flared, and always some large portion remained hidden from view. It was almost beautiful, I thought, in a distant, invisible kind of way, this mystery inside her, this perpetual secret. Whatever was rekindling between us was still too delicate to touch.

As for Peter, we barely talked. Standing at the center of the storm, holding everything together, he spent his days stalking from room to room, taking phone calls, brokering connections, easing anxieties. The best help I could offer him was simply staying out of his way, and vice versa.

Before I knew it, we were seven sessions in, only two to go before holiday break. And then, one Saturday night, I came home to find a message on the answering machine. It was Peter, saying he needed to talk first thing in the morning. He had news.

Hours later, I stood in the parking lot of the Crowne Plaza. It was before dawn, and fog filled the spaces between everything, the streetlights painting orange halos in the filmy whiteness, the rough shape of the hotel's face hovering in a state of perpetual dissolve.

A car's engine growled in the darkness and came to a halt, a door slammed and locked, muted footsteps sounded in the fog, and a moment later Peter materialized, briefcase in hand.

"Thanks," he said, swirling into focus. "Kind of short notice, I know."

"No problem," I said. "What's up?"

"How about some coffee first? You all right with that? I need it."

"Coffee it is."

I fell into stride beside him, and our double footsteps made a muffled tattoo on the damp asphalt. The hotel brightened from a dingy gray to a shimmering silver and only at the last second gained full definition, lights resolving, awnings extending, and we pushed through the glass doors into the lobby. The crystalline interior ballooned around us as we crossed to the glass elevator, which lifted us to the top floor's executive dining room, open all hours for the global workday.

The big picture windows of the restaurant normally framed a stretch of I-5 and the Kruse Way on-ramp, but today they were all packed with fog. At the bar, one of the kitchen workers was eating his breakfast, listening to a soccer game halfway across the globe. Peter and I settled into the crackling vinyl seats and opened the laminated menus in unison.

Peter put the menu aside and rubbed his eyes. The stillness of the parking lot had followed us inside. The fog pressed against the glass.

"So?" I said, getting tired of waiting.

"So Banger came to visit on Friday," he said.

"Yeah. I saw," I said. This was not news, exactly. The visit from the CEO had been planned for weeks. He'd arrived in the late afternoon, toured the rooms flanked by his minions, lurking in the back of each session for about five minutes, and left. I hadn't heard anything since. But I'd assumed it had all gone fine.

We were forced to pause when the waiter came. I ordered the buckwheat pancakes and Peter ordered a Denver omelet, and the waiter sped off through the empty tables to the kitchen.

"And? What'd he think?" I said.

"He liked some of it," Peter said. "The efficiency recommendations from Linda and Simon's group seemed practical. The one-hundred-year plan in Michael and Jaeha's group was intriguing. He thought it was all a little fruity, I guess, but not outright objectionable."

"Sounds all right."

"I'd even say the tour was going pretty well up until he got to Emilio's room. He walks in there, and Emilio's up in front talking about the enneagram."

"The enneagram?"

Peter closed his eyes and rubbed his temples. "A little improvisation on Emilio's part. The enneagram is a Sufist diagram. It goes back to ancient Damascus. Kind of a dance chart for whirling dervishes. You see it showing up in diagrams of yogic chakras, kabbalistic *sefirats*, the deadly sins and virtues, if you look hard enough."

"So Emilio was dancing?"

"No, no. He has the enneagram up on the whiteboard, with the nine points labeled with musical notations. Do Re Mi Fa. And he's talking all kinds of mystical bullcrap. 'The enneagram can do anything you imagine. The enneagram is the source of all knowledge. With the enneagram you can destroy the walls of Jericho, turn the whole organization inside out.'"

"With the CEO in the back of the room," I said.

"With Banger standing right there," Peter said. "And you know,

Banger's even okay with that. Destroying the company isn't even the problem. The problem is a minute later when Emilio starts denouncing Jesus Christ."

"No," I said.

"Yeah," Peter said. "'Jesus never existed. Jesus was an invention of the church to consolidate its power over the illiterate class.' Right in front of the fucking CEO! Now, Don Banger, he goes to church. He sends his kids to Catholic school. He almost ripped out Emilio's throat right there on the spot. Bob Doyle practically had to hold him back. Dumb fucker. I swear to God, I'm going to throttle Emilio this time. Have a brain."

The fork in Peter's fist was bending under the pressure of his thumb. He looked at it and sighed and put it down.

"Anyway," he said. "I've been on the phone with Bob about five times. Going back and forth. Maybe Banger's just looking for ways out. Anyway, the damage is done. We've got a meeting with him in a few hours. Should be quite a session, I'm guessing. He had his doubts before this, I'd say he's got more now."

"Oh, man."

"It was coming," Peter said. "I've got to remind myself of that. It's not all Emilio's fault, exactly. I just hope Banger can hear us out, is all. I hope he can see the big picture here. And by the way, you're coming. You're the one that got us into this show. I'm going to need some backup."

The waiter arrived and the coffee cups sounded dully on the fake wood, then the cream and sugar, followed by two clinking glasses of water, the ice cubes shot through with spidery branches of trapped air. Peter gazed at the window. The fog was starting to brighten as the sun ate away from above, and gradually, dim silhouettes were resolving in the nearer vicinities. The skeletons of fir trees, the electrical wires bending into nothingness, the Farmer's Insurance building on the opposite side of the freeway. We were both silent, pondering the day's coming hours.

Soon my pancakes arrived, dusted in powdered sugar, the lacy patterns almost too pristine to disturb. Peter's omelet came ruptured, spilling mushrooms. On the radio, the static roared. The commentator cried, "Gol!"

Don Banger's office was located on the thirty-third floor of the Metropolitan Insurance building in downtown Portland. Just after noon we entered the lobby, stepped into the elevator, and stepped out onto a sleekly modern reception area with a view to the shared office space, populated by a few Sunday workers, all of them ignoring the commanding views of the mountains and river in every direction.

We were led to Banger's personal waiting area, a plush chamber hung with daguerreotypes of weathered loggers in the cut mouths of ancient fir trees, and scattered with furniture of Tudor and Second Empire extraction.

We took seats on leather couches, and Banger's secretary, a time capsule from the Eisenhower era, told us he would be ready sometime soon. Peter picked up *Newsweek*; I opened *Time*, skimming articles about AT&T competing in the global information economy, and a new crop of private financiers in Hollywood. Every page seemed to offer some partial metaphor for our own situation, but none offered any clear predictions.

I put the magazine down and stared at Banger's door. All morning, I'd been trying to convince myself I didn't really care about how the meeting went. Either we kept the contract or we didn't. Either we succeeded or failed. Who cared? If we got fired, I'd go back to what I'd been doing before, writing PR and planning events. If we stayed on, I'd keep going in this direction, wherever it led.

But in fact, sitting there, looking at the daguerreotypes on the walls, gauging the tension in my chest, I realized I did care about how the meeting went. I wanted to keep this job. I'd worked hard, invested a lot of time, and I didn't want to just let it all go. I'd come to enjoy the pace, the camaraderie, the power. Most importantly, I had the sense it was helping Amy and me. Something was still wearing down in her, some hard kernel was still softening. I didn't want to stop too soon.

I looked up to find Peter staring at Banger's door, too, the morning's fatigue giving way to a more resolute demeanor. The animal intensity was returning, just in time. He glanced my way, and winked:

"I ever tell you about starting Rain Dragon?" he said, eyes returning to the closed door.

"A few times," I said.

"I told you about the voice?"

"Remind me."

"I wasn't always a food guy, you know." He rolled his magazine into a cylinder and tapped his knee a few times. "I grew up on a farm, yeah. But I was not interested in sticking around. Back in the eighties I was an investment banker up in Seattle."

"That I've heard."

"Yep. Managed a pretty big chunk of capital, too. Lived in a big rich-guy house out on the Sound. Wore tassel loafers to work every day. It was a whole different life."

"Wow," I said. "Tassel loafers."

"Yeah," he said. "I was climbing that ladder. Climbing it

fast. But then one night everything changed for me. Just like that."

"Uh-huh?" We were entering a patch of his biography I hadn't heard before.

"I was standing in front of my refrigerator one night," he said, "staring at all the food in there. Checking out the inventory. And all of a sudden this voice came into my head. It started out quiet, but it got louder fast. 'Who killed the pork chops?' it said. 'Who killed the pork chops?' It just kept bonging in my head over and over again."

"Bizarre."

"If it hadn't happened to me, I don't know what I'd think. It's hard to describe. But something happened to me that night. My mind kind of opened up. Staring at that meat on the shelf, the bubbles of blood sealed near the bone, I understood maybe for the first time it had been a living creature before. I had no idea where this meat came from. No idea where it'd been raised. No idea how it'd been killed and dressed, who'd driven it from the farm to the store, none of it. Same for the milk, the pizza, the leftover Thai in there. I just stood in the light, in a state of complete alienation from my food. And that meant from my body, too. I'd been eating animals, turning their meat into energy, with no relationship other than a second at the cash register. Something really peeled back for me that night. The next morning I walked into the bank and told them I quit, and the day after that I started on the path to Rain Dragon. I've been walking that way ever since."

Peter sat hunched on the sofa, elbows on his knees, staring at Banger's door. I could almost see the glow of his old refrigerator's light on his face.

"Who killed the pork chops," I said.

He smiled grimly. "Who killed the pork chops. I think I know who."

"Mr. Banger is ready for you now," the secretary said, rising and gesturing for us to rise, too. "Please. This way."

Together we got up and crossed the waiting area, passing into a large, dim room scented with medicine and finely aged power. The walls were decorated with elaborately framed oil paintings, many featuring a liver-colored Brittany spaniel in bucolic locales. On a low coffee table sat the most gorgeous crystal I'd ever seen, a cracked purple half-shell of dazzling facets, like an eternal burst of fresh springwater.

Banger himself was sitting behind an enormous oaken desk, his silver flattop rock-hard. His face was like a walnut, furrowed and pinched, his earlobes pendulous, his small eyes alert. Behind him floated the uppermost reaches of the city, shafts of mirrored window and concrete muted in the day's cloudy light.

"Peter," Banger said, and stepped from behind his wooden iceberg, hand extended. "Glad you could make it." He pumped Peter's hand and turned to me. "You must be Damon." His grip was strong but not showy. "Don Banger. Glad to meet you. I've heard a lot of great things about your work. Real honor."

His warmth came as something of a surprise, mostly because it seemed so genuine. For all the gravelly harshness in his voice, he had a strangely alluring tone, holding the promise of all kinds of adventure and triumph—Alaskan dogsled races, African hunting expeditions. In spite of myself, I immediately succumbed to his masculine charm.

"Beautiful dog," Peter said, admiring the portraits. "I used to have a black-and-white spaniel myself. I loved that dog. Smart, loyal animal."

"It's in the breed," Banger said. "Those are five different dogs, actually. Justice, Liberty, Freedom, Democracy, and Brotherhood. I keep going back for more. They're all exceptional."

"I liked to think mine was special," Peter said.

"I'm sure it was," Banger said. "I'm sure it was. Please. Both of you. Sit down."

By a series of subtle body movements Banger had already begun guiding us to an alcove outfitted with three high-backed Chesterfield chairs. Peter hovered before sitting, waiting for Banger to sit, and Banger hovered, too, until at last they sat at the same time.

"Thanks so much for coming out yesterday," Peter said, trying to control the conversation from the gate. "I know you're a busy man. We've been wanting to get you out there for quite a while now."

"Saw some interesting things," Banger said. "Your folks are stirring the pot, I can tell you that much."

"That's the goal," Peter said. "Stir things up and—"

"Hey, you need anything to drink?" Banger interrupted. "Water? A beer?"

"No thanks," Peter said. I shook my head, no, too. Banger asked us again and we refused again and he allowed our answers to stand. His secretary, who'd been lurking at the door, disappeared, and the conversation recommenced, but whatever leverage Peter had claimed by speaking first was already gone.

"Very interesting work you're doing for us," Banger said, leaning back and crossing his arms. "I've got to tell you, I find your line of work fascinating, I really do. I've done some reading on the methods. Shell, Procter & Gamble, they've had some great success with this kind of thing over the years. Its something we've been wanting to try for a long time here at Stanbro. Should've gotten on the ball years ago. What do you boys think? How's it going down in the trenches? Damon? What are your thoughts on the current situation? You hopeful?"

Apparently Banger's blowup from the week before had already been wiped from memory. Or at least he'd had the chance to calm himself down a few notches. Or maybe he was just warming up, luring me into a trap. I couldn't tell, so I played it safe and painted him the most blandly positive picture of our activities that I could.

"You have a lot of amazing people working for you, Mr. Banger," I said. "A lot of really smart, capable people, up and down the line. And I have to say, they're really rising to the occasion. We've had some great breakthroughs in the groups already."

"Tell me more."

"They're seeing patterns, making connections," I said vaguely, and glanced at Peter for any encouragement he might have to offer. He was looking at me like we'd met for the first time five minutes ago, though, waiting for his own chance to retake the wheel. "Recognizing old assumptions," I went on. "Glimpsing new potentials. We've generated some very simple, very effective ideas around corporate-wide conservation efforts, recycling programs, management initiatives. Last week, we came up with a concept for the particleboard processing plant's supply chain that could save hundreds of thousands a year."

"You know you're really pissing some people off."

"That's our job," Peter said. He couldn't stand holding back any longer. "We wouldn't be doing our job if everyone was comfortable. 'You have to break some eggs to make an omelet,' like they say."

"Yeah, and when there's more shit than dog, get rid of the dog," Banger replied, mugging in my direction. "That's what my daddy used to say." Whatever note of menace we were meant to hear in his voice was perfectly tuned, only the slightest edge coming through behind the good-natured bluster.

"We're engaged in a process," Peter said, refusing to be put off. "It can be messy. I'm sure you understand. Nothing worthwhile happens without some birthing pain."

"I don't care if you're pissing people off," Banger said, brushing the air with his hand. "Couldn't care less, honestly. If that's what it takes to get results, then so be it. I'm for whatever works. The thing is, what I'm trying to see is if you guys are helping or hurting at this point. To be frank, that's what I'm trying to understand. That's why I wanted you here today."

"Understood," Peter said. "And let me say: We're only just getting started. We're still just laying the groundwork here. So much of what we're doing right now—"

"Laying groundwork," Banger said. "Laying groundwork, I support. I'm not sure if that's the case here, though."

"And what's the case? In your mind?" Peter said, bristling at what amounted to an accusation of ineffectiveness on our part. If this was a trial, he wanted to hear the charges.

"I'm seeing a lot of talk," Banger said. "But none of it's really going anywhere. Nothing's catching. I see a lot of sitting and spinning wheels. I think that's what some of my people have been worrying about. This talking. This navel gazing."

"I respectfully have to disagree, Don," Peter said. "Talking in this case is a form of doing. Language is the primary tool we have at our disposal. It just takes time to understand how to use it, is all. The results aren't immediate. They show up in the long term. Some of these things, they just take patience."

"I don't know what kind of results you're talking about."

"Let me put it this way: For a company to know that it's moving ahead, it has to know where it's trying to get to. Right? It has to have a goal in mind. It has to have a destination. That takes some discussion, some back-and-forth. What is the destination Stanbro is driving toward? What is the world Stanbro is striving to create? Until your workers understand that, until they can articulate it, they can't really know if they're making any progress. And I think we're still in the process of figuring out where they're going. If you would've stuck around on Friday, we might have put the question to you, too: What do you see in Stanbro's future, Don? What is the picture you hold in your mind? I might ask you that question."

"Don't think you're putting me on the couch," Banger said, grinning. "I don't go down that easy."

"It's not the couch, Don. And the CEO should be able to answer the question. He better have a vision, right? Or else what's the point?" He leaned forward and rested his elbows on his knees. "What do you see?"

Banger rested his own hands on the arm of his chair, sensing that some kind of chase had been enjoined. He was not the kind who refused a test of wills.

"What do I see?" Banger said. "I see growth. I see increasing market share. I see measurable results." He was teasing Peter. He would not give up his vision so easily.

"That's it, just growth? Bigger is better?"

"In a nutshell."

"Not a very inspiring vision, Don. I don't know if I'd want to work at Stanbro."

"I don't know if you'll have to all that much longer."

"Here's another question," Peter said, slipping Banger's conversational half nelson. "You say you value growth. What's the difference between growth and evolution?"

"I see where you're going," Banger said, crossing his legs, resting his black sock on his knee. "Growth, you get bigger. Evolution, you change shape, you become more adaptable, efficient. How's that?"

"Would you say evolution is a goal of Stanbro's? Part of the vision as much as growth?"

"I can go with that. I accept that."

"And how does growth, or evolution, come into being, Don? What are the conditions that bring evolution into play?"

Banger was quick to reply. "Learning from mistakes. Random mutations. The power of the group mind working together. These are all elements of evolution."

"Excellent. And what allows those things to happen?"

"That depends," Banger said.

"On what?"

"On who's asking." Banger laughed, showing his fat incisors. He and Peter were enmeshed, sensing some mutual, musky pheromone in the air. Their clash had been all but preordained, and they set to the task with gusto.

For the next half hour they grappled like grizzly bears. I might as well have walked away from the room and taken a nap, for all they would have cared. The conversation ranged from DNA structures to the origins of Euclidean geometry to the teachings of Lao Tzu, with Peter probing Banger, and Banger, in answering

Peter's questions, probing Peter in return. Their powers were almost perfectly balanced. They each had their signature maneuvers to deploy. Peter played the insurgent, asking questions, stoking conflict, and Banger, the authority who reveled in the disobedience. They might have seemed like opposites, but they were more like twins.

Peter marshaled some of his best metaphors for the fight. He talked about machine thinking, and sleepwalking through history, and Planck's quantum theory of energy packets. There was nothing he could say, though, no thought experiment supple enough, to sway Banger from his conviction that the sessions were ultimately frivolous. He was unmoved by Peter's theory of a societal awakening. He did not foresee a better world of equality and justice someday. He wasn't motivated by ecological arguments. His idea of history was defiantly pessimistic and his inner compass tuned solely to family, duty, child-rearing, and self-discipline, his ideals those of masculine independence and patriotism. Peter's notions of creative self-becoming had no effect on him. The men were on different sides of a dimensional divide, hearing each others' words but untouched by each others' basic premises.

Every once in a while Banger's secretary poked her head inside to inform her boss of his upcoming appointments, but he waved her off each time, enjoying himself too much to stop. By the third visit, she was adamant that he had to move on.

"You got some funny ideas," Banger said to Peter, at last standing and straightening his pants crease. "Seems like you think there's some kind of conspiracy going on, don't you? Machine thinking. Dehumanization. There's no conspiracy, though, my friend. No one's smart enough for that. The conspiracy is just incompetence, mostly. Laziness. People fucking up and covering their asses.

You talk about command and control. No one's looking that far ahead."

"Maybe we're talking about starting a conspiracy then," Peter said. "We're talking about planning ahead for once."

"The bottom line is, you're scaring my people," Banger said. "They're not responding to your language. That's all there is to it."

"They are responding," Peter said. "They just don't know it yet. They're starting to understand each other. The energies we could tap into here are staggering. They just have to get over the hump."

"You don't understand people too well, Peter," Banger said. We had reached the door, and the two men were standing face-to-face on the threshold. Peter loomed a full head over Banger, but still the smaller man was the fulcrum of the pairing. "People don't know what they want. Self-actualization is a nice idea. I'm a member of the board for the ballet and opera. I appreciate these things. But if people can't realize their whole potential, that's okay, too. I don't need a bunch of artists in my company. I need people to try a little harder is all. What they do otherwise is their own business."

"Look—"

"I like your attitude, though," Banger said, opening the door. "I can see why Bob was so hot on this thing. You're an inspiring man. You've got a real way with words. I wasn't sure what I was gonna do when you walked in the door. I was ready to give you guys the ax. But I like what I'm hearing. You're optimistic. I like that."

This compliment was a form of sadism in disguise. To say he understood Peter's thinking was to say he had Peter figured out. But the judgment came as a relief to me.

"Let me tell you something," Banger said. "Frederick Taylor learned this long ago. What people really want is a little attention, that's all. You dim the lights on the assembly line, the productivity improves. You brighten the lights, the productivity improves. What's necessary is the proper equilibrium. The workers need some encouragement. They also need a little fear of God, honestly. I think you're right in that."

"That's not what we're saying."

Banger strode back to his desk and lifted a stack of papers. "I got this petition yesterday," he said. "Two hundred of my employees say you guys are full of shit. They don't want any part in these trainings anymore. They say I'm wasting our money. You know what? I don't care. Don't give a rip." He dropped the pile in the wastebasket.

"The woman who circulated this thing, she's done. She's fired. You don't need to worry about her anymore."

"That's not necessary, Don."

"It is necessary, Peter." Banger glared from behind his desk. "If there's one thing I'd like to teach you today, it's that you have to break some eggs, like you said. We're a good team, you and me. You're good-time Charlie. You get everyone feeling good about themselves. I'm the bad guy. I make the tough calls. If both of us are doing our jobs, we should see some real progress around here."

"I'm not—"

"Work is nothing if something isn't used up in the process," Banger said. "If some door isn't closed behind you. You want change without pain? Sorry, that's not how it is. We're a team, you and me. We have to work like a team. Now if you fellas will excuse me, I've been keeping people waiting. I enjoyed the talk. I look forward to our next meeting. My guess is, it won't be too long."

FOURTEEN

PETER WAS ACCUSTOMED to fielding a certain level of skepticism about his ideas, and he had a whole array of techniques at the ready for dealing with whatever apathy, disdain, even hostility sometimes came his way. He had durable strings of logic to trot out, compelling anecdotes to recount, and if all else failed he could usually overwhelm his doubters with an unmatchable intellectual vigor. But up in Banger's glass aerie, the CEO had presented him with a harder case, a philosophical position stubbornly impermeable to his ideals, the proverbial immovable object to his irresistible force. There had been nothing Peter could do to bring Banger over to his attitude of reform, and as such the interaction had at least momentarily stunned him. In the elevator back down, he held a look of consternation on his face. It was going to take a while to think his way around Banger. By the time we were back on the street, Peter was sunk in depression.

"We bought ourselves some time," I said, stepping into downtown's Sunday hush. "We live to fight another day."

"I guess that's true," he said, the street's foot traffic trickling around us—a fat woman with four shopping bags, a gaunt man with an orange ski hat. A distant car horn echoed in the empty canyons of downtown.

"I thought it was over in there for a while," I said, "but he came around."

"Yeah," he said, without feeling.

"The box we've opened, it can't be closed anymore," I said, using Peter's own rhetoric against him. "Banger just doesn't see the whole picture yet. That woman, she'll be back soon enough. Stanbro will be growing again soon. And she'll see what we were up to."

"Right," he said. "That's possible."

A bus plastered with the giant faces of the local TV news team squealed to a stop alongside us, and the doors opened but no one got out. A Styrofoam clamshell skittered on the sidewalk.

"The important thing is that we stay in there," I said. "We keep pushing. This is a long-term process. Nothing happens in a day."

"Mayflies live their whole lives," he said.

"You know what I mean," I said. "It's like you say, we're water and Stanbro's stone. In the long run, water is king."

I walked him to his car and watched as he pulled away into the trafficless street. I wasn't worried about him. In a few minutes the sap would be rising again. Peter was not constitutionally able to stay down long.

It was only three o'clock, and I had nothing to do. My refrigerator was well stocked. The house cleaning could wait. I wasn't ready to go back home just yet, so I decided to kill some time wandering downtown. I started out by ambling down Broadway, heading for Old Town, and as the blocks added up, I could feel my thoughts sharpening, my spirits quickening. Walking and thinking, walking and thinking, there was some correlation, some shared rhythm. Passing the Lycra-wrapped joggers, the fleece-swaddled dog walkers, I traced out the day's events in my mind, replaying the conversations, trying my best to get a fix on where it all led.

We'd dodged a bullet, of that much I was pretty sure, the weight of Banger's anger whooshing by us with only a powerful ruffle of wind. The terms of the arrangement had changed slightly—we couldn't pretend we were the catalysts of some radical change in Stanbro's culture anymore, and possibly we'd even been revealed as mercenary soldiers, agents of the very system we ostensibly opposed—but in the end, what did that matter? We were still going. We were still getting paid to do work that wasn't physically harmful to us or to anyone else. That was about as much as a person could hope for, I thought.

And maybe, just maybe, we were doing more than that, too. Maybe we were building something out ahead that we'd step into someday and feel grateful for. Maybe we were giving the world something it truly needed. It was not impossible that everything Peter believed would still be proven true. Boeing and the others would see soon enough. We'd hire more people. We'd wage battles on multiple fronts. We'd usher in a new dawn.

I ended up on the Burnside Bridge, watching seagulls mob damp bread crumbs while a freighter on the east bank named *Mega Wisdom* sucked in a load of grain, the clouds of chaff puffing around the portal. In either direction the river bent out of sight, and a tugboat pulling a load of smashed shale passed underneath, the massive power of its engine apparent only well after it was gone, in the widening wake powerfully slapping both shorelines.

I wished Amy were with me. I could have told her all about the day's adventures. They would have amused her, and she would have liked the view, too, which included not only the river but the traffic streaming off the Marquam Bridge, the barren cherry trees of Waterfront Park, and the twin glass plumes of the convention center, mounted on glass pyramids like fists, giving their perpetual double finger to the west side. We could have loitered on the bridge for a long time together, found some Bloody Marys in Old Town.

For a second I could almost hear her voice. I could smell her skin, and feel the soft pressure of her shoulder against my arm. The memory of her body surged up in me, pushing everything else away.

I leaned against the rough concrete railing, feeling gutted, and embraced the cold swelling heft. The water seemed to breathe down below. I'd been much too passive with Amy lately, I thought. I'd let things drift too far. What we needed was a new experience altogether. Some private, special event, outside the routine of our daily lives.

I needed to go to her. Maybe I even needed to commit some kind of grand gesture. I wasn't sure.

What would it be? Candy seemed so trite. Flowers. Maybe, but only along with something else, too. Maybe a vacation somewhere. That sounded all right. But there was no time, and where would we go? The coast wasn't far. We could drive out there in an hour. And with that, the idea was there, fully formed. A trip to the coast. Tonight. I liked it. It was impetuous, but doable.

I didn't make any moves at first, but just lay there against the railing and tried talking myself back down. She'd never go. And even if she did, we wouldn't have much time to spend. We had work in the morning. But the idea kept itching at me and wouldn't stop. An hour away. This was off-season, and there were plenty of cheap rooms. What could be better than an impromptu road trip?

I made my way slowly back to the car, putting calls in to beachfront properties. I put a hold on a room at Salishan, a funky resort just south of Cannon Beach, and stopped at Whole Foods to pick up some supplies: a bottle of champagne, a baguette, cheese and salami, artichoke hearts, and milk chocolate, her favorites. I also bought a few lousy movies from the discount bin near the registers, just in case. By the time I stepped back outside the ground was hidden under a light dusting of snow.

It was dark by the time I got to Linda's house, and my scheme still seemed reasonable. Tiny flakes of snow coursed through the yellow cones of the streetlights. The sound of my door slamming was muted.

I stood there on the sidewalk for a while, just watching the house—the frozen grass, the darkened windows, the ceramic coffee cup on the porch—wrestling down a last pang of doubt. The plan was so unlike me. So sudden. So romantic, even. Maybe I was doing something ridiculous. Maybe I should just go home and let the urge subside. But again I talked myself back into it. Maybe all these years had been a long windup for this kind of thing. A long fuse leading to this urgency. There was nothing to lose, anyway. She might not even be home. In any case, I knocked.

A distant clatter of kitchenware came from deep inside the house, followed by the padding of footsteps, followed eventually by the rustling of the lock. And then, abruptly, the door opened and there she was, looking lovely. Her cheeks were flushed from the heat of the stove, her hair disheveled from the day's chores, her eyes mildly surprised. She had stubble on her bare shins, visible in the blowing slit of the powder blue bathrobe she'd been wearing for at least five years, and in her hand she clutched a butcher knife with clinging bits of garlic on the blade.

"Oh," she said, tightening her robe against the cold. "What's up, Damon?"

"I was in the neighborhood," I said. "What are you doing?"

"Cooking dinner."

"You want to go to the beach?"

"What?"

"The beach. You want to go?"

I'd hoped for something like torrid, conspiratorial glee on her part, but it didn't come. Rather, she knitted her brow and querulously shook her head.

"What?" she said. "The beach? Tonight?"

"I got us a room," I said, trying to sound casual. "With a hot tub. And a fireplace. If we leave right now, we'll get there by nine. Come on. Don't think. Let's go."

She tightened her robe again, frowning further. "I'm not really following," she said. "You want to go to the beach? In the winter? Is everything all right, Damon?"

"Everything is great," I said. "Extremely great. So great I wanted to take you to the coast tonight. That's all."

She peered out into the street, like I might have a camera crew in tow. The smell of chicken and garlic wafted out behind her. She seemed unsure about whether to push me away or invite me in, and I shivered visibly on the snowy porch. Reluctantly, she opened the door for me to come in.

"I'm kind of cooking right now," she said. "And I've got a lot to get done tonight. So you can't stay that long, all right? But come on in. I don't know what you're talking about."

"Fine, fine," I said. "The beach. That's what I'm talking about."

"What do you mean, the beach?"

"It's off-season. It's so easy."

The foyer was cluttered with boots and umbrellas, and the living room was a murky cavern. We walked down a short hallway directly to the kitchen. The countertops were linoleum, surrounding a narrow island, all illuminated by the fluorescent lights in the drop ceiling. She took her place at the cutting board and resumed her chopping.

"I know it's kind of sudden," I said, "but you should just say yes."

"Why?"

"We never take vacations. We deserve one."

"You're so funny," she said. "Months, nothing. And now, hurry up, hurry up."

"All you'd have to do is get dressed. Come on."

"What possessed you today, anyway?"

"I don't know. I miss you, I guess."

"We see each other every day."

"You know what I mean."

She finished slicing the garlic and sprinkled the pieces onto a pile of carrots and brussels sprouts. I had the impression she seemed to be giving the beach idea her serious consideration, her hands dreamily sweeping up the shards of carrot into a glass tray, her body drifting to the cupboard for olive oil, but when she began pouring the olive oil onto the vegetables, chuckling to herself, I could see that her mind was made up. The momentum was already eking away from the plan. The mission was failing.

"Come on," I said.

"Not tonight," she said. "I really can't."

"The moon is full."

"Maybe another night."

I swiped a sliver of carrot from the cutting board and chewed unhappily. I couldn't say I was surprised by the outcome. I'd known all along this was the most likely response, but the rebuff was still painful. My grand gesture was not being received, and I was disappointed. To keep some dignity I pretended to inspect the litter of photos and flyers on the refrigerator.

Amy slid the carrots and brussels sprouts into the oven with the browning chicken. I heard her setting the timer on the microwave, and when I turned around she was wiping her hands on a dish towel.

"Maybe try a little warning next time," she offered.

"Yeah. Sure," I said. "It was just an idea."

"It was a good idea."

"Not good enough, I guess."

"Anyway. I'll see you in the morning?"

"Okay. Yeah. I'll be here."

We walked back to the front door, and she punched me lightly on the arm to buck up my spirits, but I didn't feel like being bucked up. We got to the door and she was already fixing her bathrobe, preparing for the blast of cold that would greet my departure, and I decided she'd have to wait a little longer while I took a quick piss. I had a long, snowy drive ahead, after all.

"Where are you going?" she said, as I climbed the stairs two at a time.

"Bathroom," I said. "It's up here, right?"

"Second door on the right. But it's not very clean . . ."

"Yeah, yeah."

Linda's bathroom was not dirty at all, it turned out. In fact, it was scrupulously clean, at least by the standards I'd let my own bathroom fall into as a bachelor. There was no darkening ring around the toilet bowl, no scurf of fine hairs and dust. Linda's bathroom smelled good, too, thanks to the copious handmade honey soaps flecked with oatmeal lining the bathtub, the perfumed lotions crowding the shelves.

In part to punish Amy, I took my time washing and drying my hands on the fresh towels. Why didn't it occur to me to clean my own house more often? I got such pleasure from the tidy arrangement of things, the gleaming, ungritty surfaces. On the windows, stars of ice were collecting. The flakes had grown to the size of nickels and almost splashed when they hit the pane.

Out in the hall, I loitered further, wanting to extend my stay just a few more seconds. I hadn't entirely given up on convincing Amy yet, and I figured a little time to herself, reflecting on the offer, might bring her around. I didn't blame her for refusing the idea outright. I'd been much too sudden, much too bold. I should have worked up to the invitation slowly. Maybe I could still rope her into the trip on a second pass. To kill time, I decided to give myself a brief tour.

The first door I opened went to Linda's room, tidy as a military bunk, notable mostly for a surprising pile of horse figurines on the bureau beside the bed.

The next door led into a study furnished with a child-sized desk and a drafting table covered in laundry.

"What are you doing?" Amy called up.

"Nothing," I called back.

I could hear her downstairs, puttering in the foyer, lining up the scattered shoes. The beach, the beach. I tried to implant the thought directly in her head. I pushed on the next knob and fumbled for the light.

The walls ignited in pale yellow. If there had been any doubt about the room's occupant, it didn't last long. Amy's blue sweatpants were wadded on the floor. A book of Cartier-Bresson prints she'd carried for years peeked from under the bed. The bureau top was a familiar cityscape of cosmetics, and her hair iron appeared to be plugged in and hot. Typical. The only decoration on the walls was a calendar of medieval illuminated manuscripts featuring brightly painted serfs planting rows of peas outside a feudal castle.

I stood there, taking in the sight. So this was her space. A part of me was pleased by the mess I found, a sure sign of Amy's fundamental inability to fend for herself in the world. Given the chance, she always slid back into this squalor. If nothing else, she needed me around to remind her to change the sheets every once in a while. But mostly I felt a sense of calm. It was almost sweet, this exile I'd fallen into. Listening to Amy downstairs, straightening the closet, so close, I could feel my love seeping back into my body. What I'd felt on the bridge was still there, still growing. It just needed a little distance to expand in.

What a trick, I thought. In her presence, the feeling had all but disappeared, replaced by petty frustration, bruised anger. And now, a few steps away, it was back again, ringing like a bell. It was like some demonic law, I thought, some inverse ratio. The greater the distance, the stronger the love. Or maybe it was even more complicated than that. It was just the right distance. Not too close and not too far. A force field. All the pieces arranged just so. Maybe I would never go home after all, I thought. Maybe I would just stand here, one floor up from Amy, for the rest of my life.

I was getting ready to switch off the light and head back down when I heard the faint sound of something moving in the room. A scratching, snuffling sound somewhere. I assumed it was a cat or a dog, not that I remembered ever hearing Linda had pets, but then I worried it could be a mouse, even a rat. I didn't want to investigate too closely, and I started to back away. It was only when the coils of the bed creaked, and the piled quilts began untangling, that I realized the sounds were coming from something larger, something human. And then a single, muscled leg emerged into view. The quilt shuddered once more and a head and torso appeared, belonging to Peter.

My first thought was he looked terrible. His eyes struggled against the light, and he raised his pale, naked arm to make a shadow. His reddish hair was thick on his chest and shoulders, and between his legs. He continued blinking in the overhead glare, propped on his elbow, the strong line of his bicep defined like a charcoal etching, and still I was confused by what I was seeing. Hadn't I left Peter on the street just a few hours ago? He was supposed to be at the mansion paying the bills or something. He blinked again and dragged a blanket over his body.

And belatedly, the recognition hit me somewhere in the solar plexus. The loss was pure, instantaneous, spherical. I was a fool.

Peter looked in my direction, trying to understand what was happening himself. Our eyes met briefly and he shook his head, pushing himself over to the side of the bed. He put his feet on the floor and started running his fingers through his hair, looking shrunken, cold. He glanced over at me one more time, as if to confirm I was really there, and looked down at the floorboards again. Whatever rationalizations he had been making to himself were not enough to absolve him from the momentary jolt of shame he seemed to feel. Soon he would have everything compartmentalized again, but not yet.

"I think my shoes are around here," he mumbled.

By then Amy had crept up the stairs and joined me at the doorway and promptly burst into tears. Peter and I both watched her, unsure anymore who had the privilege of consoling her. None of us moved, and eventually Amy wrestled herself under control. She was in the hardest spot in some ways.

"Well," I said.

"Oh God," she said.

"Yeah," I said. "Huh. I don't know . . ."

I turned and walked downstairs, unsure what else to do. Maybe I was supposed to start yelling at somebody. Or pick a fight, indulge in some kind of loud drama. But I didn't have the strength for any of that. The best I could do was go stand at the fire, poking at the orange embers, figuring I should at least give Amy and Peter a moment alone to regroup.

The snow was falling harder now. The flakes hitting the windowpanes were the size of quarters. The flames were almost dead. I tossed in the remaining pages of an old *National Geographic* and watched the paper swell and warp in the heat. The pages charred and the dark parts of the pictures turned silvery black, and finally the whole spent carcass ascended the spiraling air into the flue.

Maybe I should just walk away, I thought. I could walk out

the back door and keep going and disappear into the swirling white snow. If I could just keep walking, I thought, I might somehow escape this moment. By heading out into the trees, never stopping, I might get free, and end up traveling in a world of pure light and sound, a being of heat surrounded by cold. The idea had its appeal. I found it impossible to take the first steps, though. I didn't want to leave Amy just yet.

A baseball team and a Nissan Pathfinder turned into red constellations sparkling on black ash. A sunset browned and evaporated. I added another page and watched the heat tease the air out of shape, stretching the fabric of space with its furious ascending. People, animals, words, all disintegrating and dispersing into the cold air. I did love Amy. I loved her almost wildly when I was all by myself.

I didn't hear anything upstairs, but apparently Peter got dressed in a hurry. It was only a few minutes before he descended the stairs, buttoning his shirt to the top stud, and without looking at me proceeded to the closet and retrieved his coat. Amy followed a few seconds later, and stepped outside with him to the porch.

I waited. Soon the door opened and Amy reentered. She came into the living room and sat down on the couch with her knees pressed together, rubbing her left palm with her right thumb. Her eyes were red, her nose swollen, and more than once it seemed like she was about to tell me something but then didn't. The oven buzzer went off, three beeps floating through the room like an ellipsis, and she went to the kitchen. I heard the sound of the oven door flopping open, the bubbling of the chicken fat, the glass sliding onto the linoleum countertop. She came back empty-handed and sat down on the couch.

We didn't say anything. We sat in the living room surrounded by the smell of her chicken dinner. I detected rosemary, a hint of lemon. I put a new log on the fire. When the fire was burning steadily again, the red embers throbbing, I stood and pulled on my jacket. I waited, hoping for some final reprieve, and then walked the narrow chute of the hallway. The finality of the walk was harrowing. Once I exited the house there was no coming back. Our life was ending. The grand spinning wheel was grinding me under.

Amy followed me to the door just as she'd followed Peter a few minutes before, but this time she stopped on the threshold. The door opened onto a cold, wintry scene. The snow was collecting, and already it was marred by the tracks of walking neighbors and dogs. I turned around to say good-bye.

"I don't know if I'm going to see you again," I said, choking, and then I turned and stumbled down the steps into the night.

FIFTEEN

I STAYED HOME from work the next day. I didn't bother calling in. I figured someone would take my place in the group, maybe Peter himself. It would only be right. With me at home, he and Amy could sneak off during breaks and fuck each other in the janitor's closet. They could grope each other in the halls and hold hands under the table. They could laugh and tease. I lay on the couch and imagined a thousand humiliating scenarios. Peter fucking Amy on her creaking box frame. Amy stroking Peter's aged cock and balls. Peter fingering the star of Amy's ass. I drank in every image like sweet poison, writhing in a state of pure exile, pure love, total, clarifying expulsion from everywhere I wanted to be.

All day long, the time crawled. By nine o'clock in the morning I'd been awake for five hours, and I couldn't force myself to keep my eyes closed any longer. Ten miles south, the day's participants were just assembling in the lobby of the Crowne Plaza. By ten, they were breaking into small groups, running through their introductions.

In the afternoon I slept a few more hours. And when I woke up I regretted not having gone in to work after all. I wanted to be there, making everyone as uncomfortable as possible. I wanted to stand next to Amy and observe her presentation of the energy pyramid, knowing what she had done the night before and judging her.

For some reason, the betrayal on Peter's side seemed less profound. What had he done to me, anyway? Did I own Amy? No. I didn't care so much about Peter's role in the humiliation.

By early evening I was feeling almost hopeful again. Maybe I'd overreacted to the situation of the night before. Maybe I still hadn't lost hold of Amy after all. We'd come through some bad episodes in the past, hadn't we? And in the bigger scheme, what was the crime? I knew couples who had divorced five and six times. Couples who had split up and gotten back together forty years later. I knew a man and woman who lived in houses down the street from each other and only stayed over if explicitly invited. By some standards, our relations were still perfectly healthy, or at least far from permanently broken. What was infidelity, anyway?

I waited for any contact from Amy, or from anyone else for that matter, but no one called. Dinnertime came and went, and I ate a boxed pie from the convenience store. The sun set in a bath of silver through the electric lines. I tried to keep myself from picking up the phone and calling her, hoping to preserve some sliver of dignity, but there was no way to hold back. Around nine, I dialed her number.

Amy picked up on the third ring. I didn't say anything, and neither did she. I was a little bit surprised she was home, and suddenly all the anxiety rose to my skin's surface again. My whole consciousness poured into my ear. I missed the old hiss of the wire, like wind on the frozen tundra. The cold digital silence was too complete.

We sat there for a full minute without saying anything, just waiting for the other to speak.

"Damon?" she said at last.

"Yeah."

"You're there?"

"Yeah."

We listened to each other breathing for another half minute.

"How was it today?" I said. I couldn't think of anything better to start with than work.

"Okay," she said.

"The new group's okay?" I said.

"About the same."

"So . . ."

"Yeah . . ."

We sat through another long pause. A rattling engine passed a few blocks away. A weird metallic bang happened somewhere outside, without consequence.

"I'm sorry, Damon," she said. "What can I say?"

"I just wish . . ."

"What?"

"I don't know . . ."

"Come on, what?'

"Why couldn't it have been somebody else, that's all?"

She didn't answer. By then we'd been on the phone so long, the hot plastic of the receiver was making my ear ache.

"You're not going to say anything?" I said.

"What am I supposed to say?"

"I'm supposed to tell you what to say now, too?"

"Oh, Jesus," she said.

"Ahhh, here we go. Blame the victim."

More silence.

"You make it so fucking hard, Damon. I mean, what are you

holding on to anyway? What are you so afraid of, that you can't see when it's not working?"

That wasn't what I wanted to hear, so I hung up, hoping she would call back immediately, but she didn't. I lay in bed, weeding through our conversation for hidden clues, secret codes, inadvertent confessions of some kind. I turned everything she said inside out. Was this really about Peter? Or was this about me? Did she love Peter? What did that mean, even, love?

In one of my more elaborate convolutions I got to wondering if perhaps Amy's behavior was not what it seemed at all, not a method of severing relations with me, but rather the exact opposite, the ultimate test. Maybe this was my invitation to prove my devotion once and for all, the prelude to some spectacular reconciliation. Maybe her feelings were just so powerful and consuming that she needed hard evidence before allowing herself to take the next step. I tried in every way to convince myself of this interpretation, but it never quite stuck.

At two o'clock in the morning, I couldn't stand being in the house anymore. I had to know what was happening across town. Was Peter with her? Some other, unknown third party? In the back of my mind I wanted to believe a visit might change something. If I was just humble enough, if my love was pure and strong enough, I still might perform some heroic act.

I got dressed and drove across town. It was a longer drive than usual. The distance seemed to double with every block, space accordioning in time. I didn't know what I hoped to find, but I imagined some kind of confrontation taking place. Maybe I would catch her at something sordid, kneeling in front of Peter in the window. Or better yet, I would find her waiting on the front porch, wringing her hands, needing me and knowing I was coming.

I passed the Arco station, Red's Barbeque, the curl of highway bending over the warehouses of the industrial east side. At last I funneled into Southeast, the windows blurring, the road itself drawing me onward. At the end of the tunnel I came to Linda's house, still stolid and tight-lipped in the darkness, splashed with the same white streetlight as the night before. The windows were all black. The same book was on the top stair, beside the same ceramic teacup.

I sat there, sending telepathic signals through the air molecules. "Amy, Amy," I thought. "Appear in a window. Flash on a light." But nothing happened. Nothing was revealed. The house failed to ignite into fire. A few minutes later, exhausted, I drove home and slept.

The next day I didn't call Amy. I did talk to Linda, though, thinking she'd have some insight, and to Jaeha, hoping he'd have some advice, but they had nothing beyond sympathy to offer. Linda said she thought Amy was trying to take some control over her life, and this was the only way she could imagine how. It was a form of self-determination, and I wouldn't do her any good by pushing too hard.

From Jaeha I learned the affair had been going on longer than I'd thought. He said Amy and Peter had first begun laying the groundwork back in the summer, and over the fall the first illicit contacts had occurred. This knowledge caused me to recoil, and revise every conversation with both parties in memory. Where had the deceptions come? Where were the missed cues? The details were all maddeningly hazy, already lost to memory's incinerator. The more I thought about it, the worse I felt, and yet I still needed whatever grains of information I could get my hands on.

The day ended in another burst of cold, white sunlight. Night came quickly, and still I tried not to call her. One day without contact would be fine, I told myself. One day wouldn't hurt anything. No ground would be lost. But again I couldn't help myself. I picked up the phone around nine o'clock, and this time she didn't answer. Nor did she call me back. The rest of the night some phantom organ throbbed inside my chest.

In the morning Jaeha called to check in. I hadn't showered for days, and all I'd eaten in twenty-four hours was a bag of barbeque corn nuts. It wasn't hard for him to hear the torpor in my voice.

"You okay?" he said.

"Yeah."

"Do you need anything? I could bring you something. Some soup?"

"I don't think so."

"Okay. You coming to work?"

"No."

"You're sure?"

"Yeah."

"Well. I'm calling because Amy wanted me to tell you something. You're sure you're okay?"

"What is it?" I perked up. Maybe this was the message I'd been waiting for.

"She wanted you to know she's leaving town for a while," he said. "She said she'd be in touch."

"Leaving?"

"That's all I know."

"Oh," I said. "So she's gone?"

"Yeah. I think so."

"Oh."

"You're all right?"

"Yeah."

"You're sure?"

"Yeah, totally."

"I could come over. Bring you some soup."

"No, I'm fine."

I hung up, my heart soaring. Thank God. Peter was abandoned, too.

I skipped the Rain Dragon holiday party that weekend, and heard from Michael the next day that the spread was opulent. Caviar and truffle pâté, entertainment by some jug band with washboard and stand-up bass. I spent my own Christmas at home, eating an Entenmann's pound cake, watching old episodes of *Entourage*.

The Stanbro job went on hiatus between Christmas and New Year's. No one knew exactly what would happen when the contract came up for renewal in the new quarter. It was still too early to see quantifiable results, so the decision would revolve on more subjective claims. Did the employees believe this was a worthwhile experience? Did the cost seem too extravagant? Peter was probably in meetings with Stanbro's executives on a daily basis, going over the exit surveys, discussing the content and time frames. They were meetings I would have attended in a different life.

But these issues had no impact on me anymore. I'd fallen suddenly and entirely out of the loop. Whatever phone calls were taking place, whatever back-channel communications were going on, I was not part of them. Instead, I busied myself taking hikes in the woods, watching TV, haunting coffee shops. I went to the grocery store numerous times a day, roaming the aisles, one day stumbling across a newly designed package for Rain Dragon's honey mustard. A dragon with bee's eyes. I had helped guide it through development months ago.

Jaeha wanted me to come back, regardless of the social awkwardness that might entail. They needed me, he said. Emilio was leaving the company at the end of January, pocketing his earnings and putting a down payment on a house on the coast that he intended to turn into an ashram. Simon was jockeying to take over my job, Michael was moving ahead on the methane digester, having collected the first major disbursement of Stanbro funds. Linda was lobbying for her beekeeping operation to be the next recipient.

"Come back," he said.

"Maybe," I said. And in truth, the longer I waited, the more likely that option became. I had no other plans. And there was no way I'd ever find anything that paid as well.

A few days into the new year a letter from Amy arrived. I re-read her blocky handwriting at least nine times, trying to decipher the subtext. The slant of the writing leaned to the left, indicating what? Her t's were crossed high on the stem, which was significant, but how? I had no idea. The subtext unknowable, I had to settle for the text itself. She claimed she was sorry about everything that had happened, but she had to get away from all the noise and clear her mind. She said she would be in touch.

I filed the letter in a desk drawer, a little gift to myself, a gem of pain I could take out and scrutinize one day. As the weeks passed, I could feel my love binding itself into an ever smaller, more compact object. It was getting hard to see how it ever would have worked.

Still, whenever the phone rang it was like a bolt of lightning in the house. I jumped from the couch and ran for the kitchen, disappointed whenever the voice on the other line was not hers. I watched the street from the front window as the mailman dawdled his way from door to door, his three-wheeled sack resting on the sidewalk as he stepped heavily onto the porch of the yellow house, the brown house, the duplex, chatting with the old man in the blue flannel pajamas.

Up above, a line of birds on the phone line looked like musical notation. The neighbor girls were washing their car. The sun crept on the wall.

Finally the mailman climbed my stairs. The creak and flop of the metal mouth came next. Then the receding footsteps. I waited as long as I could before making the move, about twenty seconds, usually. Scattered on the floor were the water and garbage bills and a postcard from a new pizza place in the neighborhood. Nothing from Amy.

My final consulting check arrived, though, for $9,000, and that offered some consolation. I went out and bought new tennis shoes.

As fate would have it, I ran into Peter by accident one morning in mid January. I was driving down Powell and pulled up next to him at the stoplight, and we caught each others' eyes. His face brightened, and quickly darkened as he remembered the issue between us. He waved gravely, and pointed over at the parking lot of the International House of Pancakes, and we piloted our cars to places side by side.

We shook hands like distant relatives under a billboard for Z100, its electrifying logo still livid in the day's damp light. The undercurrent of distrust between us was so deep, so still, as to be unnoticeable. He seemed chastened, though, and to his credit he tried to apologize right away.

"You know, Damon, I feel terrible about how things—"

"It's all right," I said, cutting him off.

"I just need to tell you, though, I thought you two were over—"

"Really," I said. "No need." I took some pleasure in robbing him of clean forgiveness. Time would tell if we ever got back on solid footing again, and meanwhile I didn't want past events to affect our day-to-day business dealings. I wanted my job back, and whatever advantage I'd been given was best left unstated.

"You want to get some coffee?" he said.

"Sure."

It was Sunday, and all the tables were crowded with plump families, elderly couples, and all-night partiers on their way home to sleep. The sweet smell of cinnamon and sugar enclosed us and we joined the mellow circus, taking a window booth. I asked him about the farm, and he told me Michael was indeed moving ahead on the methane digester at last, the down payment on the turbine paid for with proceeds from Stanbro. All the digging I'd done over the summer was finally coming in handy, and by next year they would be sending electricity back into the grid. Some cows had gotten sick, but they'd recovered.

We were silent, watching traffic, the boxed life of each driver zooming by, replaced by the next. Peter fumbled with the foil covering the tiny half-and-half container and poured the load into his cup. A baby cooed.

"And what about Stanbro?" I said.

"What about it?" he said.

"When does the next session start?"

"Oh, you haven't heard?"

"Heard what?"

"I thought you'd have heard. They pulled the plug."

"What?"

"Yeah, couple days ago, real surprise," he said, and added another container of cream. "I thought we were on the glide path. Banger was with us. But the board voted. That's it. The board decides."

"But why?" I said.

"I think it was the floor workers," he said. The coffee didn't seem to please him, and he set it aside. "They came in with pitchforks and torches. Practically lynched us. It's a shame, too. But I guess we were just moving too fast. Stanbro wasn't ready for what we were showing them."

"So, what now?" I said.

"Consulting-wise?" he said. "No idea."

"What about Boeing? Hewlett-Packard?"

"We're not too high on anyone's list right now," he said, chuckling. "Word gets around fast."

"So there's nothing? "

"Yogurt. Butter. Cheese."

I stared at the menu. The photos of enormous breakfast plates looked grotesque, and although a part of me relished Peter's misfortune, the failure of his ideas, another part mourned my own fate. I didn't want to go back to doing PR. I didn't want anything to do with the farm without Amy. Where would I go?

"So there's nothing?" I said.

"I've been talking to some people down in San Jose," Peter said. "Nothing major."

"Oh?" I said.

"Software company," he said. "The founder is a very interesting guy. He thinks the speed of light is getting faster. He says it has ramifications for information retrieval. Anyway, it's a much better fit than Stanbro. Knowledge workers. They're already halfway there." He seemed eager to talk about the new gig, but reined himself in, remembering our problem. "Anyway. We'll see what happens. How about you? What are you up to? What's next?"

The cars on Powell sped by soundlessly.

"I don't know."

I woke up to white light in my eyes, raw sunlight streaming through the fresh snow piled on my windshield's bowed, fogged glass. The light was blinding, like milk pouring over the cold dashboard, turning everything in the car luminous and unearthly.

My breath wisped in the air as the last shreds of a dream faded from mind. Something about an enormous plain of cracked earth, and me, cleaning the entire expanse with a push broom. It was a happy dream, though, a dream of completion.

For a woozy moment I clung to the image, viewing my sleep with peaceful satisfaction. I didn't know where I was, or even who, exactly. I was just a body strapped into a 1996 Camry, facing the nubs of the steering wheel's handgrip. The orange needles of the dashboard lay flat and my pants glowed like phosphor inside the bubble of trapped light. The grain of the snow on the windshield shivered, flashing pink and blue and yellow facets. I found my hands balled in the pockets of my brown corduroy jacket, clutching the car keys. And then, gradually, the memories of who I was spilled back into me.

The car was parked in the woods east of Bellingham, Washington, a few hours north of Seattle. I had on the same faded blue jeans and no-longer-new Adidas I'd been wearing for the past three days straight. The rest of my belongings were now in boxes in Portland. In the bank, I had enough money for a year, most likely. Maybe longer up here, nowhere.

I cracked the door and a sheaf of snow fell from the window. I pushed against the soft snow bank. Funnels of cold air shot up my pant leg. And then I stepped out into the day.

I'd arrived in the middle of the night, so this was my first real look at the property. Fiery mulberry bushes edged a clearing in the Douglas fir trees under the shining blue winter sky. Off to the left, the land dipped and a short meadow ran to a break of naked maples. Directly in front of me was an old RV, its roof a perfect plane of white icing. Everything was shockingly white and motionless in the mountain landscape.

First things first. I pissed onto a buried juniper shrub near the car's front bumper, burning deep chasms into the snow.

I'd barely zipped up when I heard the noise of a laboring car engine coming closer. Soon a blue Ford pickup chugged into view, parking at the mouth of the clearing. The driver was a burly man in an orange down coat, with many days' beard on his fat face. He sat in the cab, heat on high, shuffling papers, until he noticed me and rolled heavily out the door. He had red shoelaces in his round-toed boots, and a black tattoo of a diamond on the back of his hand. The snow squeaked like Styrofoam under his heavy feet.

"Damon?" he said. We shook hands. He had rough, meaty fingers and a soft grip.

"You're Chris?" I said.

"Yup," he said. "I guess you want to look at the RV." That was one good thing about the Northwest and its old Norwegian stock. No one asked any questions. He had an RV to rent; I wanted one. That was enough.

We crossed the clearing and he twisted the lock's face, then pushed the door open. The air inside was cold and stale. The walls were paneled with fake wood, the carpet was thin and chartreuse. There was a narrow cot set up near a propane stove, and a half-size refrigerator holding an old can of RC Cola and a molding, deflated orange. I turned on the water and brown, brackish fluid came out, then sputtered to a trickle, and stopped.

"Hose is frozen," Chris said. "It's fine when the weather clears, though."

"Okay," I said, and I paid him the first and last month in cash, barely denting my savings.

Chris was happy with the negotiation. He shook my hand and took off, laying a double track of tire tread that seemed to vibrate against the severe whiteness of the ground. As his truck disappeared, a cloud passed over the sun and everything turned dingy gray and then, a moment later, it came back again, radiant, pristine white.

Unpacking took all of twenty minutes. I hadn't brought that much. A down quilt, a few bags of clothes, a laptop, a printer. There was a grocery store a few miles away, and a shower at the YMCA, but I wasn't in any hurry to get into town.

There were two items that I made sure found a place. One was a photograph of Amy, a Polaroid she'd included with her last letter, showing her in a blowsy yellow sundress standing near an adobe hut. On the ground were what looked like handmade mud bricks and far in the distance the pink and brown hills of the desert catching the last of the day's sunlight. The light was hitting her face, too, and her left hand was raised, one finger holding a strand of hair from her cheek. She was living with her friend Rosa, the letter said, thinking about acupuncture school. The photographer was a glassblower named Richard.

I taped Amy's picture to the window. I was happy for her, and beneath the lingering burn I could glimpse a wistful, almost innocent affection coming into view. In time, we'd love each other again, in a new, almost purer way.

The other item was a small wooden box that Peter had given me, a polished, lacquered cube with tidy black nails limning each seam. I turned it over in my hands and shook it a few times, listening to the soft rustle of a substance inside. He'd given one to everyone before Stanbro, and never told us what was inside. I placed it beside Amy's photo for safekeeping.

I heated some water on the propane stove and made coffee. The oily, earthy smell turned the RV almost cozy. I switched on the space heater and watched the black coils brighten into hot orange threads, passing my hands nearby until my skin seemed to soften on the bones. The whirring machine was reassuring somehow, a semblance of breath in the dead locker of the RV.

Out the window a pathway led into a stand of blue spruce trees. I followed it, entering a grove of naked birch, and continued alongside a stone fence that crumbled in places and then picked up farther along. I kept going into a fir forest, passing muddy milk containers, an empty bag of SunChips, the plastic noose of a six-pack.

I came to a set of boulders scrawled with graffiti: "Class of 89 Rules," "Fuck Andy," "Tina Rocks Josh."

The mountain air stung my nose and cheeks, and I fell into a brisk walking rhythm, letting my muscles find their pace. Clean air. Quiet trees. Hard earth.

Beyond the graffitied rocks another hiker appeared, an older woman with white hair and high, flushed cheekbones, descending the hill in clean Gore-Tex and fleece. We passed within arm's length, nodding hello.

"Bald eagle," she said, panting, and jabbed her thumb over her shoulder. Then she was gone.

I kept climbing until I arrived at the edge of the trees. The woods opened onto a wide burn field, a scene of mauled trunks and uprooted stumps, pulverized earth and thrashed rocks. At the top of the slope some trees lined the ridge, slivers of sky showing between their trunks. A single aluminum shack anchored the field, surrounded by the crazy threads of wide-gauge tire tread in the thick bandage of snow. I scanned the sky, but no eagles were flying.

My face was numb. I could hear a faint ringing sound in my ears, the high-pitched whine of the city's electricity still singing in my nerves. From my pocket I pulled Peter's wooden box. I tried prying it open, but it didn't come easily, so I bent down and broke it on a rock. It took a few bashes to crumple the walls, but once they got going they splintered easily. I tipped the mangled box, and some reddish powder spilled out. It took a few moments to recognize what it was. Plain, dry dust from the farm.

I laughed, and turned the box upside down, letting the fine grains blow away in the wind. Then I sat down on the rock to watch the sky change. Far in the distance, a beam of sunlight was passing slowly over the hills, raking the trees, some of which swayed and some of which didn't. I sat and watched the scene, waiting, ready, looking everywhere for some kind of sign.

ACKNOWLEDGMENTS

This book took a bit longer than expected. In that time, many readers offered their thoughts and encouragement, and my deepest gratitude goes out to all of them. Special thanks must go to Jennifer Carlson, Ben Adams, Kelly Reichardt, Todd Haynes, and Emily Chenoweth.

A NOTE ON THE AUTHOR

Jon Raymond is the author of the novel *The Half-Life*, a *Publishers Weekly* Best Book of 2004, and the short story collection *Livability*, winner of the 2009 Ken Kesey Award for Fiction. He is also the writer of several films, including *Wendy and Lucy* and *Meek's Cutoff*, and co-writer of the Emmy-nominated screenplay for the HBO miniseries *Mildred Pierce*. Raymond's writing has appeared in *Bookforum*, *Artforum*, *Tin House*, the *Village Voice*, and other publications. He lives in Portland, Oregon, with his family.